A TIME OF WITCHES

AF843336

Also by Madeline Martin

The Last Bookshop in London

The Librarian Spy

The Keeper of Hidden Books

The Booklover's Library

The Secret Book Society

A TIME OF WITCHES

A Novel

MADELINE MARTIN

HANOVER
SQUARE
PRESS

HANOVER SQUARE PRESS™

Recycling programs for this product may not exist in your area.

ISBN-13: 978-1-335-00267-9

A Time of Witches

Copyright © 2026 by Madeline Martin

Stock Images: © Oleksandra/stock.adobe.com (Moon); © Anja Kaiser/stock.adobe.com (Celestial design elements); © Paolo/stock.adobe.com (Stars)

All rights reserved. No part of this book may be used or reproduced in any manner whatsoever without written permission.

Without limiting the exclusive rights of any author, contributor or the publisher of this publication, any unauthorized use of this publication to train generative artificial intelligence (AI) technologies is expressly prohibited. Harlequin also exercises their rights under Article 4(3) of the Digital Single Market Directive 2019/790 and expressly reserves this publication from the text and data mining exception.

This is a work of fiction. Names, characters, places and incidents are either the product of the author's imagination or are used fictitiously. Any resemblance to actual persons, living or dead, businesses, companies, events or locales is entirely coincidental.

The recipes at the end of this book are for informational purposes only. The author and publishers are not engaged in rendering medical, therapeutic or other services in this publication. They are not intended to provide a basis for action in particular circumstances without consideration by a competent professional. The author and publishers expressly disclaim any responsibility for any liability, loss or risk, personal or otherwise, which is incurred as a consequence, directly or indirectly, of the use and application of any of the contents of this book.

TM and ® are trademarks of Harlequin Enterprises ULC.

Hanover Square Press
22 Adelaide St. West, 41st Floor
Toronto, Ontario M5H 4E3, Canada
HanoverSqPress.com

HarperCollins Publishers
Macken House, 39/40 Mayor Street Upper,
Dublin 1, D01 C9W8, Ireland
www.HarperCollins.com

Printed in Lithuania

MIX
Paper | Supporting responsible forestry
FSC® C021394

1 2 3 4 5 6 7 8 9 10 LIT 29 28 27 26

For those who still believe in quiet magic—
there's a little witch in all of us.

A TIME OF WITCHES

Lilith

Present Day
Savannah, Georgia

Every night, Lilith Legare burned alive at the stake. The recurring dream was inevitable, unstoppable, and she was powerless before its fury.

Each time, she braced for the assault as she was dragged under: smoke choking her lungs, splintered wood biting her bare feet, the rough rope rasping over raw wrists. And the flames. Blistering hot, licking at exposed flesh.

The dream tossed her into a landscape she'd never seen, yet somehow remembered. A preternatural storm roiled above stretches of green hills, a town at her back, a horizon of slate-roofed homes. Eighteen figures swayed by their necks from a beam of wood, tainting the smoky air with the stink of death.

A crowd churned before the woman, spitting accusations, seething with bloodlust.

Witch.

The dream tonight, however, was different. This time, Lilith was not the woman tied to the stake, but a spectator.

A teenager at the front stood apart from the mob with gleaming red-gold hair that hung in a heavy braid down her back.

The air crackled with tension, a charged energy that drew the throng closer, pushing Lilith forward. A man wearing black robes strode toward the woman on the pyre—the woman who had taken Lilith's place. Wind snapped at her plain white shift, revealing the harsh lines of her emaciated body. Her eyes were bright with fear. With hate.

The man gripped a torch in his fist which he unceremoniously flung onto the pyre. A moment of collective awe silenced the crowd. A sputter followed, a whisper of hope that the fire would not catch.

But Lilith knew it would. She *knew*.

Horror gripped her throat as light glowed within the kindling. All at once, the embers erupted into a blaze of demons. The flames clawed toward the woman, clambering over the shift's hem and up thin, dry fabric.

Lilith relived every sensation the woman experienced. How quickly that linen shift singed away, the agony of those white-hot flames, the effort of dragging burning air into starved lungs. Even now, Lilith found herself sucking in a hard inhale, ash gritty in her mouth.

And yet she could not look away.

Her gaze locked on the woman as the intense heat warped her vision. But the woman did not scream as Lilith had in her dreams.

The sky blackened with rage and lightning speared through the clouds. Rain spat fat, angry drops on the earth and the woman lifted her face as if to savor the cool splash against her skin.

Suddenly, the teenager with red-gold hair turned, her eyes narrowed as they locked on Lilith with fierce determination.

Her lips moved and Lilith caught the words as they were torn away by the wind.

"Help her."

Lilith wrenched her gaze back to the woman standing on the pyre as the conflagration whipped around her. And that's when Lilith saw it, branded on the flesh in the crook of the woman's right arm: the shape of a crescent moon.

The exact replica of Lilith's own birthmark.

CHAPTER ONE

Lilith

Four cups of coffee brought no relief. The dream clung to Lilith like a cobweb, the odor of smoke lingering despite the humid July morning air. She perched on the bottom step of her back porch and pulled in a deep breath to clear the phantom smell. The dream always left her disoriented and weighted with an ache over her mother whose death had changed everything.

The sun's brilliance hummed within Lilith before the golden light filtered through layers of draped Spanish moss to splash across the lawn. Beneath her feet, the earth vibrated with life and vitality.

She'd always been sensitive to the rhythm of the moon and the sun as day blossomed and then rolled back into night. Never with such intensity as now though. Not until Mama's death only months before.

Guilt tugged at Lilith. Mama had never been kind, not even

when Lilith dropped out of college to care for her. Still, she had expected grief.

Instead, there was only that heaviness in her chest and something she hated to name.

Relief.

After four years of cancer eating away at her mother, after her meanness curdled into cruelty, after Lilith's self-confidence had been whittled to nothing, Mama had finally died.

That's when the strange happenings began.

Frustration crowded Lilith's thoughts and the clouds swelled overhead, blotting out the sun.

As soon as the life sighed out of Mama, something snapped inside Lilith, a cracking dam that sent a current of energy roaring through her veins, amplifying everything in nature. Suddenly animals followed her in adoration, plants stretched toward her as she passed, and the earth's pulse thrummed in an ever-present lyrical tune just for her.

Lilith pulled in another breath, forcing her clenched muscles to loosen. The clouds overhead broke apart.

The rest of the world had become amplified as well. The sun imbued her with vigor, and the moon gave her strength. The breeze whispered in her ear, guiding her in a way she could understand, but couldn't explain.

That had been three months ago.

The same time the nightmares had started.

A shiver squeezed down Lilith's spine despite the muggy heat. Her gaze wandered to the honeysuckle, the hardy wooden vines coiled tightly around the fence sending tendrils threading through the garden, lush with healthy green leaves and bristling with brilliant red flowers. It hadn't always looked that way.

Her heartbeat spiked.

A thrill. A jab of curiosity.

A needling of fear.

All this weirdness creeped her out. Nature stalked her, injecting itself into her every thought, every breath.

Why couldn't she just have her quiet life back and be boringly normal again?

The rattling of her phone on the painted boards next to her drew her attention.

A text showed on the screen from Essie: Amara's already up. Did I ever sleep in before motherhood?

Lilith snorted and tapped back a reply. You've always been too much of a go-getter to sleep in.

Essie: What a waste. I want those mornings back.

A smile pulled at Lilith's lips. Her best friend could never not be a go-getter. She'd even tried to get the elementary school to have a student counsel when they were in second grade, launching a one-person campaign that had been vastly ignored by the administration and their fellow students alike.

Lilith's fingers flew over her phone screen: Coming to story hour?

Essie: We wouldn't miss it!

Lilith's job at Shelver's Books was a great opportunity to see Essie and Amara regularly despite their packed schedule. Lilith set her phone aside and the smile melted from her face.

A soft breeze swept behind her. A distinct nudge toward the honeysuckle.

With a sigh, she pushed to standing and strode over dew-damp grass that prickled against her feet. Memories of the dream flooded back, a reminder of how the splintered wood stabbed against her soles.

The heady fragrance of the honeysuckle mingled with the redolent notes of smoke. The vines quivered as she approached.

As though excited she was near.

But that was ridiculous, right?

Just like the plant itself, being so unnaturally wild and healthy.

The honeysuckle had been a nub of a thing for almost two decades, since Mama hacked it down to the roots when Lilith was a girl. When Lilith had claimed the plant had stretched itself toward her.

The sad remnants of vine remained in the backyard, a memory of its former glory, like a Christmas tree tucked away after the holidays. But after Mama's death, after the hum of the earth filled Lilith's veins, vines had regrown overnight, scaling the fence and pushing out beyond the barrier of the garden.

Her head ached, exhaustion blunting any logical explanation of how the plant could have grown again after all these years.

She reached for a leaf and the vine stretched to her fingertips; red flowers sprouted outward like a series of small fireworks.

Her hand jerked back and an icy breeze lanced through the thick humidity.

The hair on her arms stood on end.

Plants grew all the time.

Not like that though. Not that fast.

Surely, she hadn't imagined that the plant had just grown toward her.

Like when she'd been a little girl. Back when Mama said there was no such thing as magic, that Lilith was being foolish.

But if she was a fool, why had she suddenly been cursed with all this...strangeness?

And why did she feel like the world and that dream were trying to tell her something?

CHAPTER TWO

Lilith

Lilith sagged against the counter at Shelver's after showing the fourth customer that day where *Midnight in the Garden of Good and Evil* was located—in the section conveniently titled "Local Interest" where stacks of the popular book were on prominent display.

She scrubbed a hand over her face, as if she could swipe away the veil of fatigue.

Lord, she needed sleep.

One of the resident cats padded to the front room and looked miserably up at her, his stomach gurgling audibly. She knew that sound when it came to Fred.

A noxious odor filled the room.

Suddenly wide awake, Lilith snatched him up and rushed him to the back room where she discovered his food bowl was full of the crunchy X-shaped cat food. Not his prescription food.

"No, no, no, no..."

She quickly swapped out the food as the new girl entered the back room. Debbie's nose wrinkled. "What's that smell?"

"Fred got the wrong food." Lilith dumped a couple scoops of Happy Gastronomy into a fresh bowl. "I left you a note about it last night."

Debbie shook her head. "I didn't see a note."

Tamping down her frustration, Lilith replied, "I left it on the counter."

Like, smack dab in the middle of the counter, written in thick black sharpie.

"I'm sorry. I didn't see it." Debbie frowned down at Fred and gave him an apologetic stroke. He nuzzled against her and all was forgiven.

Lilith set the right bowl of food in front of him and left them both to return to the cash register.

Guilt trailed after her.

She *had* written the note, right?

In her mind's eye, she recalled the bold black letters on a hot-pink sticky note. But at the counter, there was no note. Not on the floor or stuck to a nearby book or even crumpled up in the trash can.

Maybe she hadn't written it after all...

Her sleepless nights were getting the better of her.

"Hey, Lilith," Essie sang out as she navigated her stroller over the threshold of the store. Amara jostled in her seat, unperturbed as she plucked a Cheerio from a spill-proof plastic bowl.

Lilith glanced at her watch and grinned at her best friend. "Exactly 2:30 on the dot."

Essie pumped her fist victoriously. "Right on time."

From the stroller, Amara lifted her hands to Lilith, who obliged, pulling the girl into her arms. Little beads at the ends of Amara's braids clacked together as she did so.

"Your braids are so beautiful." Lilith snuggled her goddaughter closer.

Amara beamed at the praise. The story time bell chimed and she wriggled out of Lilith's arms, making a beeline for the children's room.

"That girl knows what she wants." Essie shook her head, even as her warm brown eyes glowed with pride. Together, Lilith and Essie followed Amara's quick steps to the back of the store.

A pulse of longing echoed in Lilith's chest. She ached to know her own place in the world as surely as her friend did. As even little Amara seemed to. Essie had always been driven to achieve what she wanted for as long as Lilith had known her, back when they became neighbors after Essie's parents died and she moved in with her grandmother. Her childhood hadn't been easy, but now Essie had it all, and she'd *worked* hard to have it all: a handsome husband, a loving child, a flourishing law career.

"Aren't the braids just so cute?" Essie settled onto the colorful carpet with Amara in her line of sight.

Lilith recalled Essie's hair in those same braids, pink and white beads clicking melodiously every time she moved her head. Her hair was natural now, a halo of curls worn like a regal crown on her head. Lilith glanced at where Amara sat with her back straight, full attention fixed on Debbie who cradled the day's book in her hands. "I can't believe how big Amara is getting."

Essie folded her legs crisscross. "And I can't believe how tired you look."

Lilith shot her friend a look of playful injury. "Ouch." She sank to the floor beside Essie, unable to ignore the slight hum of the earth beneath her, even through the flooring and the kid-friendly carpet.

"You know I'm all honesty and tough love," Essie said with a beatific smile.

And she really was. She always had been ready to offer advice at any moment throughout their friendship. Whether wanted or not. Advice that was, in hindsight, always needed.

From the front of the room, Debbie opened a book about a pig wearing a raincoat and began to read.

"Is it the nightmares?" Essie asked quietly.

Lilith nodded.

Essie frowned. "Still?"

Another resident cat slid against Lilith's shin. Brutus was an orange tabby who liked to chase his own tail and tease the kids desperate to pet him before he performed a disappearing act. She stroked a hand over his face and rubbed behind his ears as a purr rumbled to life. "The other things too," she added in a soft voice. "Like the honeysuckle bush and the weird weather. It's all since Mama died."

"You need to get out from under her control, Lil." Essie set a hand on Lilith's arm, her nails a freshly painted coral red. "She's gone. She can't hurt you anymore. You need to move on, make a plan for your life."

Lilith sucked in a breath, hating how even the reminder of her mother's rage could sting. How much she still let those biting words crumple her confidence.

"There's a full-time position available here." Essie bumped her shoulder against Lilith's. "I saw the flyer when I walked in."

Amara looked over her shoulder through a crowd of other children and found her mother's gaze. Essie waved and Amara grinned before turning back to the story.

"Several people have already interviewed for the position." Lilith shrugged and scratched Brutus under the chin. "I didn't feel like throwing my hat in the ring. Besides, I like working part-time here. It's about all the people-ing I can stand in a week."

"Well, you don't need the money." Essie winked. "Maybe you should consider going back to school?"

It was true—between both parents' life insurances and a terrific financial planner, Lilith didn't have to work. Ever again, if she didn't want to.

Still, she hated this conversation. The gentle, nudging reminders of how her life had stagnated.

At twenty-six, she had no purpose, nothing to aspire to. Honestly, she didn't even want a husband or kids. A decision that everyone had an opinion on, which they had to voice. As if her sole purpose as a woman should be to get hitched and pop out babies.

Kate Chopin's *The Awakening* always blossomed in her thoughts during such moments. "The bird that would soar above the level plain of tradition and prejudice must have strong wings."

Only she didn't have strong wings. She had little chicken wings, plucked bald by Mama.

Being a godmother was as close to motherhood as Lilith cared to be. And before Mama got sick, Lilith's pathetic time at Georgia State University had only amounted to wasted money and precious few passed classes. Mama was right, she didn't have the chops for pre-law.

But without Mama to care for, without school to attend, Lilith was unmoored, floating through life without purpose.

Essie patted Lilith's hand and took a deep breath, as if she meant to say something, but decided against it.

"What?" Lilith asked.

Indecision crossed Essie's features. "I have a suggestion, but it's..."

"It's what?"

"Woo-woo."

Lilith cut a side glance at her friend.

"I know, I know." Essie held out her hands, palms up in acknowledgment. "There's a fortune teller on Montgomery Street."

Lilith immediately shook her head. "You know how I feel about that."

That.

The supernatural.

Magic.

"Because your mama made you feel that way." Essie's expression softened. "She's gone now, Lilith. Maybe you should lean into it a little more. Remember how when you first told me about the honeysuckle, how you thought there might be purpose in it? That all this weirdness happening to you is like the world trying to tell you something?"

Lilith rolled her eyes before sliding a grin toward Essie. "I really should stop oversharing with you."

But the playful comment didn't put Essie off. Not when she knew Lilith so well.

Essie glanced around before speaking in a whisper. "Do you remember how the wind would pick up when you were mad? How you always knew the moon was out, even if we weren't near a single window?"

Lilith scoffed. "We were kids, hopped up on stories like *Bayou Magic* and sneak watching *The Craft*. Which, by the way, we really were way too young to be watching. Our imaginations were on overdrive."

"Oh, we were definitely too young to be watching *The Craft*." Essie gave a wicked grin. "But it wasn't just our imaginations." Her smile slipped away. "What about that honeysuckle growing back as soon as your mama died? What about how you said you can *hear* the earth? What about… What about your daddy?"

The pain at those words was as fresh and raw as a decade before when Daddy had gone to work and never come home. When Mama had blamed her.

Essie pulled out her phone, glossy nails catching the light as her fingers flew over the screen. Lilith's phone vibrated in her back pocket.

Essie casually slid her phone back into her purse. "I just sent you the link for the store."

Lilith pulled out her phone and glanced at the screen with a groan. "'Enchanted'? Really?"

"Those dreams don't sound natural, and there is a part of yourself you've been denying your whole life." Essie shrugged a shoulder. "Maybe it's time to explore now that your mama isn't here to stop you."

Before Lilith could argue again, story time ended, and Essie was already helping Amara into her stroller. A quick hug later and they were gone, bumping through the doorway, Cheerios sprinkling out like confetti. Not to be seen again until story time next Saturday.

A young woman approached Lilith with a book in hand. "Can you ring me up, please?"

She handed Lilith a copy of *Practical Magic*, the very title she and Essie had pored over their freshman year in high school. The cover was warm, a slight unmistakable tingle against her fingertips.

Recognition stirred, delicate as the brush of a butterfly's wing. Maybe it was nothing. But maybe it was everything.

Because with that whisper of recognition came the tease of hope, that she might explore what had for so long been forbidden.

"Of course." Lilith ventured back to the cash register to ring the woman up, working around Brutus as he tried to rub his face against her hands.

When the customer left, Lilith glanced down at Essie's text again.

Enchanted.

She was right—of course—maybe there was something to the dreams. And if so, maybe the time had come for Lilith to finally explore the supernatural.

CHAPTER THREE

Sybil

July 1645
Bury St. Edmunds, England

The candles whisked out. All three at once.

Sybil Brantham froze, quill poised above the parchment.

There had been no wind in her bedchamber at Brackenmere Manor. No movement. No breeze to cause even a flicker.

A chill crept up her spine like something living, icy tendrils ticking each vertebra.

An omen.

Light limned the heavy curtains, indicating there was no longer a need for the candles. In Sybil's former life, she would not have been so wasteful. She could not have afforded to be. And certainly, she would not have had beeswax candles, but ones made of tallow, the odor oily and rancid.

Smoke curled from the blackened wicks, cast in a shard of light where the curtains had not been fully closed. Sybil's gut knotted with anxiety.

A gentle knock sounded at her door.

She set aside her quill, clinked the cap onto the pewter inkwell, and closed the ledger. There would be time for noting the monthly stores and expenses later.

"You may enter, Bess," she called out.

The maid bustled in and set to yanking back the curtains. Daylight streamed in and motes that had clung to the heavy velvet frolicked in a wild frenzy that left the air feeling charged.

"Anne can tend to the garden," Bess said disapprovingly as she withdrew the brown worsted dress from the carved oak coffer. "Goodness knows the lass needs more to do."

If Bess let the other servant share her tasks, the girl *would* have more to do. On an ordinary day, Sybil might have reminded Bess of that fact. But those candles snuffing out…

Sybil could not clear them from her mind.

A warning to be sure.

But of what?

There was much to fear in this world where political turmoil tore the country in half, rife with religious persecution, where women were so oft the brunt of the world's injustices with so many of their menfolk at war.

Only a sennight before, four women in Manningtree swung by their necks after an accusation of witchcraft. Sybil scarcely bothered with newsbooks, finding the content more scandal and drivel than actual news. But this one she'd purchased for a sixpence, waiting until she was home to read the horrors.

They had all been women. Women without men to speak for them, to rein them into the boundaries of society, especially prone to such danger. Women, after all, had no voice on their own.

Bess frowned. "Is something amiss, mum?"

Sybil blinked. "No, I… I'm not myself this morning." She offered a pleasant smile in the costly Venetian looking glass on the dressing table. "Working in the herb garden will set me to rights."

Bess helped Sybil into the plain garment, brushing at the

coarse fabric as she would the finest silk. A faint scent of lanolin clung to the woolen gown, reminiscent of Sybil's childhood when no finer fabric could be had.

"Anne seems amiss lately, too." Bess swept Sybil's hair back to plait into a long braid. "I do wish you'd allow me to create more elaborate updos."

The light gleamed against Sybil's rich, black hair. Though she was no great beauty, her features were handsome enough—hazel eyes that were often called clever, and a jaw that was a mite too hard. Her one true glory was her hair, thick and luxurious, dark as velvety night, falling well past her waist.

While Bess would delight at a more stylish fashion, the heavy Puritan population of Bury St. Edmunds frowned upon such extravagance and Sybil had learned well from her mother to maintain a muted existence.

Fully dressed, Sybil left Bess to tend to the bedchamber, but paused outside Jacinda's door. The image of the extinguished candles intruded Sybil's mind like a warning bell.

Was Jacinda the one at risk?

Fear prickled over Sybil's skin.

Quiet as a thief, she pushed into Jacinda's room and let her eyes adjust to the dark. The girl—for she would always be a girl to Sybil—lay sleeping, red-gold hair splayed over her pillow, mouth slack with sleep and slightly agape.

In the corner of the room, away from the window, Jacinda's beloved kestrel sat, tufted into its black speckled feathers. Absent jesses or bells or even a hood, the obedient pet kept watch over the sleeping girl, gleaming black eyes fixed on Sybil.

At Jacinda's wrist was the band of decorative iron, a gift from Sybil earlier that year to mark her sixteenth year. When, ignorant to the power of her bourgeoning abilities, Jacinda had nearly caught the manor on fire. The curtain nearest the hearth still bore a singe from the last time Jacinda had been impassioned with rage.

Some of the tension ebbed from Sybil's shoulders at the sight of that bracelet pressed against Jacinda's skin, quieting her gifts. The girl would come into her knowledge of the earth soon enough. But now was not the time. Not when a threat tainted the air with the odor of ash and death.

Again, Sybil thought of Manningtree, of those women perceived to be so dangerous.

The kestrel shifted on his perch, restless, anxious. As if he too sensed the threat.

She had thought Jacinda protected after Henry and Sybil wed. And there *had* been safety for years. Until his death and the slander suggesting Sybil's elevated widowed status was temptation enough for her to kill her husband.

That the gossip was false made no difference. A rumor once spoken could not be recalled.

And only one single spark was needed to light a pyre.

No, now was not the time for Jacinda to step into her legacy.

Sybil turned away and let the door close silently behind her. If she was going to harvest herbs, she must do so soon, before other demands required her time.

How pleased Mother would be to see Sybil taking to the various tinctures and salves she had spent her stubborn youth turning her nose up at. Just as she would be pleased to see Sybil accepting the earth's power and seeing to Jacinda's care.

Sybil had spent a lifetime promising her mother she would never attract attention, that she would keep them safe.

Whatever portent of ill tidings had whisked out those candles told her such vows—despite her arduous efforts—might well be broken.

CHAPTER FOUR

Sybil

Hours later, Sybil rode the path oft taken between her home and that of her neighbor, the first stop of several for the day. While her neighbor required a willow bark tincture for her headaches, Mr. Cooper needed some nettle tea for his gout, and some feverfew for the Daniels' boy. Even after all these years, her mother's herbal aids for fevers, agues, and everything in between were sought by the community. While Henry hadn't been a lord, his vast fortune put Sybil in a position to help those in need. These days, there were many.

Cloth manufacturing had once been plentiful in Bury St. Edmunds. Before taxes and regulations devoured profits. Before the Dutch came in with the lighter, more modern new draperies that turned everyone's heads.

In times of such strife, Henry's family made wise investments that withstood the test of time. Following his death, Sybil utilized the profits from those investments to ensure his employees remained cared for and well paid.

Her horse's head bobbed aggressively as he walked, riled by her disquiet. But then, Brixton was always in tune to Sybil's moods. He had been ever since she saved him from slaughter after his final failure at the Newcastle racing grounds the king had established not far from Bury St. Edmunds.

Were it not for the lashing scars upon Brixton's pale glossy coat, one would never know how easily life had once discarded him. He was powerful, muscular, and had a fine, superior attitude to match his outward demeanor. At least to all but Sybil, whom he trotted to meet like an adoring pup.

She patted his strong neck. "Don't let my nerves vex you."

A woodlark landed in the middle of the path.

Brixton's ears went back, and he picked up his pace. The poor little bird was forced to hop up and flutter back several paces before returning to the road once more.

"Be kind," Sybil chastised.

Brixton immediately stopped and she dismounted, mindful of her skirts, and approached the familiar little bird.

Behind her, Brixton stamped his hoof with impatience, as he was wont to do when she gave her attention to anything but him.

The bird held a fragrant honeysuckle blossom in its beak—a summons from the other women.

They too must be plagued by the threat of danger.

"Anon," she replied softly.

The little bird dropped the flower and fluttered off.

Brixton grunted out a huff behind her but was too late with his warning.

A steed rounded the corner and she went stiff. The horse's coat was as black as the robes of his rider, both immediately recognizable. They traveled too quickly to allow Sybil time to sweep onto Brixton's back and so she remained standing helpless in the road.

She squared her shoulders, invoking the stoicism of the Roman women in *Plutarch's Lives*. Women who refused to be intimidated by men. Or even by their own fear.

"Good morrow, Magistrate." Sybil kept her tone civil, without warmth.

A man like him needed no encouragement.

"A gentlewoman such as you should not be alone, Mrs. Brantham." His lips curled in an oily smile that made her flesh want to peel away from her body. "Is there something amiss with your steed?"

Sybil tipped her chin with pride for Brixton. "There is not."

"Then I can assume you stopped for some provincial matter." He lifted a brow. "Rustic learnings you acquired from your mother, no doubt."

Ah, he was bringing up her past.

How he would hate if she did likewise. For she recalled the many years when he did not stand a head taller than everyone else, before he acquired that glint of hatred in his eyes. When he was diminutive, and weak, and cowed by the boys who threw mud upon him—and the girls who laughed.

They did not laugh now.

But she would use his excuse to her advantage and approached a silver-green plant rising from the earth like a sharp-petaled rose. "Mullein." She plucked a few velvety leaves. "A simple salve made of this, and a bit of nettle can do wonders for a sore back."

The magistrate's eyes darkened. "It is not my back that is sore."

Sybil clenched her teeth, willing the rise of bile to ebb.

"I seek a wife, as you are well aware." His gaze slid down her body, as if penetrating the layers of cloth and linen. As if he could touch her as easily as he could see her.

Panic sliced through her stoic determination, shattering her resolve with memories of the last time she'd been alone with him. "Doubtless there are many women who would be honored for such a role."

She backed toward Brixton. This far from Brackenmere Manor, there would be no one to hear her scream.

Not that her screams had enlisted help before.

The memory clawed at her throat.

Brixton's tail flicked.

The magistrate's cheeks splotched red beneath the black stubble of his beard. "You know I want you."

She tensed in preparation for a conversation they'd had far too many times. Yet with each rejection, he returned, as if planning to wear her down.

Sybil propped a foot in the stirrup and swept into her saddle. "I will never marry another." Brixton's strong body beneath her was all the assurance she needed that she was safe. For now.

"Because you loved that decaying old man?" The magistrate scoffed in disgust.

She took the reins. "I will not stand idly by as you insult my husband."

"Henry is dead."

The very mention of his name lanced through her chest, his loss as sudden and hot as the fever that had claimed his life.

The magistrate hopped from his saddle and Sybil flinched.

She hated the reflex, but her body reacted on its own accord.

Worse still—the magistrate clearly witnessed her reaction, that one show of weakness. He approached, his boot crushing the honeysuckle blossom into the dirt.

Though Sybil was on horseback and he was not—though she was in a position of protection and power—the moment held breathless terror.

His nostrils flared, as though catching the scent of her fear.

He reached for Brixton's bridle, but the horse snapped his head round and bit the hand that meant to grab him.

The magistrate's howl pierced the air.

"Leave me be, Robert." Sybil clicked her tongue and Brixton tore off, but not before she caught sight of the magistrate glowering after her.

A gust shoved at her back, making the leaves tremble overhead, the pitch of warning heightening.

Whatever danger approached, she had just made things worse.

CHAPTER FIVE

Lilith

A low rumble sounded overhead as Lilith stepped out of Shelver's Books that evening. An impending storm to mirror her churning emotions.

Not that the rain would offer a reprieve from Savannah's July heat. If anything, a deluge thickened the humidity, turning the air into hot sludge, which she struggled to drag into her lungs.

She locked the door behind her, leaving the three bookstore cats happily lapping at their freshly filled bowls—Fred's proper diet restored.

Rushing to avoid being caught in the rain, Lilith ignored her usual inclination to stroll through the city squares and instead dashed down Liberty Street to Montgomery Street as droplets flicked at her in warning. Enchanted blended innocently among a row of shops despite what the store represented to Lilith.

Her steps faltered, weighted by the sight of black candles and tarot cards displayed in the window. Mama would not have approved.

But Essie was right. Mama wasn't here anymore.

Still, Lilith hesitated. The dark interior implied the store was likely closed. She glanced at her watch. Quarter past six. Most stores in the historic area were closed by now.

Ah, well. She'd tried.

Lilith turned away from the store when a clap of thunder reverberated through the sky and echoed in her solar plexus. Wind pushed at her, shoving her back toward the door as fat, angry drops pelted with stinging force.

A wave of tourists erupted from City Market, heads covered with bags and jackets. Lilith turned to the shop, grabbed the handle and pulled. The door flew open, and a little bell tinkled above her head. She stepped into the sweet, smoky fragrance of incense and a blast of cold air that raised goose bumps along her damp skin.

The door closed behind her and silence heightened her awe as she took in the curio cabinets filled with neat rows of tarot cards, candles, and crystals. Art depicting skeletons, witches, and crows lined every square inch of the walls and a chandelier of horns and feathers swayed languidly overhead.

This went against everything Lilith had been taught. It was wrong. But it was beautiful and fascinating. An ache broke open within her, a longing she had repressed for far too long.

Warmth blossomed in the crook of Lilith's right arm, just over her birthmark.

Oh, Essie was going to *love* hearing about this.

Every item in the shop lured Lilith closer, from the images of witches with dark hair wild and spilling over their pale shoulders to the silver moon trinkets in the curved glass of the display case.

Curiosity fed her excitement like a familiar drug, making her blood go hot and her breaths shallow.

Mama had called magic an obsession, one that had made Lilith responsible for Daddy's death.

A knot too large to swallow ached in the back of her throat.

Shoving aside the allure, she retreated toward the door.

"Haven't you spent enough time running from what makes you afraid?"

Lilith jumped. She turned to find a woman in a loose black velvet dress, her long gray hair twisted with raven's feathers.

The woman smiled, revealing teeth that were slightly too crowded. "May I help you?"

Lilith swallowed, the words stuck in her throat.

Yes.

She needed help. Answers. Explanations for why plants stretched toward her, why animals wouldn't stop fawning over her. Why the earth called to her. She needed to know what all this meant.

Especially that nightmare.

The gritty taste of ash filled her mouth.

Her eyes burned with tears and she shook her head with a self-deprecating laugh. "I don't..."

"It's the dream, isn't it?"

Every hair on the back of Lilith's neck stood on end. "Excuse me?"

The woman smiled and curled her fingers gracefully toward herself. "Come."

Lilith's feet moved obediently, following the woman to the rear of the shop where a round table was draped with a paisley silk scarf. Her pulse tap, tap, tapped with apprehension.

Still, she sank into the plush burgundy chair opposite the ornate wooden one where the woman sat.

The table between them was small, but the decision that lay before Lilith was vast.

The air in the rear of the shop pulsed with life. With secrets.

"This is a sacred space," the woman said, as if by way of explanation. She held her hand out in silent request. "May I?"

Lilith's mouth went dry, but she stretched her arm out, settling her hand into the woman's warm one, palm up.

The fortune teller's extraordinarily green eyes glowed in the candlelight as her focus shifted to the crook of Lilith's elbow. "Some believe birthmarks tie us to the past, to our ancestors."

The birthmark tingled, as if stroked.

Lilith tried to swallow. Before she could muster anything to say, the woman leaned over her palm and sucked in a breath.

Lilith sat forward. "What is it?"

"All women have magic within them," the fortune teller replied, her fingertip whispering over Lilith's palm. "But the power in you is exceptional. Your gifts have reawakened. They are raw. Wild. They *must* be tamed." Her voice held an edge.

Lilith shook her head. "I don't—"

But the fortune teller was not done.

"You are stuck in the past. You cannot be free until she is. You must help her."

Air fled Lilith's lungs. "What did you say?"

"The woman from your dream. You must help her." Those strange green eyes found Lilith's. "Or you will unravel, one thread at a time, until you are gone."

The world around Lilith shrank away, leaving her too large, too exposed. "Excuse me?"

The fortune teller did not blink. The flat monotone of her voice resonated in Lilith's soul. "You will cease to exist."

"Cease to exist?" Nerves pitched Lilith's voice. "I don't understand what that means."

"Look into your past. The answers of the present are always in the past."

Panicked frustration surged in Lilith. "That isn't an answer. It's a riddle."

The woman stood. "That is all I have for you."

Lilith didn't move from where she sat, gaping at the woman who spoke in riddles and threats. "That's it?" Lilith asked, a worm of fear eating its way into her heart.

The woman did not appear perturbed at all by Lilith's lack of composure. "You must find the answers soon."

"How soon?"

The fortune teller lifted her shoulder with casual uncertainty. "You have as long as she does."

Another riddle.

Her birthmark burned hot enough to make Lilith flinch. "Who?" she demanded. "Who is *she*?"

The woman closed her eyes, her lids shiny and threaded with blue veins. "Sybil," she breathed.

"How do I—?"

But the woman rose and walked toward the door.

Lilith did not move from her seat, not even as the woman opened the door and offered a sweet smile. As if she had not delivered a cryptic fortune to Lilith and told her she would soon be dead, assuming that's what "cease to exist" meant.

"I don't..." Lilith stood and slowly approached the door, as hesitant to leave as she'd been to enter. "I just don't understand."

"You will." The woman's eyes squinted into half-moons with her deceptively kind smile. She cupped Lilith's cheek in a maternal way. "May the earth guide you."

Lilith had never liked people touching her, the intimacy of a stranger's hands infiltrating the barrier of her personal space. And yet what should have been awkward was instead curiously comforting, a moment of connection between her and the peculiar fortune teller.

Reeling, Lilith stepped outside and the door closed behind her.

The rain had stopped and night had descended, but clouds still gathered overhead, swollen and shifting over the moon.

How long had she been in there?

A sudden realization gripped Lilith. She hadn't paid.

She spun back to the door, but when she pulled at the handle, it did not budge. Locked.

Frowning, she peered into the window, but the shop was completely dark behind the thick plastic. Not a single candle lit.

Closed.

The dream was more intense that night, keeping Lilith from sleep, leaving her to run over the fortune teller's words until they blurred in her mind.

When morning finally came, she looked up Enchanted's phone number. The phone rang several times before a gentle voice answered.

"I had a reading yesterday," Lilith began. "I forgot to pay. And I… I also have some questions."

"Yesterday? The man who does our readings on Saturday called out."

"But I had one last night, around six."

"Honey, we close at five. At least until I can hire someone new." She paused. "Hey, you lookin' for a job?"

Lilith frowned against her phone. "But I was there. Last night. The woman had feathers in her hair."

"No one I know looks like that," the woman said distractedly.

Lilith's heart beat too fast. Her mind racing to keep up. She hadn't imagined the fortune teller. Had she?

"But what she said was so real," Lilith's words were almost a whisper. "That I had to help someone…"

A soft whump came from the other side of the line, like something heavy being set down. "Look…" the voice was slower now, measured "…I don't know who you spoke to or if you maybe had a dream and thought you were here, but the world speaks to us in strange ways, telling us things we need to hear." There was a pause. "Maybe you should listen."

CHAPTER SIX

Sybil

The sweet scent of sun-warmed honeysuckle in the clearing hung incongruously amidst the bitter warning in the air. Sybil rode Brixton through the curtain of weeping birch trees, into the open clearing where the earth's energy pulsed with an undeniable force.

The two women waiting near the honeysuckle ring were the only other ones the birch branches would part for.

"'Ere she is now." The one with thick flame-red hair spilling from beneath a cap waved at Sybil. A swaddled infant lay in the crook of her arm, the newest of Kat's brood. A squirrel chittered on her shoulder, his red fur blending with her brilliant curls.

Edith, the oldest of the three by a few decades, leaned forward, concern darkening her blue eyes like an approaching tempest. "Did you sense danger too?"

Sybil sank onto the ground, completing the circle. Brixton

stayed at her side where he nipped at the grass. "Three candles blew out this morning with naught a whisper of wind."

"I was sewing this morning, a lovely brocade I got my hands on," Kat began. They all nodded encouragingly, knowing she could go on and on about the creations she stitched. "A knife I dropped landed blade first in the floor, straight as the stick stuck up the magistrate's—"

Her daughter fussed and she broke off, jostling the swaddled infant.

"This one's been following me around all morning." Edith looked up where a magpie sat on a sagging branch, feathers iridescent in the sunlight. "Ever since I went out to my garden. Had a fine harvest of beans and parsnips today though."

That harvest would go far in feeding the poorest souls in the surrounding area, the ones so often forgotten. Those too old to walk to the town, or too ill. Edith ensured they all had a full belly and a full heart. That they were never forgotten.

In *The Book of the City of Ladies*, Lady Reason taught that a kind woman is stronger than a roaring man. In that regard, Edith was the strongest soul Sybil had ever met.

Above them, Edith's woodlark who had summoned Sybil earlier sat beside the magpie, chest puffed out and chattering bullishly at its stubborn companion.

They all knew the ditty about the magpies, taught to them since they were babes.

One magpie for sorrow.

Two for joy.

Three for a girl.

Four for a boy.

On and on the rhyme went to thirteen.

"It's the witch trials…" Kat smoothed a lock of red hair from her daughter's brow. "There have been other arrests. Three in Chattisham. Two more in Halesworth."

"And they mean to do more?" Edith asked, her ruddy face going pale. The woodlark flew down from the branches and hopped anxiously at her feet.

Kat nodded. "They say he's coming here next."

"Do you think he's the cause?" Sybil asked, unable to feel her lips as they moved. "Do you think the threat is..." She hesitated, hating to even voice the man's name, as if doing so gave him power. The very man who committed those poor women in Manningtree to their deaths by accusing them of witchcraft. A man whose bloody hands were not wet enough.

The man who called himself the Witchfinder General.

Sybil swallowed and tried again. "Do you think the threat is Matthew Hopkins?"

All at once, a cloud of magpies erupted from the weeping birch trees, an ominous cast of iridescent wings whipping feverishly against stark white bodies.

Thirteen.

Eleven magpies for health,

Twelve for wealth,

Thirteen beware, it's the Devil himself.

Sybil sat transfixed as the odd-numbered cluster of birds soared overhead, then landed in a perfect circle around the women and their animals. Brixton flicked his tail at the one nearest him and stamped a hoof into the soft earth. The birds did not move.

"We must prepare, my sisters," Edith said. "We must protect ourselves."

For they were indeed sisters, chosen by the earth to share the power from the deepest roots in the ground to the crest of a watching moon.

Kat lay a blanket on the ground before her and transferred her sleeping daughter to the soft surface. The red squirrel hopped from Kat's shoulder and sat before the sleeping infant, tail twitching with alert vigilance.

Each woman then turned to the baskets at their side, all filled with innocuous items for their tasks. Items that could draw the power of nature for any spell required.

From Sybil's basket of herbal remedies, she withdrew several sprigs of rosemary. Edith produced a small sack of salt while Kat studied a sprinkling of several polished jet chips that could be easily sewn into a garment. "We could curse him," she suggested.

"That is not our way," Edith reminded her gently. "Work with love, not hate."

Kat gazed down where her sleeping daughter lay nestled beside the little red squirrel. "Oh, I've got love aplenty." But when she looked up, her eyes hardened. "But I've hate aplenty too, especially for men the likes of Matthew Hopkins and the magistrate."

Kat was always willing to push a little too far, to go beyond what the earth wanted to give.

But Sybil did not want either of those men in her mind as they worked the charm. "Let us clear our hearts and minds."

She filled her lungs with fresh air and exhaled away all thoughts of witch trials and wicked men.

"We seek protection." Edith sifted a pinch of salt into the grass in the form of a circle.

The wind stirred, bowing the grass and ruffling the feathers of the tiding of magpies surrounding them.

"Protection for ourselves." Kat laid the black stone chips among the dots of salt in the grass.

The honeysuckle perfume in the air intensified.

"And protection for our loved ones." Sybil scattered the needlelike rosemary leaves across the sacred circle.

The hum of the earth vibrated as power gathered around them.

Each woman grasped the hand of the woman next to her—

palm to palm, fingers entwined. A current of energy ran through them, cold and hot and charged with a unified strength.

All at once, the magpies burst skyward in a wild disarray, as if the ground burned them.

"We seek protection, for ourselves and for our loved ones." They spoke in unison, bound together through age and love and the magic of the earth.

The small pile of salt and rosemary and jet emitted a subtle glow, the way light catches a reflective surface.

Together they closed their eyes, yielding to the earth, giving the whole of their focus to the charm.

Sybil's pulse quickened and they spoke the final line, "We seek protection, for ourselves and for our loved ones."

A cyclone whipped around their circle. An answer to their collective plea.

Sybil's hair lashed against her face and her skirts billowed and flapped at her legs. Despite the chaos of the charm working, a sense of peace washed over her.

All at once, the world went quiet.

They opened their eyes to find the circle of protection gone, absorbed into the earth. Their words had been heeded.

A hushed moment fell over the women. No matter how many spells they performed, they were always awed with wonder and gratitude after.

They rose in silence, each collecting their baskets, Kat gathering her daughter into her arms. Then they bid farewell and departed amid a favorable wind.

As Sybil ducked back under the birch branches, she continued to focus on the protection spell. Not for herself, but for Jacinda.

The girl could not control her gifts, and power in a woman—especially one as extraordinary as Jacinda—was the swiftest path to ruin.

Sybil could take whatever persecution came her way, but she would sacrifice anything to protect Jacinda.

Even her own life.

The remainder of the day whirled by in a frenzy of preparation, of whispered charms and focused intentions to ensure a protective seal on the house. They wouldn't be as powerful as the rite performed with her sisters and could be easily blown away by a strong gust, but still better than nothing.

The harvested herbs that morning were needed to replace the dried stock those charms required.

She climbed the stairs to the topmost floor of Brackenmere Manor, the area set aside for drying herbs. The capacious room remained dark enough to protect the herbs from having their powers leeched away in the sun. Meanwhile, slats beneath the eaves could be opened to allow wind to circulate, preventing mold and rot.

A breeze sifted through, setting the carefully bundled herbs swinging on their strings.

The shush of dried leaves whispered against one another overhead as she gathered what she required into a basket made of twisted weeping birch branches from the clearing.

Laurel leaves to safeguard against evil influences.

Angelica to ward off what was undesirable.

Nettle to create a boundary to keep unwanted intruders at bay.

Rosemary for protection.

As she lifted the bundles of rosemary, the sharp scent washed over her, dredging up memories from seven years ago of the great plague. She'd been able to push away those thoughts earlier in the clearing, when her focus had been on Jacinda's safety. Now they assaulted her.

The recollections of the pest houses, the floors littered with the weak and dying so thickly that she had to pick her way over them with care. Bodies burning with fever, blackened with sores, the air thick with their wet coughing and the odor of impending death.

Sybil's thoughts flinched away from such memories. Her wits were needed for the tasks ahead.

Once the herbs were gathered, Sybil carried them down to her bedchamber and secreted them in her coffer. Later that night, while the household slept, she would sneak into the hidden room within the library.

When Sybil first wed Henry and came to Brackenmere Manor, the library had been her refuge—a place of knowledge, illumination, empowerment. All things women were never supposed to want. All things that terrified men. At least all men, except Henry.

He indulged her curiosity, introducing her to *Plutarch's Lives* where Rome's women taught her courage, then later *Heroides*, which laid bare the hearts of mythic heroines and the wrongs wrought upon them.

His first anniversary gift, *The Book of the City of Ladies* was one she especially cherished. In those pages, she found validation and appreciation for a woman's strength, where a woman's virtues were built prioritizing kindness, intellect, and courage.

In later years, the library offered a place of sanctum as well.

A hollow space was set deep beneath the hearth, unseen to ignorant eyes. What had been built to save priests from the flames of persecution became Henry's ultimate gift to Sybil. Once he understood her knowledge of the earth, that she had been given gifts she could manipulate to help others, he had fortified the room, ensuring its presence would be never be unearthed by others.

He had always been good to her. First saving her and Jacinda from a life of poverty by wedding Sybil after Mother died, a woman whose understanding of the earth's healing properties he had so greatly respected.

Within the safety of that secret room, Sybil hid her mother's grimoire, the one that imparted the knowledge Sybil had been too green and foolish to appreciate in her youth. Her mother had foretold such information would be needed.

Sybil hadn't listened, but her mother had been right.

Mothers so often were.

Sybil understood that now. She only hoped she was not too late.

CHAPTER SEVEN

Sybil

A knock at Sybil's bedchamber startled her. She closed the coffer, sealing away the inventory of herbs she would need for protective charms, and called for the person to enter.

A young maid stepped hesitantly into the room, her clean brown hair pulled back beneath her white cap. "Supper is ready if you please, mum."

Supper? Already?

Sybil looked out the window, surprised to see the sky gilded with the reds and golds of a day dissolving into night. The setting sun never escaped her notice, but then she had been out of sorts the entire day. Ever since the whisked-out candles announced their warning.

"Forgive me, Anne." Sybil pushed to her feet. "I have lost track of time."

Anne's fingers twisted together. "Mrs. Brantham, I..."

She had been an anxious soul since the day Sybil had hired

her ten years earlier—a desperate girl with eyes far older than her scant years and too much family burden on her slim shoulders.

The last time Anne had appeared this overwrought was during the pestilence when her youngest sister came home with a wet cough. Sybil had allowed the child to remain in the manor, keeping her from Anne's ailing parents, likely saving all the lives in their family.

Henry had already been gone by then, no longer at risk.

Sybil went to the young woman. "What ails you, Anne?"

"I..." Anne bit her bottom lip, reddened from her persistent worrying.

Sybil settled a hand on the young woman's arm. "You can tell me."

Anne flicked a nervous smile. "It's my da. He's hurt his back, trying to make himself useful. You know how the menfolk can be."

Sybil relaxed. "I do indeed. In fact, I just found some mullein leaves earlier today. I'll put together a salve for him."

The tension melted from Anne's young face. "Thank you, mum."

If only all of life's problems could be so easily solved.

"There's one more thing..." Anne hesitated, as though debating what to say. "Jacinda has lost another pair of shoes."

Sybil frowned, not simply at the lack of care for expensive wares, but for what Jacinda's bare feet meant. The earth's pulse was stronger against naked soles, the hum intoxicating.

"Thank you for letting me know." Sybil made her way downstairs to the Great Hall where Jacinda already sat at the long table.

At the rear of the room, the fireplace glowed with a fire in the cool summer evening, golden light flickering off the Grecian statues on either side of the hearth. They had been a gift from Henry when they'd wed. Penelope poised mid-step, face tilted with dignity—the queen of Ithaca from *The Odyssey*, a resilient and powerful woman. And Sappho with a scroll in her hand—a poet from the isle of Lesbos, a woman of intellectual curiosity.

Both women Sybil had profound respect for after reading Ovid's *Heroides*.

Such gifts were constant reminders of Henry. Of what Sybil had lost.

She joined Jacinda and made a point of looking under the table. Jacinda's toes wriggled against the rushes, dirt creasing the dimples between her toes.

Sybil sighed as she straightened. "Another pair of shoes?"

Color touched Jacinda's cheeks. "I don't like wearing them. I can't..." She chewed the inside of her cheek. "They are too heavy."

What she meant, of course, was that she could not sense the power of the earth through the thick leather soles.

In truth, Sybil ought to be teaching Jacinda the ways of their gifts. She ought to have years ago, the way Mother had with her.

But Sybil recalled all too clearly how such powers had been difficult to control, how easily life's struggles could be swept away with the right spell. And her abilities were a mere fraction of what Jacinda possessed.

No, such teachings were far too dangerous.

"I think my shoes are near the stables," Jacinda hedged.

"Are you wearing your bracelet?" Sybil asked. If Jacinda was vexed about not feeling the earth beneath her feet, she clearly was not wearing the iron jewelry, which silenced her gifts.

Jacinda slid her hazel eyes to the side, as if the conversation were as easily averted as her gaze.

"Jacinda, you know you must." Sybil's words were harsher than intended, infused with a frisson of fear.

"I know only what you tell me," Jacinda shot back.

The hearth spit out a shower of sparks.

One of the servants entered, a middle-aged widow Sybil had

hired the previous year when the woman's husband—one of their best weavers—had passed.

At least Jacinda had the good sense to quiet in the company of others.

The woman brought in a platter of roasted chicken along with potatoes and string beans. A second servant followed with bread and wine, spiced by Sybil herself with ginger, cardamom, and cinnamon to aid with digestion.

When they left, Sybil regarded Jacinda with a stern expression. "I tell you what you must know to ensure your safety. It is why I insist you wear the bracelet and why I must now tell you to remain indoors."

Jacinda's pretty mouth gaped with outrage and the candles flickered in their sconces. "Indoors? Why? For how long?"

"I'm not certain."

Jacinda shook her head, splotches of red blossoming on her neck and chest. "Henry always said knowledge was power, and yet, you see me disarmed."

The words were a barb and they struck home in a tender place within Sybil's breast. How could Jacinda throw Henry's words at her like a weapon?

"You tell me it is not safe, but you do not tell me why." A spark snapped in Jacinda's expression. "You know I am different, but you do not explain."

A peal of thunder rumbled outside, and sparks floated up from the glowing red logs in the hearth.

"Jacinda…" Sybil said in a warning tone.

"How do you know about the iron?" Jacinda demanded. "Why do you make me wear it?"

"You aren't ready."

"I *am* ready," Jacinda cried.

There was a strange shift in the air, a weighty pressure, and flames burst to life in the hearth, sending a wave of heat washing toward them.

Sybil stood abruptly. "Enough."

Jacinda was right. Henry touted learning and knowledge, and he would have encouraged Sybil to instruct Jacinda. But Sybil knew the girl too well. Knowledge would only whet her appetite for more. Jacinda would fall upon her gifts with an unrelenting zeal—pushing, testing, taking—all with a force that challenged anyone to stop her.

Power gathered and vibrated within Jacinda, unlike anything Sybil had ever witnessed. Greater even than what Sybil drew with Kat and Edith. Jacinda veritably crackled with the energy that swirled around her, a vortex barely tethered and desperate to be unleashed.

What would such strength do?

As a child, Jacinda had been precocious, eager to absorb everything from Mother that Sybil had so readily ignored. Now as a teen, the girl brooded with sullen anger, begrudging her sheltered life. Not understanding the dangers.

Not realizing how readily women with strength were silenced. How often they were seen as a threat.

That had been Sybil's fault.

In fact, so much of Jacinda's hardships had been Sybil's doing.

But in a chasm of regret, where was Sybil to begin in setting things right?

Especially now when the earth continued to warn Sybil that they were at risk.

How easily it would be for Jacinda to be discovered. Arrested. To dangle from the end of a rope.

Everything in Sybil flinched back in horror from the mental image.

"Now isn't the time." The protest was weak, but all she could offer.

"You are my sister, not my mother." Jacinda's eyes glinted with the fire of youth and naive ignorance. "Mother would never have handled me with such disregard."

The room was suddenly too stuffy, the aroma of roasted chicken overpowering and unappealing. Sybil was desperate to be outside. To breathe. To let the wind speak to her, to guide her.

She mumbled an excuse and pushed back from the table, leaving Jacinda glowering after her, eyes boring into her back like burning embers.

The night embraced Sybil, cool and welcoming. Dampness hung in the air from an incoming storm, one dredged up by the mix of the roiling emotions between Jacinda and Sybil both.

Sybil closed her eyes and breathed in the rich scents of fertile earth and fragrant blooms and herbs. Eager to drink in the moon's strength, she tilted her face upward.

But instead of fortitude, she was imbued with a sense of unease, as though her skin fit too tightly.

Her eyes flew open, staring into the sky. She staggered back, her knees soft with shock.

Staring down at her from between the churning clouds was not the beautiful full face of a silvery white moon, but one cast in a violent red hue.

A blood moon.

One that bespoke impending misfortune and doom.

CHAPTER EIGHT

Lilith

Rain pattered against the windows and the old wooden floors groaned beneath Lilith's pacing from room to room.

The house embodied her past, handed down from mother to daughter since the nineteenth century. Mama had wanted to escape the legacy, always seeking something more before she was tethered by Lilith's birth.

Was *this* what the fortune teller had meant when she said the answers to the past were always in the present? Was there really a clue in Mama's unwanted inheritance?

Lilith drifted into the study, the room that reminded her most of Daddy. Books filled the mahogany shelves, legal texts long out of date. She'd just dusted the day before, but old houses weren't airtight, and a thin layer of dust dulled the glossy surfaces. The lightest scent of sandalwood still clung to the room, a reminder that her father's presence had once been there, the only warmth that house had ever known—at least in Lilith's lifetime.

This was the only room that hadn't been touched by her mother, the only one not smattered in an explosion of florals and ornate gold-painted frames and brass fixtures. Boutique buys did not equate to good taste. The gaudy decor hemmed her in as she continued her aimless pacing.

She stopped, pausing in front of the door she seldom entered, and her heart gave an involuntary lurch.

Hesitant, she settled her fingertips on the cool brass doorknob. Gritting her teeth, she opened the door.

Darkness blanketed the room. Mama's presence lingered there—suffocating, oppressive, absorbing whatever light eked into Lilith's life. The odor of lilies was still pervasive, a flower Lilith had always despised.

They'd been Mama's favorite. She'd ordered bouquets of them for herself, adorning the house with crystal vases bursting with their aggressive blossoms and sprinkling the table with thick orange pollen.

Stomach swirling with unease, Lilith stepped into her mother's room. The bed was piled with floral pillows, positioned exactly as Mama preferred.

Lilith opened the closet, devoid of all the designer clothes once crowded within. Donated to Dress for Success to help women reenter the workforce—a way for Mama to do some good in the world, even if it was post-mortem.

At the top of the closet was a box labeled "Ancestry."

Lilith pulled the hatbox down and hurried from the room, slamming the door shut behind her. As if the memories could be as easily sealed away.

The box was heavier than expected, weighted with Mama's hopes that they were related to a Hollywood star, or even nobility in some distant country with an inheritance that could have made them rich.

They weren't.

All those years of Mama wishing for wealth, and it finally did come—in the form of an insurance payout.

Guilt squeezed Lilith's chest.

Daddy had died when she was in high school. His life was worth more than his outrageous insurance policy, and though Mama enjoyed spending that windfall, she never forgave Lilith. As if sensing his death made Lilith responsible.

She'd tried to stop him from going into the office that day, begging him to see a doctor instead.

She shoved the memory from her mind and sank onto the stiff couch. Suddenly the moment seemed too poignant, like she was standing on the edge of a cliff knowing once she leaped off, she could never go back.

Desperate for a mindless distraction, she picked up her phone.

Essie's last text was unanswered: How did it go at Enchanted? Please don't tell me you chickened out.

There had been too much to say via text.

She wished Essie was there with her, to rehash the entire weird scene from Enchanted, to get Essie's real-world advice paired effortlessly with her easy humor for a bit of levity.

If Lilith texted her right now, Essie would be on the doorstep in less than fifteen minutes.

But Sundays were family days for Essie, a chance to enjoy her husband and Amara without phone calls and courtroom drama. Given how hard Essie worked, Lilith would never pry her from that special quality time.

With a sigh, Lilith set the phone down and flipped the top off the hat box.

Sepia-toned photographs stared up at her. Several faded documents, thin as onion skin, and more than a few printouts were piled haphazardly inside.

Mostly documents tracing the women who had owned the house on East Waldburg Street before Lilith's grandmama, who'd died before Lilith was born. A lineage with wealth that peaked in the 1800s before eventually crumbling into poverty along with most of Savannah.

That is, until *Midnight in the Garden of Good and Evil* came out and breathed life back into their sleepy Southern city. Lilith had been a girl then, when the historic district was transformed into a line of high-end stores, quaint boutiques, and fine dining, and the squares were reinvented with colorful splashes of azaleas and camellias.

She continued to riffle through the box, finding a handful of census printouts and various documents with approved requests to alter the exterior of the house. You couldn't paint a shade off from the current house color or replace a spindle on the balcony without approval from the Savannah Historic Association. Lord, did she know that…

At the bottom of the pile was a journal.

Floral, of course, blooming with Victorian roses.

The moment Lilith's fingers grazed the cover, warmth tingled from her fingertips to her birthmark.

The opening had several paragraphs crossed out. Lilith skimmed the writing beneath the bold X of dark ink.

How Mama had always felt she'd been missing something in her life, the same as her mama had felt.

How she thought she could fill that void with money—until Lilith's father died, then she realized maybe that void could have been filled with love.

Lilith doesn't have that emptiness in her.

Lilith's pulse stuttered at the sight of her name in her mother's journal.

She thinks magic completes her, and maybe it does. We didn't imagine that honeysuckle vine growing toward her.

Most likely, I resent her. Because I know I'll never have that. I tell her the magic is all nonsense. Maybe it's my way of protecting her from being hurt like I have, but part of me realizes I might be making her feel small, the way Mama did with me. To make her feel the way I always have.

The journal almost slipped out of Lilith's hands. Mama hadn't feared magic—she'd feared Lilith, been jealous of her.

Resentful.

Something painful twisted in Lilith. Something she didn't have the time, energy, or capacity to unpack.

She returned her attention to the journal, this time her mother's crisp handwriting detailed their ancestry, dating through Savannah's existence and reading like a history lesson from school.

Their family had been one of the first to relocate to Savannah after it was established as the first city in the newly claimed thirteenth colony of Georgia. There was a grandfather killed in the late eighteenth century while trying to reclaim the city from British rule. More than a few ancestors fell victim to yellow fever.

Before Savannah, the family had been in Maryland.

Lilith continued reading, skimming Mama's handwriting. A strange scent caught Lilith's attention. Lavender and…hay?

Brackenmere Manor—Bury St. Edmunds, England.

An image flashed in Lilith's mind, a Great Hall with glossy wood paneling, a hearth that covered almost the entire rear wall, carved with two women standing on either side adorned in Grecian attire. Overhead, beams arched like a ribcage, stretching above straw-like rushes that were slick underfoot. The scent of hay and lavender grew stronger, revealing something else.

Meadowsweet.

How could she identify an herb she didn't even know?

Lilith blinked herself back into her living room in Savannah, her heart slamming.

What the hell was *that*?

She hadn't imagined that room. She had *been* there.

Even now, the redolent fragrance of the floor rushes still lingered.

Fingers trembling, she turned the page…and froze.

Sybil Brantham.

Burned as a witch.

The fortune teller's voice hissed in Lilith's mind, "*Sybil.*"

Thunder cracked outside, lightning flashed, and the entire house went dark.

CHAPTER NINE

Sybil

Over the years, Sybil learned that Jacinda's disposition improved when given time alone.

Sybil had not been such a child at Jacinda's age. No—at sixteen, she had fallen in love and had her life planned out. A familiar pain flared within her, one old enough that it ought to have calcified by now.

Never would she love a man the way she had John Griffin. Two years her senior, he had given her his heart. They'd pledged their undying love to one another, vows that made John's father balk. After all, a landowner's son could not wed the peasant daughter of the local healer. In all Sybil's life, she had never been made to feel so low as the day John's father looked at her, lip curled in disgust.

A woman silenced by the world and crushed under the heel of the rich. She had turned away John's affection, refusing to spend her life treated with such disdain.

That day, she made a different vow—that never again would she allow someone to treat her as less than. And though she'd intended to improve her station, even she had not expected to rise so high as when Henry proposed.

What's more, he understood that her heart was not hers to give. He himself had lost a wife who'd died birthing a stillborn child two decades before and declared he, too, could never love again.

Theirs had been a marriage of respect. Rather than silence her questions, he encouraged them. He offered her education and knowledge.

She had been scarcely twenty when she first met him in her mother's hut, when he'd come to learn from the local healer. Back then, Sybil had been filled with more questions than answers. While he was content to have her mother explain the creation of tonics and tinctures, Sybil had wanted to know the intricacies of the world.

He had gifted her with responses to all she'd asked.

Now she had even more questions, but had also gained the knowledge to understand that one would never live long enough to see them all answered.

No, Sybil had not been like Jacinda, who should be an adult, yet sulked like a child.

The hour was past noon, far beyond when Jacinda ought to be awake.

How she could sleep past the sunrise baffled Sybil. As soon as the brilliance of the sun peeked over the trees, the energy in Sybil's body forced her awake.

But Jacinda needed to rouse. They had to discuss their argument the prior evening.

Sybil strode across the Great Hall, her shoes whispering over the rushes when a hard object underfoot hissed metallically beneath her shoe.

Sybil lifted her foot and bent to retrieve the item.

A single band of iron curled and twisted into a fine bracelet.

Even touching the thing made the world around Sybil go uncomfortably quiet.

Was it any wonder Jacinda refused to wear the bracelet?

Mayhap Sybil ought to confess all to Jacinda.

But then the memory of the blood moon surfaced in Sybil's mind.

Ominous. Threatening.

A warning to heed.

Sybil glanced to the hearth, recalling how the fire mirrored Jacinda's rage.

No, teaching Jacinda was far too dangerous. She would push past every boundary, eager to explore a power greater than Sybil had ever known.

With an irritated huff, Sybil climbed the stairs.

The fragrance of rosemary and sage hovered throughout the manor, notes of protection adorning every window and doorway, discreetly sprinkled by Sybil in the middle of the night. The barrier of those enchantments lent her a sense of peace.

The door to Jacinda's bedchamber was closed, and dread slowed Sybil's steps. There would be an argument, of course, the hurling of painful words, the frustration of Sybil trying to infuse sense into the girl. Before the ordeal even began, Sybil was exhausted.

Walking away would be so easy, so effortless. If she did not love Jacinda so much, she would have. The time had come to have a conversation with the girl, to finally admit the truth. About everything.

With the weight of what she must do upon her shoulders, Sybil pushed the door to the room open. "Jacinda, I..."

The bed was rumpled, unmade, but devoid of its occupant. Sybil glanced about the room with a frown. "Jacinda?"

No answer followed.

The kestrel's perch sat empty, a single speckled feather resting beside the base.

Unease coiled low in Sybil's stomach. "Jacinda?"

There was no answer.

Sybil swept through the house, calling for the wayward teen, until the entire household rushed about with her name on their lips. Not that their efforts mattered. Sybil already knew the truth.

Jacinda was gone.

Not only was she outside the manor, but she was also not wearing her bracelet.

All that wild energy fueling her gifts could alter the weather, bend nature, and even change the course of the heavens. She once held night off by an hour, hanging the sun in the sky a full hour beyond its time.

The Witchfinder General was coming. He could be anywhere, and Jacinda was reckless. Careless.

If he caught her. If Jacinda were arrested. If she were convicted of witchcraft…

The frantic staccato of her heart left no room for breath and Sybil fought to keep her panic at bay.

Wherever Jacinda had gone, Sybil must find her.

Which meant leaving the house. Putting herself at risk.

But Sybil would do it.

She would sacrifice all for Jacinda.

CHAPTER TEN

Lilith

The electricity did not come back on in the next half hour, but Lilith's laptop was able to connect to the internet through her hot spot to search for Brackenmere Manor.

BrackenmereManor.com was the first hit on Google.

That was easy.

Lilith clicked the link and was met with a clunky website. The neon-blue background featured a picture of a dilapidated three-story Tudor manor–style house. Though ivy crawled up the parchment-colored exterior and the house sagged in on itself, Lilith recognized the estate as if she'd been there.

She could recall the original glory so vividly with its stone path leading to the entrance, framed by manicured bushes shaped like giant gumdrops.

A lightheaded sensation swept over her, the same as when she was sucked into the dream. She paused for a steady breath, grounding herself like Essie always encouraged.

"I'm in Savannah," Lilith said aloud, feeling silly. "I'm sitting in my living room on a hideous couch Mama bought when I was ten."

She scowled at the floral couch.

It really was a crime against upholstery.

Essie was right, there was a lot more life to live now that Mama was gone. Maybe Lilith might start by replacing the furniture.

If she *existed* long enough.

Whatever that meant.

Still, her pulse raced a little faster. Because regardless of what "ceasing to exist" meant, it sounded ominous.

"I'm in Savannah," Lilith repeated loudly to absolutely no one. "Sitting on this floral monstrosity I need to replace."

She lowered her gaze to the website, this time without the disorienting thought of its former appearance.

Essie really was right about everything. So unfair.

There were three drop downs available on the site. One for more pictures, of which there were none. Another with a history of Brackenmere Manor, detailing the construction in the mid-1500s by a wealthy wool merchant. And a third with a Contact Me form along with a broken link to a bed and breakfast.

Given the website's ancient design, the Contact Me probably would disappear into a dusty old AOL inbox no one had checked in a decade.

Still, nothing ventured, nothing gained.

Lilith filled out her contact information and jotted a quick inquiry about the property's history, adding Sybil's name for good measure. She didn't mention the broken B&B link. No sense in riling them up before they even replied.

If they replied.

Lilith hit send and closed her laptop.

Hands shaking slightly, she poured herself a glass of chilled Chardonnay and pushed out the back door, into the garden. Into the night.

The rain had stopped, but the earth was wet beneath Lilith's bare feet, and the cool caress of waterlogged grass sent a sense of peace up her legs and through her entire body. Moonlight peered through curtains of hanging moss draped over the gnarled branches of their single live oak. She closed her eyes and tilted her face to dappled beams, bathing herself in silver light.

Her nerves calmed and a sense of strength washed over her.

She set aside the wineglass, no longer wanting the dulling effects of alcohol. Emboldened, she approached the honeysuckle vine.

Rather than fight the allure, she inhaled the sweet fragrance and gently stroked one of the leaves. The vine grew toward her, sprouting tender green leaves.

"Are you trying to tell me something?" she whispered into the quiet evening air.

Red honeysuckle blossoms flared open in reply.

But rather than surrender to the weight of her confusion, Lilith basked in the beauty of the garden. In the exquisite impossibility of something so otherworldly being *possible.*

Surely all of this could not be for nothing.

"Will you help keep me from ceasing to exist?" she asked.

A breeze blew through the warm, still night like a reassuring caress.

"Thank you," she mouthed. Her gratitude was for no one in particular, but for everything. For the earth around her, the wet soil under her bare feet, the garden with all its powerful secrets, and the honeysuckle that made her believe it was okay to hope.

She returned inside with a profound sense of peace and opened her laptop to find a reply waiting for her from Asher@BrackenmereManor.com.

She clicked the email and read.

Miss Legare,
Thank you for your interest in Brackenmere Manor. I'm afraid it's in a sorry state at present, and I don't have as much history as I'd like. I do know that the estate has been in my family for several generations, sometime after your ancestor, I believe. With apologies, there is little else I can offer.

Another email had arrived one minute later from Asher@BrackenmereManor.com, this one with a curiously different tone.

My dear, I have failed to mention there is a fully operational bed and breakfast on the property. If you come stay with us, you are welcome to explore the old manor house whenever you desire. For your convenience, I have attached an updated link with information on our accommodations. Guests have been quite happy, as you can see from our stellar reviews!

Yet another email arrived ten minutes later, from the same email address.

Miss Legare,
Apologies, I forgot my aunt still has access to this email address and apparently, we have both emailed a reply. She is quite proud of her bed and breakfast as you can tell. Do not let her badger you into coming.

Lilith could picture a stodgy old Asher and his even older aunt in separate rooms, pinging emails back and forth in an internet-fueled tete-a-tete.

The link Asher's aunt sent worked, revealing a modern, ready-made website depicting three simple bedrooms, each with an en suite, all done in neutral-colored furnishings and decor. Judging by the booking calendar, the property did not appear popular, but Trip Advisor's dozen reviews confirmed the beds were comfortable, the breakfast was delicious, and the entire thing was legit and not some trap for a serial killer to lure in victims.

But travel to England?

Could she do that?

She did have a passport—from the trip to Italy she'd planned with her last boyfriend. He'd been her waiter at Local 11 Ten restaurant one night and had offered to walk her home after his shift. They'd taken go-cups of merlot and strolled Forsyth Park, outlasting dog walkers and even the art students out for late night sketches. From there, she'd pictured a life with him, maybe moving in together, getting a cat…and they'd booked the trip to Italy.

He'd been a reprieve from Mama until the pandemic, when the trip to Italy had to be postponed and the roommate he swore was "just a friend" turned into something more.

Forced proximity. Even now, Lilith rolled her eyes at her own stupidity. She knew better. After all, how many books featuring that trope passed from her hands to eager customers at Shelver's Books on a regular basis?

The thought of Shelver's brought up another obstacle. She couldn't go anywhere until they hired their full-time employee.

Her birthmark grew warm, the skin tingling.

There was a certainty in her gut that this was the past the fortune teller had meant, that this Brackenmere Manor could help answer the questions she didn't even know how to ask.

For all the excuses she found to remain comfortably at home in Savannah, everything in her demanded she hop on the next plane to England.

Lilith picked up her phone, finally replying to Essie: I think I need to go to England.

She replied immediately: If that fortune teller told you to take a trip to Europe, I need to book an appointment stat!

Lilith bit her lip, weighing whether to elaborate on her visit to Enchanted. Mentioning the whole thing felt a little heavy, a lot strange, and way too underexplained to even begin to describe.

Especially when she didn't even understand exactly what happened herself. But whatever was pulling her toward England, she needed to give in, to find answers.

For Sybil.

For herself.

For that horrible warning hanging in her thoughts like a curse.

You will cease to exist.

CHAPTER ELEVEN

Sybil

Sybil didn't spare a thought for her own safety as she swept onto Brixton's back and left Brackenmere Manor in search of Jacinda. Her horse required no guidance as he trotted onward with purposeful intent. Like Kat's little red squirrel and Edith's woodlark, Brixton was imbued with the same gifts as the daughters of the earth.

He thundered down the path of his own accord, his pace every bit that of a horse once employed at the king's races. As Sybil feared, they turned toward Bury St. Edmunds. The sky above the town congealed in a dark, angry storm, wind tugging in every direction as they neared.

This was no ordinary squall, but one manipulated by a woman of great power.

One who did not know how to control what roiled inside her in a blend of unfettered strength and unbridled emotion.

Sybil only hoped she could find Jacinda before others took notice.

Even before Sybil crossed the town gates, she caught the angry cries of a mass gathering.

Memories of the pestilence slammed into her. When barley was needed to feed the poor and too many brewers were forced to shutter their doors. A mob gathered, angry, violent, in want of ale, the potent sort from brewhouses that numbed their pain, dimmed the brilliance of their loss.

Homes and shops were ruined that day, and more than a few people injured.

A mob was a dangerous thing indeed.

And now they had gathered once more, the jostling swarm visible as Sybil traveled through the massive arch of Eastgate Street.

People clustered the trail to Angel Hill before the crumbling abbey, torn apart by King Henry's wrath against the Catholic Church a century before. Where once pilgrims gathered to witness St. Edmund's relic, now a new crowd formed. One inflamed by a handful of desperate years plagued with pestilence, low harvests and starvation, religious strife, and political upheaval that left their country warring against itself.

Witch.

A word cut clearly through the din. A single, simple word, barbed with a need to control any woman who lived her life without a man to keep her in order. Women who learned too much, whose wealth and land were their own, women with tongues that would not still when challenged.

Hag.

Devil's servant.

Witch.

Lightning split the sky above.

Brixton remained steadfast despite the chaos and the unnatural storm whipping the world into confusion. Sybil was not so calm, her mind racing through the horrors of the past and what could unfold in the present as she frantically searched every face they passed.

Where was Jacinda?

A kestrel sat atop a cart, shifting restlessly from foot to foot.

And where there was the kestrel…

A glint of red-gold hair showed in the crowd.

Sybil leaped from her steed, leaving him where he stood, secure in the knowledge he would not wander off, and hastened toward Jacinda.

She grabbed the girl's arm, and Jacinda turned to her, eyes wide in her small pale face.

"We must go," Sybil said quickly.

Jacinda shook her head.

Kill the witch.

Thunder growled overhead and lightning flickered in the rolling black clouds.

"Cease at once," Sybil said under her breath.

"I can't." Jacinda's lower lip trembled. "I can't."

She reached for the girl's hand. A current buzzed over Jacinda's skin with an energy that nearly burned Sybil's fingers. Sybil did not let go. Instead, she pushed her focus into feeding her own energy into Jacinda's.

The connection between them opened Jacinda's emotions to Sybil, the same churning wild storm inside as brewed in the sky above.

"Concentrate," Sybil soothed.

Jacinda's shaky breath grew even and the burning power on her skin cooled.

With a low rumble of protest, the clouds slowly broke apart.

The kestrel made a soft chittering from where he remained perched on the cart.

But even as the intensity of the storm abated, a new charge

crackled in the air, and the crowd surged forward. Jacinda dropped Sybil's hand as they both followed the stares.

A woman staggered down the middle of the street. Her bare feet caked with dirt, her face obscured by strands of stringy gray hair. Mud coated her cloak, making its color and design indistinguishable.

Sybil gaped in mute horror at the poor woman bent beneath her suffering, wilting beneath the hatred of the inflamed mob.

"Hang her," someone shouted.

Cheers of approval chorused the suggestion.

A man beside Sybil lobbed what looked to be a potato toward the woman. It exploded with slick brown rot. "Hag."

The kestrel turned his head toward a lone bird following the woman's progress.

A woodlark.

Recognition slammed into Sybil.

The persecuted woman turned, revealing a familiar face, confirming what Sybil already knew.

Edith.

A hand gripped Sybil's arm, so tight, so fearful, it could only be Jacinda. "Help her."

Temptation ensnared Sybil—to do something brave and stupid. And entirely useless.

No.

The word resonated in Sybil's mind, Edith's voice as clear as if she'd spoken aloud.

"She's hideous," a woman cried. "Foul creature, lured by Satan!"

And there it was, the accusation that homely features were manifested by the evil inside.

Edith had been plagued by warts from an early age, immune to every application she tried. Vinegar washes in moonlight, garlic and bacon and pig's blood, even potatoes that had been rubbed over her skin and then buried. Those potatoes decayed into the ground long ago, but the warts remained.

As a result, the world had been cruel to Edith for her lack of beauty, and that viciousness bore its mark upon her, leaving her withered.

But for all that hatred, she gave only love.

The gnarled hands that curled around her filthy cloak had tended to those forgotten by the rest of the town. The gaze that had lowered in shame at the crowd's jeers looked upon others without malice or judgment. The back bent protectively forward had toiled in a garden for those who could not provide for themselves.

Witch.

Hag.

Sinner.

On and on, the accusations flew as the pitiful progression of a good woman being defeated by the evil of a mob slowly crept by.

The weight of a stare pulled Sybil's gaze across the street where Kat stood, her flame-red hair bright against an emerald green bodice. Like Sybil, she did not move.

One of her children had his face pressed into her skirts, her hand secure on the center of his back. Protective.

The sheen of Kat's tears mirrored Sybil's own turmoil. Guilt. Shame. Horror over the necessity of their impotent silence.

Down the road, someone shoved Edith, sending her sprawling. A man lunged forward—not to offer aid, but to land a kick to her ribs before the guard could issue a lazy threat to leave the prisoner be.

Then they turned up Cook Row, toward the old jail, and Edith was gone.

The crowd dispersed and Sybil clasped Jacinda's hand in a

way she had not done since the girl had been a child, yet Jacinda did not protest as she would on any normal occasion. Together, they picked their way through the lingering crowd until they reached Brixton.

Sybil turned to Jacinda to lift her onto the horse. But the girl did not move and instead choked out a sob, beginning to cry in earnest.

Overhead, the sky split open and rain poured down as the earth wept for Edith.

As it would soon weep for the many women who would follow, for Sybil understood more than she wished to share with Jacinda.

The arrests had only just begun.

CHAPTER TWELVE

Lilith

Lilith turned down Brackenmere Manor Lane on the wrong side of the road, at least compared to what she was used to in America. The rental car jostled over the barely paved path toward a rooftop peering above the overgrown trees in the distance.

A thick forest of oak trees crowded the fern-strewn ground in a way that was strangely, intimately recognizable. That familiarity pressed at the edges of her awareness, demanding her attention.

"If adventures will not befall a young lady in her own village, she must seek them abroad." Lilith had always been intrigued by that line from Jane Austen's *Northanger Abbey*. Too bad, in this case, fate had decided there were not enough adventures to befall Lilith in Savannah.

Just over a week had passed since her discovery of the manor. In that time, Shelver's Books had hired a full-time employee and generously allowed Lilith to take two weeks off to explore Bury St. Edmunds.

Flying in an airplane wasn't as terrifying as she'd thought—at least once the slight issue of her missing ticket had been resolved, thanks to the email she'd saved with her flight information. The stomach-dipping disorientation of takeoff and landing, however, was not dissimilar to what she experienced when she fell into the nightmare.

Those dreams had become more frequent since visiting the fortune teller, more vivid and insistent, as if something dormant had been awoken.

Traveling to England was only the first step. The next would be to visit Brackenmere Manor in the hopes she could pull a Nancy Drew and uncover something that would crack the mystery open, so any of this made sense.

Lilith slowed the car, tires crunching over the gravel driveway as she parked before the two-story home.

The building was likely constructed within the last few decades, with creamy walls and slate-colored shutters. An arching trellis of roses framed the door with pink blossoms big as dessert plates.

Mama would've killed for roses like that.

Lilith climbed out of the car and paused at the trunk, immediately regretting her heavy suitcase with all that gravel to contend with. Before she could haul it from her trunk, the front door opened and a man about her age strode out.

A boxer loped along at his side, face tucked into grumpy folds that matched his owner's stern expression.

The man's gait was sure and confident as he approached, his blue eyes bright against the navy T-shirt that stretched over his broad shoulders and revealed a muscular physique she couldn't help but notice.

"Lilith, I presume?" he asked in a posh accent. But then, to her, all the accents in England so far had sounded posh.

Not only was he ripped, his head was as clean-shaven as his jaw. She'd been a sucker for bald men since that drummer she'd had a fling with during her first year of college.

She had assumed Asher was an old man, living alone with an even older aunt, but apparently she'd been wrong…

"That's me." Lilith smiled at him. "Asher?"

He gave a nod. "And this is Toby." He stroked a hand over the boxer's crinkled head.

While his welcome could use a dose of Southern hospitality, Essie would be delighted to hear the report on the hot bed and breakfast owner.

"Hi, Toby." Lilith beamed down at the boxer, who sat back on his fleshy rump and stared at her.

Asher reached for her luggage, biceps bunching as he lifted the suitcase like it wasn't full of books and way too many creature comforts. The red HEAVY tag fluttered from the handle.

He hesitated, still holding her bag. "I hadn't anticipated you would be here so quickly."

Lilith glanced at her watch. Half past eleven in the morning. "I'm actually an hour later than I said I would be."

"I mean, from the time of your inquiry on the website to your decision to come to England." He narrowed his eyes and the corners crinkled in a way that suggested he might be slightly older than her twenty-six years. "Coming to Brackenmere Manor must be very important to you."

"Practically a matter of life or death." Lilith gave an awkward chuckle.

His brow furrowed in what might be concern, but was gone in an instant. "I imagine you'll want to see the manor today then?"

"If that's okay?" She hated the question in her tone when her need to see the old house was borderline desperate.

Asher turned toward the bed and breakfast, and Toby grunted up, toddling after him.

Feeling a little unsure, Lilith followed them beneath the trellis where the scent of roses pulled at her and the leaves quivered in her direction.

The house inside was light and airy, with sunlight spilling in through large picture windows. Potted plants were scattered in various corners and on tables, their leaves lush and verdant. The scent of cinnamon clung to the room, as if a pot of tea had been freshly brewed.

An old woman sat in a recliner with a green caftan draped over her lap, so only her blouse was visible. There was a slight red stain near the top button. Her gaze caught Lilith and the clicking needles stilled in her hands.

"Lilith, this is my Aunt Jacqueline." Asher spoke louder than he had earlier, likely for the benefit of his aunt. "The one who so eagerly welcomed you to come." He slid a glance at the older woman. "This is her establishment, but I've been persuaded into helping her." He said *persuaded* as if he really meant *forced*.

Asher's aunt smiled. Her eyes were the same shade as her nephew's, albeit with more warmth. "Welcome to Brackenmere Bed and Breakfast." There was a thready frailty to her voice. "I must say, we don't have as many visitors as we used to. You're here for family history, correct?"

"Yes, ma'am," Lilith replied. You could take the girl out of the South, but you couldn't take the South out of the girl. "My ancestor lived here back in the seventeenth century before it belonged to your family."

The old woman's face suddenly appeared stricken, but she blinked and recovered quickly. "Ah yes, I recall from your electronic mail."

"She means email," Asher said under his breath.

"Legare..." His aunt tilted her head, pronouncing Lilith's last name like Luhg-aire. "I don't recall any French having owned the manor."

"We pronounce it La-gree," Lilith replied, saying her name like she always had.

The older woman grinned and set her knitting needles down. "Oh, I do love your Southern accent. Where are you from in America?"

Lilith suppressed a frown. Not everyone in Savannah had an accent. She thought she didn't either.

Daddy had moved all over when he was a boy, never staying anywhere long enough to absorb an accent before returning to Savannah, where he'd been born. But Momma liked to talk like she was old Savannah nobility, and Lilith had done everything she could to sharpen the soft drawl from her speech.

"I'm from Georgia," Lilith replied with careful enunciation. "But apparently, a Jacinda Brantham moved to Maryland in the mid-1600s."

Asher's aunt nodded in understanding, as if this were the most natural thing to know. "Likely with the colony founded by Bartholomew Gosnold. He was from Bury St. Edmunds."

"Who is he?" Lilith asked, intrigued to learn more.

Asher reappeared in the doorway without her realizing he'd even left. He handed her a set of keys with a brass plate labeled "Brackenmere" with the number one. "Aunt Jacqueline, I'm sure our guest would like to recover from her travel."

"Actually, do you think we can see the manor?" Lilith asked, more intrigued to visit Brackenmere Manor than to learn about someone who moved to America.

"You don't want to unpack first?" Asher's eyes narrowed slightly.

"Of course she can go to the manor right now," his aunt

scolded in a light tone, even as she smiled at Lilith. "Why, that's the sole purpose of your trip, is it not?"

Asher shot his aunt an irritated look, but Lilith grinned at her. "Thank you. It's so nice to meet you."

The woman nodded sagely, eyes twinkling. "And I've been waiting to meet you."

CHAPTER THIRTEEN

Lilith

Lilith followed Asher down a worn footpath in the grass, grateful to be in the sunshine after being locked within a plane for hours and then a car for a couple more. "What did your aunt mean when she said she was waiting to meet me?"

Asher shrugged. "She's eager to have a guest at her bed and breakfast. Business never really resumed after the pandemic." He paused and regarded Lilith, his expression inscrutable. "My aunt is rather aged, as you can see. What she says doesn't always make sense, so I wouldn't think on it too heavily."

Other questions crowded Lilith's tongue, but were immediately forgotten as the dilapidated manor from the website came into view.

The world went still. Her breath froze in her lungs and her eyes locked on Brackenmere Manor. Its windows were dulled by dust and time, several broken like jagged teeth against a stained exterior tangled in ivy.

The manor had clearly suffered at least another decade or so of deterioration since the pictures on the website were taken.

Her birthmark tingled beneath her long-sleeved shirt.

A brilliant light flared and faded, revealing the manor transformed to the way Lilith had seen it in her vision in Savannah. Gone were the layers of grime and abuse. The house stood upright once more, windows gleaming, exterior clean and creamy white in the sun. The bushes were landscaped to identical wide domes and the clean fragrance of rosemary wafted from an unseen garden.

She blinked and the image cleared, returning to the abandoned manor house.

Her heart lurched.

What had she just seen?

"You all right?"

Asher's voice broke through her shock.

"Did you see that?" she asked.

He lifted a brow and regarded the house before looking back at her. "What did you see?"

"I thought I saw a flash of light." She shook her head, not about to get into what she'd *actually* seen.

He withdrew an old-fashioned skeleton key and slid it into the ancient lock. The door clicked and groaned open, revealing the Great Hall.

Light struggled in through the windows, illuminating a long table splitting the center of the capacious room. Swords were crossed in X formations on the wood-paneled walls, and curtains hung from the tall windows, their color obscured by shadows. Dust sifted over the stone floors, fine as baker's flour, and she vividly recalled when it had been strewn with fresh rushes, mixed with lavender and meadowsweet.

A voice echoed through the room, foreign and familiar at once, muffled as if underwater.

The clatter of a pan hitting the floor sounded distantly, followed by a glass breaking.

Lilith startled and gave an anxious, self-deprecating smile as she glanced at Asher to see his reaction to the sudden sound.

He arched that same eyebrow at her, making her feel as weird as she always feared she was.

Clearing his throat, he said, "Well, this is the manor."

Lilith stepped hesitantly forward. "Can I explore a little?"

He thrust his hands into his pockets and gave a little shrug. "Just not the top floor or the attic."

"Why not?"

A muscle flexed in his jaw and he hesitated for more than a beat. "They're not safe."

His delayed reply nudged at Lilith's awareness. He was lying.

Still, it was his house and she'd play by his rules.

She explored the downstairs area, going first to the marble hearth carved with a pair of Greek goddesses on either side, one holding a scroll, the other with her head lifted in pride. Exactly like the vision she'd had in Savannah. Heat blossomed in the crook of her arm near her birthmark.

Her gut told her this manor held the key to what she needed.

Asher followed a foot behind her, studying her every move. Unsettled by his apparent distrust and the idea of being so thoroughly micromanaged, she kept her hands tucked behind her back.

The kitchen had an island with a blue flecked Formica countertop, a jarring difference from the stone hearth with an ancient iron crane-looking apparatus on the side. She could envision a massive pot hanging from its hook.

She blinked. Actually, she truly *could* see the outline of a pot hanging from the hook, the rich aroma of stew flavoring the air.

She breathed in the savory scent. "Do you smell that?"

He frowned. "Smell what?"

Lilith cringed. He must think she was a few peas short of a casserole. "Nothing."

Old wooden cabinets lined the wall, their scalloped edges dating them to a time decades before. An avocado-colored toaster sat in the corner, as if it'd been used recently and not returned.

"Does anyone live here?" Lilith asked.

"Of course not," Asher said abruptly.

"They did," she countered.

"Not during the time of your ancestor." The retort was clearly British for "not your business."

Lilith wandered into the Great Hall once more, her vision wavering. The figure of a woman in a pale green dress swept into the room, appearing as gauzy and transparent as cobwebs swirling lazily in an unseen breeze.

Her long hair was unbound, but unmistakable, even in her translucent state. Red-gold hair. Like the woman in the dream. The one who continued to beg Lilith for help.

Lilith's birthmark blazed with sudden heat, making her hiss in surprise.

The woman spun around, revealing a face Lilith recognized immediately.

The air shifted, becoming heavy in Lilith's chest, filling her with unspeakable terror.

A thundering bang reverberated from the front door.

Boom, boom, boom!

Lilith jumped at the sound, dread turning her veins to ice.

The young woman's eyes locked on Lilith's, as if they could see one another from a place that blurred between two worlds.

Nausea surged, spiraling through Lilith with the same awful pull as her dream. Her nightmare.

And everything went black.

CHAPTER FOURTEEN

Sybil

Boom, boom, boom!

Sybil stiffened at the insistent knock thundering through Brackenmere Manor. Her hand remained poised over her ledger. An ominous silence followed.

Anne abruptly stopped dusting the bookshelves and turned to Sybil, her eyes wide.

The entire household had seemed jumpy that day. Earlier, the scullery maid had dropped a pan with a great clatter that upset the kitchen maid, who knocked over a goblet made of precious Venetian glass.

Anne flashed a nervous look toward the doorway from the library, then in Sybil's direction. "Are you well, mum?"

Was there a tremble to her voice?

Sybil pulled a fortifying breath and addressed the young woman. "I am."

She wasn't.

Her heart was beating too fast. Her lungs working too hard to draw in air as she recalled the storm Jacinda had summoned, and the protective herbs likely swept from every entrance to their home.

Sybil did not need foresight to tell her what the authoritative knock meant. Everything inside her screamed to run, run, *run*.

But she would never leave Jacinda.

As lady of the manor in her own right, Sybil would perform her role to the bitter end. With the comportment of a Roman wife, she exited the library and descended the stairs, approaching the entryway, where a servant opened the doors to the magistrate.

Robert Walsingham locked eyes with Sybil, his gaze going dark. "Mrs. Brantham, I require a moment to speak with you."

"You may do so here, before my servants," she replied in a manner she hoped appeared unaffected.

"I should think you would like to converse in private," he pressed. "Such measures would be in your best interest."

Fear prickled at the back of her neck as she recalled the last time she had been trapped alone in a room with this man.

When she had gone to his home to speak with him about her stable hand, who had found himself in a bit of trouble. When Walsingham had cornered her in his study.

Though she had not issued the command, her servants now fled the room, leaving her alone. With *him*.

Walsingham stepped closer. This time, they were not outside where the breeze mercilessly swept away his scent. The noxious blend of ambergris and musk he wore in excess flooded her senses, filling her mouth with water and her mind with unwanted memories.

She had once scrubbed that odor from her body until her skin was raw.

Her fingers wandered to her pocket where she'd kept a penknife ever since that day.

"Marry me." His demand was guttural, insistent.

"No."

He stepped closer, but she held her ground, refusing to be cowed into the corner again. Where there was no escape.

"You are to be tried as a witch," he said, his tone velvety, almost cajoling.

In truth, she had expected this.

As Christine de Pizan so eloquently stated, "For even if some men will not tolerate women to be learned, they cannot prevent them from having intelligence."

She had always been at risk.

"I'm to be tried as a witch under what grounds?" she demanded.

"This poppet." He lifted a crude cloth doll, its limbs and head knobby with bits of rags stuffed inside sausage-like casings and bound with red string.

She scoffed. "Lies."

"This poppet is enough to warrant a guilty verdict."

She clenched her teeth, hating that he was right. The poppet was not even truly necessary. Even a word against her would be grounds for condemnation.

"The Witchfinder General is in Bury St. Edmunds, seeking witches." Walsingham gave a subtle shrug. "I ought to show him this, as I am a magistrate…but I don't have to."

"Sybil." His expression softened, reminding her of the boy he'd been. Back when they'd been friends, before teasing twisted him into someone cruel. "I could protect you." He'd dropped the authority from his voice, sounding more like the Robert she'd known so long ago. "No one would ever hurt you again."

Except he had hurt her.

A rush of anger flooded her cheeks with fire.

Except that protection from him would sentence her to a life of obedience, of silence.

"Never."

Magistrate Walsingham's face hardened. "The accusation includes more than just the poppet..."

Sybil lifted her chin with the indignity. "Who has accused me?"

"I cannot say." Walsingham shifted, putting his weight on the foot nearest her. "Do you want to know the other charge against you?" His eyes gleamed, a cat enjoying batting around his mouse.

She remained silent, refusing to feed his excitement.

"Your husband," Walsingham said.

"What of him?" Sybil snapped. Too abrupt. Too harsh.

The show of her emotion was a weakness the magistrate would not miss.

"Being a widow is rather convenient for you, is it not?" He tilted his head. "You have too much power, too much wealth, especially for a woman with no husband." He stepped even closer, obviously trying to force her backward against the wall.

Rather than yield to him, her hand slid into her pocket, fingering the cold, sharp steel there. Her salvation.

The magistrate looked down at her. "His death was rather convenient as well, wasn't it?"

She stepped forward, antagonizing her antagonist. "Was it?" she asked, heady with determination. With terror.

Walsingham narrowed his eyes. "You deny me still?" he breathed.

Disgust slithered over her skin. "I do."

His stare glided down her body and came to rest at the bulge of her hand in her pocket. "Guards," he shouted.

Half a dozen men poured into the grand entryway of Sybil's home, boots scattering dirt upon the gleaming floor, the thunder of their heavy tread reverberating off the walls. Behind her, more people emerged—her servants, hands twisting in aprons, shoulders tensing with uncertainty at the desire to protect their mistress.

The guards surrounded her, shackles clanking.

"Sybil?" Jacinda's soft voice sounded behind her, but Sybil refused to turn. To do so would be her undoing. She could not look upon Jacinda and bear witness to the vulnerable fear and unanswered questions in those large eyes.

This was not a time to crumble, but to remain ever strong.

"Mrs. Henry Brantham, you are hereby arrested on the charges of witchcraft." Walsingham's declaration resounded in the entryway. "A felony that has been raised to petty treason for using witchcraft to cause your husband's death."

Sybil's knees went soft with horror. A felony would result in being hanged. But petty treason meant she would burn alive at the stake.

"No," Jacinda cried out. "She would never."

"I am no witch," Sybil said fiercely. "And I did not murder my husband."

The magistrate narrowed his eyes. "I heard of the storm you brewed up when we arrested the witch three days past. How the clouds crowded the sky with an unnatural ferocity."

The fight bled out of Sybil at the reminder of the tumultuous weather wrought by Jacinda's unbridled power. At how Sybil's preoccupation with Edith's capture had caused her to forget to reapply the protective barriers on the home.

Jacinda ran to the magistrate. "That wasn't her. That—"

"That was the weather being as mercurial as weather so oft is," Sybil said in a tired voice. "Bess…" Before Sybil could speak her order, the maid was there, pulling Jacinda back, cajoling the girl in soothing tones.

Sybil did not look at them as the guards closed in around her, jerking her hands roughly in front of her. Iron clapped over the tender skin of her wrists, cold and weighty. All at once, the world around Sybil went still.

The steady hum of the earth's power, as familiar to her as the throb of her own heartbeat, went quiet, its song abruptly cut short.

That silence bore the weight of an eternity.

The charge of witchcraft, she could endure. Indeed, had expected. Especially if her arrest might somehow keep Jacinda safe.

But the accusation that she had killed Henry…

Henry, her revered husband who had loved her as a scholar adored his star pupil, whose long, tapered fingers elegantly crawled over script as he patiently instructed her in the ways of philosophers, theologians. He had so readily accepted Jacinda into his life as another student, treating her as a daughter rather than a sister-in-law and educating her like a son.

And now Sybil would be tried for his death, this man who had cared for her with unending patience and understanding.

Guilt dragged at her with the weight of a millstone.

Because she knew the truth in her heart. If not for her, Henry would still be alive today.

His death had indeed been her fault.

CHAPTER FIFTEEN

Lilith

Lilith blinked her eyes open as the ribcage of a great beast bloomed into focus, the timbered support beams of the ceiling of Brackenmere Manor's Great Hall. "What—?"

She tried to sit up and was rewarded with a flash of pain at the back of her head.

"Don't sit up too quickly." Asher's large hand went to her shoulder, his touch surprisingly gentle. "You fainted and hit your head."

She gently lay back down. "You didn't catch me?"

"You weren't close enough."

She gingerly probed the back of her skull, where a lump was beginning to swell. "My hero."

His mouth hitched up at the corner. Was that…almost a smile?

"Stay there a moment, yeah?" He pulled his phone from his

pocket and a brilliant light cut through the dark, straight into her brain.

She flinched away.

"Shh," he soothed. "I know it's uncomfortable but look at the light."

Ever the trusting lamb, she steeled herself against the pain and looked directly into the phone's flashlight. Behind the penetrating glow, he studied her eyes.

The light mercifully clicked off.

"Now follow my finger." He moved his forefinger side to side in front of her face, then up and down. "Good. Are you well enough to stand?"

"I think I'll just keep lying on this dusty floor, thank you."

He tilted his head. "Sarcasm will get you a cold night's sleep."

"Is that a threat?" Lilith allowed him to guide her into a sitting position.

"How do you feel?"

Oh, what a question.

Like she had just stepped into a time warp haunted by translucent memories of the past. Like she had no idea why she was even here, aside from a weird tingling birthmark. Like maybe she might have just seen a ghost.

Oh, and like this all might somehow kill her—make her cease to exist—whatever—at some point.

But ladies weren't supposed to say things like that. Instead, she replied simply with, "Fine."

Asher watched her in silent expectation, clearly skeptical of her glib brush-off. "Any feelings of unsteadiness?"

"No."

"Would you like to try standing?"

Lilith almost nodded, but the throb in her skull had her murmuring her assent instead.

The skin around Asher's eyes tightened. "Maybe wait another moment. Don't want you standing up too soon."

Lilith offered a smile of relief, hating how much this small show of attention made her feel more cared for than she'd been in years.

There had been so much time tending to Mama when she was sick, and being lambasted with abuse for her efforts. Even before the cancer, Mama had been about as cuddly as a gator.

But Asher was genuinely concerned.

For Lilith.

Warm tears pricked her eyes, and she lowered her face in horror.

Was she really about to cry?

Here this guy was trying not to get sued when she almost concussed herself in his ancient manor house, and she was dissolving into tears because his modicum of attention made her finally feel like she mattered.

"Are you a doctor?" she asked, distracting herself from being so ridiculously pathetic.

"A vet, actually."

She lifted her head in surprise, and he gave a single shoulder shrug. "I'm not really the best with people."

"Oh?" She kept her voice light, teasing. "Imagine that…"

That little quirk at the corner of his mouth made another appearance.

"I've always done well with animals though." Asher offered a bemused smile, the first she'd seen since her arrival. "And if you're in need of a distemper vaccine, I can be of assistance."

"My temper is perfectly fine, thank you."

"It's actually a common vaccine for dogs, to keep them from a deadly disease."

Lilith's face went hot. "Sorry, we never had pets."

Asher pulled back a fraction of an inch, enough to reflect that Lilith was suddenly not to be trusted.

"It was my mama." Lilith looked at the floor where her jean-clad legs lay stretched out against the dirty stone tile. "She didn't want pets in the house. Afraid they might get mud all over her floral furniture."

"Animals do have an affinity for destroying floral furniture, I'm afraid."

Was he flirting?

"As well they should," Lilith offered. "It's all hideous." She looked shyly up at him. "I've always wanted a pet though. Guess I can have one now."

Asher's mouth opened, likely to ask what she meant. She hadn't meant to drag the conversation into Mama territory. That whole mess was supposed to stay back in Savannah.

"Tell me more about the manor," she said quickly. "I'd expected the inside to be empty, but there's all this furniture. And so much is modern—unless Formica existed in the seventeenth century." She grinned.

He didn't.

She cleared her throat. "Is it like that in the rest of the house?"

Asher nodded.

"When did people stop living here?" Lilith noted the room's disuse. Not only the velvety layer of dust, but also the distinctive musty odor permeating the air. The scent was one she was familiar with in her old home with the rooms she seldom entered.

"We should put some ice on your head to minimize the swelling," Asher said abruptly.

Was he avoiding answering the question?

But the mention of her head made the pain intensify, pulsing in time with her heartbeat, and she conceded defeat. For now.

Asher put one hand between her shoulder blades and offered her the other. She accepted, unable to keep from noting the heat of his fingers against her own. He lifted her easily to her feet, his touch lingering. "Are you steady?"

"Yes, thank you."

He nodded and dropped his hands, turning for the door, clearly eager to leave.

And could she blame him? She'd just passed out on the floor.

"I don't usually do this," she called, rushed after him. "Fainting, I mean. I…I thought I saw something."

He stopped and looked over his shoulder at her. "What do you mean?"

"A figure?" She sifted through her memory, trying to decide exactly how to reply honestly without seeming like she'd lost her mind.

He turned toward her and frowned.

"There had been a sound before that," she added.

His frown deepened. "There are a lot of broken windows. Sometimes the wind makes strange noises as a result."

"It was a banging."

"Probably the wind knocking a broken window frame against the wall."

Lilith wanted to press, to know what he'd witnessed.

But she'd been raised not to push or pry into other people's affairs. No one liked a nuisance. Instead, she seized the opportunity for an excuse to drop the subject. "Yeah." She gave him a sweet Southern smile. "That was probably it."

He nodded, the matter resolved, and strode to the door. Once outside, he flicked the key in the lock with a firm twist of his wrist and led the way to the house at a quicker pace than they'd arrived.

As if he wanted to get far away from Brackenmere Manor.

CHAPTER SIXTEEN

Lilith

Asher's aunt was no longer in the recliner when they returned to the bed and breakfast, her knitting neatly tucked into a wicker basket.

Lilith trailed after Asher into the kitchen where he dug in the freezer. Straightening, Asher handed her a freezer pack filled with blue beads. "Put this on your head."

Lilith accepted the ice pack, the frost melting against her fingertips. "Is this for animals?"

"And humans."

Toby trundled into the kitchen, toenails clicking on the terracotta tile. He gazed up at her, eyeing the ice pack curiously.

The ice pack was most definitely for animals, but beggars couldn't be choosers and she put it to the back of her head.

"It's best you stay put until we know you don't have a concussion." Asher opened the fridge. "Do you like lasagna?"

"You don't have to—"

He lifted his brows, clearly wanting an honest reply rather than an objection.

Lilith grinned. "I love lasagna."

"It's leftover."

"Even better."

He plated two squares from a white-and-blue casserole dish that looked like a '50s housewife's prized possession.

"If I promise not to faint again, can I go back to the manor tomorrow?" Lilith didn't bother to keep the hope out of her voice.

The kitchen filled with the scent of warming herbs and tomato, and her mouth watered.

"I don't think that's a good idea," Asher said with obvious hesitation. "I'll be at work."

"I promise to be *very* careful."

The microwave dinged and he pulled the plates out to cool on the counter. Melty cheese oozed from between the noodles.

"I'd prefer you didn't," he replied.

Ah, the polite British way of issuing an emphatic "no."

She bit back her protest. The next day would be a great opportunity to go into the town of Bury St. Edmunds. There was a museum there with an exhibit on witch trials that might offer some new insight.

Asher handed her the plate and a set of silverware wrapped in a cloth napkin. "There's a table in your room. I'll collect your plate in the morning."

Ah, they weren't eating together then. To be fair, it probably would have been awkward.

Why then did the reminder of the table in her room carry the sting of rejection?

Once in her room, alone, she found several messages from Essie.

Did you land OK?

Is England amazing?

I'm literally sitting here eating oat bran for lunch thinking about the great food you're enjoying for both of us.

If you don't tell me you're safe soon, I'm going to call Interpol to do a wellness check.

Lilith chuckled to herself, hearing Essie's voice in her head, and typed back: Does Interpol even do that?

Three dots immediately appeared, followed by the message. They'd do it for me. You know I don't take no for an answer.

Lilith replied: I'm at the bed and breakfast and already saw the manor. It was amazing.

Her thumbs hovered over the keyboard, considering whether to tell Essie she'd fainted.

But that would make Essie worry. Knowing her, she'd book the next flight to England and there already was way too much going on in her life to worry about Lilith.

That and Lilith had been keeping her at arm's length about the full truth of what was happening. She'd told her the fortune teller suggested digging into her family's past to understand the nightmare and how Mama had the hatbox full of old ancestry research that led her to Bury St. Edmunds. But Lilith hadn't explained the warning or the strange mystery she needed to somehow solve.

Or what failure might mean.

Instead, she typed out: The guy who runs the bed and breakfast is younger than I thought.

Essie: Hot?

Lilith smirked. Classic Essie.

Essie: OMG he IS hot! You hesitated, which is quite clearly a yes.

Lilith: OK, he's hot. But he's not super friendly. Kind of cagey.

Essie: Oooooooh—a Mr. Darcy type?

Lilith: Just because I'm in England doesn't mean there's a Mr. Darcy waiting to sweep me off my feet.

Essie: But you're SO Elizabeth Bennet!

Lilith: You read way too many romances.

Essie: You sell them to me.

Lilith: Fair enough, but I'm only appealing to your romantic sensibilities.

Essie: Which is why you're totally going to end up together.

Lilith shook her head, smiling at Essie's eternal romantic optimism for her future.

Essie: Gotta get Amara from daycare. Keep me posted on Mr. Darcy. ♡

Still smiling, Lilith set aside her phone and shoveled a very unladylike forkful of lasagna into her mouth, grateful she wasn't eating in front of Asher after all. She hadn't realized how hungry she was.

But even as she dug into the cheesy, savory goodness of homemade lasagna, she couldn't help but think of Asher. Not how very Mr. Darcy–like he was, but how he'd followed her so closely when they were at the manor, how he'd avoided her questions.

How he didn't want her going to the manor without him.

Like maybe there was something hidden.

Something he didn't want her to discover.

CHAPTER SEVENTEEN

Sybil

Sybil was marched down the streets of Bury St. Edmunds as Edith had been. Mud streaked her ruined silk gown, one sleeve torn where she'd been roughly grabbed and thrown to the ground.

They spat in her face and hurled accusations, citing her as the source of all their pain. She stirred the civil unrest that led the country to war. She summoned the pestilence and robbed Bury St. Edmunds of so many lives. She killed the babes who had not been born strong enough to endure this life.

These men and women whose children she had helped through fevers and whose agues she'd soothed with salves and poultices, they called her Jezebel, a liar, a murderer. A witch.

She did not care what they called her. The only power they had was in their cruelty. She cared for nothing so long as they did not mention Jacinda.

Beleaguered, wet with filth, and thoroughly abused, Sybil staggered toward the old jail.

The exterior of the centuries-old building rose before her, crumbling and chipped, a place meant to be uninviting. A damp chill greeted her inside as she was led down a set of pitted stone stairs, worn smooth with a dip in each center.

Darkness pressed in as she descended into the depths of the prison. Her pulse quickened with the realization—they meant to keep her there. To try her. To kill her.

To burn her alive at the stake.

And who would protect Jacinda if Sybil was dead?

Sybil found strength in her connection to the earth, the ever-present hum and the beauty of nature around her. But the silence of the iron manacles was deafening. She was alone and would need to lean into her own strength.

A wall of odors hit her. Unwashed bodies, damp hay, refuse, all catching in the back of her throat.

Her heart pattered around in her ribcage like a frantic moth.

Great cages lined either side of the large room, like massive pens for holding chickens at market. But instead of hens, scores of people were locked within. Mostly women, with one cell containing a few men.

Narrow rectangles were cut into the stone near the top of the wall—too high to reach, and too small to climb through. But enough to allow a weak stream of sunlight to filter in, revealing the turn of curious faces in her direction, eyes wide and haunted.

The jailer, a short man with a chest like a barrel, unlocked a gate unceremoniously and waved the prisoners back with his cudgel, despite the women already cowering.

With a hard shove at Sybil's back, she stumbled forward, her legs too weak to bear her weight as she pitched to the floor. The rushes were wet and foul smelling, and she wrenched her face aside. The clang of metal on metal rang out as the door was latched, followed by the click of a lock.

And just like that, she was a prisoner.

★★★

"Oh, Sybil." The voice was familiar.

Gentle hands curled around Sybil's shoulders and helped her sit. She looked up into Edith's bruised face.

"Edith." Sybil caught her friend's hand, chains clinking where they draped from their wrists. She squeezed her friend's fingers. To give and to receive comfort. To rein in her growing terror.

"I'm sorry to see you here," Edith said mournfully. "The magistrate was responsible for this, I presume?"

Sybil nodded.

Edith sighed. "I regret I stopped Kat—"

"No." Sybil would not let her say she regretted discouraging Kat from cursing the magistrate after learning what he'd done to Sybil.

What he'd likely done to many of the women in Bury St. Edmunds. Including Sybil's own neighbor, leaving a babe who was spirited away in the middle of the night to a childless couple three towns over.

"Never apologize for not wishing ill on others," Sybil said weakly as she allowed Edith to help her to her feet and guide her toward the rear of the cell. They both gratefully sank to the floor where they had a wall at their back.

The rushes beneath them had not been changed in some time. Dark flecks moved about on the hay, and something large and unseen shuffled beneath.

"More women will be accused." Edith lowered her voice. "They encourage us to speak against one another, name new victims for them to arrest."

A wail broke through the prisoners' shuffles and murmurs, a low, defeated keening that made Sybil's chest ache.

"I did not denounce you," Edith said quickly. "But they will take you to be questioned."

"I never assumed you would." Sybil leaned her head against the wall. Dampness from the old stone bled into the cloth of her dress. The wet chill crept into her bones and left her skin pebbled with gooseflesh. Exhaustion weighted her limbs, a demand for sleep after what she had endured.

Her mind, though, was a hive of activity, a constant buzz of worry.

Jacinda.

Jacinda.

Jacinda.

If Sybil had been arrested, would she be next? Would Magistrate Walsingham use her to get to Sybil? Could the girl manage without Sybil there to protect her?

She had been left vulnerable and Sybil was helpless to offer any aid.

Tears burned in Sybil's eyes. Not fear, but fury. The indignation that she could not be with Jacinda to ensure her safety. Sybil blinked until her vision cleared.

She had to be strong.

"What can I expect when they examine me?" Sybil asked.

"The inquirers are insistent, spinning such stories when they bid our confessions, encouraging us to admit their preposterous tales are true." Edith patted Sybil's arm. "You have always been strong, my friend. You have naught to fear."

Sybil nodded and a silence settled over them, each lost in the horror of their own thoughts. Finally, Sybil had a chance to catch her breath, to truly take in her surroundings. Her gaze drifted toward the men's cage and caught sight of a familiar face: Edward Morris.

He was a shadow of the youth he had been the year before, back when he was a staunch Parliamentarian. Then, he'd been vociferous in his protestations to the king's rule. Especially the preposterous taxes, like Ship Money dues when they did not even live near the coast.

He'd gone to the battle of Marston Moor charged with a need for vengeance. While he returned a hero, the light in his eyes had been snuffed by the violent slaughter of so many Royalists. In the month following his return, his wife died in childbirth along with his firstborn, a little girl.

His fragile soul had perished along with them, leaving him a husk of a person, hollowed out by loss. Now he sat in the prison, gaze fixed on nothing, face slack, as if already dead.

"Poor Edward Morris," Edith tutted. "They say men plagued by melancholy are as subject to the Devil's influence as are women with our weak minds."

"Weak minds indeed," Sybil scoffed.

"And that man, the vicar." Edith nodded to a frail old man. "He escaped the noose when he spoke up for a woman accused of witchcraft some thirty summers ago, but there's no one to help him this time round. He's already confessed."

"A vicar confessed?" Sybil studied the elderly man in surprise.

Age had leached all color from his hair, as well as from his grizzled beard. Still, even as he wavered on his feet, he held the hands of two men, his head bowed, lips moving in silent prayer.

"They swam him," Edith whispered. "The water trial broke him, that dear man. He confessed." She drew in a shaky breath. "They mean to break us all."

"Then we must be strong."

Sybil looked at those in the cage with them. Most were as old as Edith, their faces creased with age, their hair wispy shades of gray and white. Women who society felt no longer offered value to the community. Women whose presence would never be missed.

Such women were so easily discarded.

But there was also a child, a little girl tucked in a dark corner, as if trying to wish herself unseen. She shrank back from Sybil's observation, the poor chit.

The iron door grated open with a shrill cry, and the barrel-chested guard shoved the women back with his cudgel before depositing a young woman inside.

Her unbound hair spread about her shoulders like a thick golden cloak, and even in the dark, dismal light, her beauty was unmistakable. She wore a shawl dyed in Lavenham blue from the nearby town, which obtained the distinct color from their use of woad.

"My husband," the young woman whispered. "Please send him word. Oh, my husband, my husband…" She buried her face in her hands and wept. One of the older women approached and patted her shoulder. A woman who had naught to give but comfort and offered it readily.

"Sybil Brantham," the guard's voice rang out through the sound of the woman's quiet sobs.

Edith tensed beside her.

"Sybil Brantham," the guard called again. "Come forward."

"Be cautious." Edith locked eyes with Sybil. "He is cruel."

And as brave as Sybil wished to be in that moment, she was terrified.

Not so much for herself, but for what her incarceration might mean for Jacinda.

CHAPTER EIGHTEEN

Lilith

Lilith woke to the sound of barking, followed by Asher's insistent hush. A glance at her watch illuminated 8:18 in white numbers.

She had slept that morning. Like *actually* slept.

The nightmares had started early on in the night with Jacinda begging Lilith to hurry, to help save Sybil, but then finally left her alone long enough to get a few hours of uninterrupted sleep.

Her stomach rumbled, reminding her that staying at a B&B meant there would be breakfast.

Knowing she'd likely see Asher, Lilith took a quick shower and added a bit of mascara, blush, and pink lip gloss.

Lord, Essie was getting to her with all that Mr. Darcy nonsense.

She left her room and entered the glass-walled patio where a wrought iron table awaited her with a single plate setting.

She slid into the chair, and everything suddenly seemed too still. Too quiet.

She'd always hated iron. Such a heavy, unforgiving metal that left a tinny scent on everything. But now, it seemed almost oppressive. Even the sun outside lacked its usual hum that she'd grown accustomed to.

Strange.

Asher entered the room wearing pale blue scrubs with "Kindred Creatures" stitched in black above a paw print on his right pec. An impressive pec, at that. Not that Lilith ought to be noticing.

"I forgot to ask your breakfast order last night, so a full English breakfast it is." He set the loaded plate in front of her. The briny scent of ham mingled with the sweetness of baked beans, setting her stomach rumbling in anticipation.

"About Aunt Jacqueline." He cast about the room, appearing almost helpless before his features set in that stern expression. "I have been considering hiring a nurse to tend to her, but didn't have the opportunity before you arrived."

Lilith recalled how caught off guard he'd seemed when she'd arrived so soon after his aunt's invitation to come to England. Perhaps this was why. That made more sense than him just being a jerk. Lilith nodded, eager to please, especially after having put him out. "I can help with her during the day."

"That isn't necess—"

Lilith waved him off. "I really don't mind."

He nodded, the tension from his face relaxing somewhat. Toby plodded into the room with a red leash dragging from his mouth.

Lilith chuckled. "I think Toby says it's time for a walk."

"Actually, it's time to leave for work." Asher threw a look at his dog and grinned, transforming his face into something boyish and so handsome, it would have given Essie *way* too much hope.

With a wave, he was off, and Lilith devoured her first-ever English breakfast, deciding she might need another one the next day. Even as she ate, a restlessness rattled through her as she thought back to the previous day.

Had she really seen the young woman with red-gold hair from her dreams in the manor? Had she really heard the clatter of a dropped pan and smelled food cooking?

Surely that was all just a byproduct of a near concussion and jet lag.

Everything in her yearned to return to the manor, to confirm that what she'd experienced had real explanations.

But she couldn't just go there after Asher told her not to.

Dang her Southern manners.

Maybe if she just looked around at the house from the outside… She could peer into a couple of windows. Technically that wasn't going *in* the house.

Resolved, Lilith dashed outside and came to an abrupt halt as she caught sight of Asher's aunt kneeling on a cushion before a flower bed, wearing a pale pink blouse with white flowers, a smudge of dirt visible on one shoulder. A musky animal smell lingered in the air.

She called a bright hullo to Lilith.

Movement shifted beside the older woman as a small black and white animal clawed aggressively into the soil.

"Miss Jacqueline, ma'am…" Lilith said awkwardly.

The older woman waved a hand. "Oh, do call me Aunt Jacqueline."

Lilith pointed to the skunk. "Um, Aunt Jacqueline…"

"Isn't he such a good little digger?" Aunt Jacqueline beamed down. "He always helps with my gardening."

That was…not normal. And didn't skunks carry rabies?

Did they have animal control in England?

"Is this safe?" Lilith asked.

Aunt Jacqueline laughed. "Oh, heavens, yes. He does it all the time." She said that like having a skunk at her side was a perfectly normal, not at all bizarre occurrence. "Are you going to the manor?"

Lilith stiffened. "I... Well... Asher said he preferred I didn't go."

Aunt Jacqueline threw her hand in a dismissive motion. "He doesn't understand like you and I do." With a grin, she reached into her pocket and withdrew the old iron key.

Lilith's pulse skipped.

"Take it." Aunt Jacquline waggled the key at her.

Still, Lilith paused. What if Asher found out and got so steaming mad that he made her leave? Then she'd never see Brackenmere Manor again.

Aunt Jacqueline gave a little whistle. The skunk withdrew its head from digging detail, took the key from her with its sharp teeth, and trotted over to Lilith like a puppy.

She jerked back instinctively.

"He won't hurt you." Aunt Jacqueline nodded, as if this was the most normal thing ever. "Go on, open your hand."

Everything about this seemed like a horrible idea.

Still, Lilith hesitantly extended her hand and the skunk dropped the key into her palm before returning to Aunt Jacqueline. "Did you train him to do that?"

"No," Aunt Jacqueline replied airily. "He just knows what to do because he's such a good boy, aren't you?"

The skunk opened his mouth in a snaggle-toothed smile.

Well, that was weird as all get out.

Aunt Jacqueline waved at Lilith. "Go on, go on."

Lilith looked at the skunk skeptically once more.

"I may be old, but I assure you, I know what I'm doing." There was an impatient chastisement to Aunt Jacqueline's tone, one that spoke of a lack of others' faith in her. "I can be trusted."

Lilith understood having her ideas muted, like with a male

manager she once had in her teens when she worked at The 5 Spot. Or with how many times Mama told her an opinionated woman was a nuisance.

Lilith nodded and left Aunt Jacqueline to her skunk, setting off for the manor with a whoosh of excitement flooding her veins.

CHAPTER NINETEEN

Lilith

Brackenmere Manor appeared to be an entirely normal dilapidated old house upon Lilith's arrival. There was no flash of light, no altered reality with the manor restored to its former appearance.

Her shoulders relaxed.

Jet lag, or maybe some strange migraine, had likely altered her vision yesterday.

She unlocked the door, which creaked open with an ominous groan that scraped up Lilith's spine.

Had it sounded like that before?

She stepped inside and was met with the now-familiar fragrance of rushes, meadowsweet, and lavender. A hint of their existence hovered atop the dusty floor, like a vellum overlay on the present.

Lilith blinked her eyes hard and regarded the floor again.

The image didn't clear. In fact, now she could make out

ghost impressions of images all around the room, heavy wooden furniture, tapestries hanging on the walls.

Voices snagged the air in thready whispers. Just like before, only this time they were louder.

More insistent?

Chills prickled over Lilith's arms.

Was she entirely losing her mind…or was this what she needed to help her figure out answers?

She focused, trying to look beyond the modern-day furnishings to the translucent past beneath. The image wavered and the birthmark at her arm tingled with warmth.

Several figures bustled about the room in long heavy skirts, hair covered beneath white linen caps, their words a muffled jumble as they set to tasks performed centuries ago.

That familiar lightheadedness crashed over Lilith, and she reached for the table's edge for support.

"I am in England in a creepy old house that might be haunted," she said aloud. Her fingertips gripped the cool hard surface, centering herself. She was *not* going to faint. Not when she was here alone.

And not when Asher specifically told her he didn't want her in the manor without him.

"Get it together," she hissed to herself.

She had to be here. Whatever the fortune teller meant, the answers—ensuring her future existence—were somewhere in this house.

A gauzy figure strode into the room, gown shimmering in green silk, dark hair swept back from her face. Though her features were indecipherable, Lilith *knew* her.

Through the pull at her gut, a certainty in her soul.

The noncorporeal figure was the woman standing on the pyre in Lilith's nightmares.

This was Sybil.

The woman opened her mouth, and her voice came like a soft exhale.

Jacinda.

Onward, she strode, directly toward Lilith.

Through Lilith. Passing through skin and bone and organs, leaving a cool, damp imprint on Lilith's lungs and heart.

She shuddered at the sensation, then spun to follow Sybil, refusing to let the woman out of sight. Together, they climbed the stairs, steps tandem with a muted pat of Sybil's leather heels and the thud of Lilith's Brooks.

A sound came from below, the clatter of a pan in the distance, followed by breaking glass.

Heat blazed at Lilith's arm.

The same sound as yesterday.

Without thought, Lilith glanced at her watch.

12:03.

Had it been the same time as the day before? They'd gone to Brackenmere Manor around noon.

Before she could ponder it further, Lilith found herself at the landing of the second floor, looking into an open space where the apparition of portraits from the past hung on wood paneling against the current state of empty walls with peeling yellow paint.

Lilith swayed, torn between two worlds.

Sybil rounded a corner, disappearing out of Lilith's line of vision.

No.

Lilith followed Sybil into a sprawling library filled with shelves of books that stretched from floor to ceiling. The past and present cluttered together in a dizzying blend with the tease of a low fire flickering within the hearth. The smoky scent lingered in the air from another time and mingled with the mustiness of ancient books now tilted crookedly against one another on sagging shelves.

When Lilith turned around, Sybil was gone, but another woman was in the room with her. A young woman with red-gold hair. She was bent over the bookshelf on the opposite side of the hearth from Lilith, searching for something.

Jacinda.

The voice came from another room, too distant for Lilith to identify.

The young woman leaned her head back in exasperation and looked toward the door. Her gaze caught Lilith's, and she stiffened.

So did Lilith.

None of the other figures in the house appeared to see her. Certainly, Sybil hadn't before she'd walked through her.

"You're Jacinda?" Lilith asked, her voice hesitant.

The teen's hazel eyes narrowed, then wandered down Lilith's body, taking in her T-shirt, jeans and messy bun. "Yes."

The word was soft, a whisper of the past filtering into the present.

Heat radiated from Lilith's birthmark through her entire being. "You were in my dream."

Jacinda's brows clenched and she shook her head. "I don't understand."

"I think I need to help Sybil."

"Help her?" Jacinda frowned. "With what?"

"I don't know," Lilith admitted. "I think maybe keep her from being burned alive."

Was she really having a conversation with a ghost right now?

Jacinda paled. "I don't understand." She shook her head. "Is something going to happen to Sybil?"

Lilith recalled Mama's ancestry notes.

Sybil Brantham—burned as a witch.

"I believe so," Lilith replied slowly.

Jacinda took a step back, as if Lilith brought ill fortune, then glanced at the bookshelf. "I think…I think Sybil's been hiding something from me." She gestured to the bookshelves. "Mayhap something here? Can you look for it?"

"What do you think I'll find?" Lilith asked.

Jacinda worried her lower lip with her teeth. "A secret Sybil doesn't want me to know about."

"I brought peppermint tea." The voice was so loud behind Lilith that she nearly leaped out of her skin.

Aunt Jacqueline appeared in the doorway, the knees of her white slacks stained with dirt. Her feet were bare and muddy, and at her side was the skunk.

"Are you okay?" Lilith gasped. "Are you supposed to have the skunk in here?"

"Tea." Aunt Jacqueline panted, clearly exerted by her efforts even as she extended a mug toward Lilith. "To open your eyes. The house has been waiting so long."

Before Lilith could ask what she meant, the mug tumbled from Aunt Jacqueline's hand, liquid spilling, darkening the floor to its original stained color beneath the dust. The wet scent of steeped peppermint tea filled the room.

Lilith lunged forward, catching the frail woman before she landed in the growing puddle.

She had to get Aunt Jacqueline back to the manor immediately. Questions for whatever just happened could come later. So, too, would searching the library.

Aunt Jacqueline came first.

Lilith glanced over her shoulder to seek out the young woman before leading Aunt Jacqueline from the room, but Jacinda was gone.

CHAPTER TWENTY

Sybil

Sybil was led to a room in better repair than the rest of the prison, long and narrow with wood paneling that likely masked crumbling walls beneath. A great desk sat at the rear, where a sconce provided ample light. Behind that desk sat the man she could only assume to be Matthew Hopkins.

The Witchfinder General himself.

He looked up when she entered, studying her as she formed her own assessment of him. His broad linen collar and wide-brimmed hat with a polished silver buckle spoke of a man who believed himself significant.

A mean little mustache traced the hard line of his mouth and glistened with oil. His hair was likewise well-groomed, having been brushed to a shine that fell in gentle waves about his shoulders.

This was a man who cared greatly for how others perceived him.

Such men were dangerous.

Men who knew how to get what they wanted, to ensure they received the praise and approbation they craved. At any cost.

He set aside his quill. "Mrs. Henry Brantham," he said by way of greeting.

She notched her chin at a haughty angle. "Mr. Hopkins, I presume?"

He flushed with prideful pleasure. "I have not had so esteemed a person on the other side of my desk as yet."

Ah, then she was a grand prize.

But Sybil would not be taken in so easily. Christine de Pizan's words came to her at once. "There is no man so valiant that he cannot be wounded by a woman's heart and courage."

The line bolstered Sybil, arming her with that very heart and courage. "I fail to understand why I am here at all."

His smile was mirrored by his oiled mustache. "I should like to ask you some questions." He indicated the chair.

She did not sit.

His nod was directed behind her, and the guards who'd escorted her into the room gripped her by the shoulders, shoving her down until her knees buckled. In the end, she was forced to sit on the hard-backed wooden chair whether she wanted to or not.

"Please, Mrs. Brantham." He said her name like a disappointment. "You are a gentlewoman. Surely, we can speak as equals, me being elevated from my birth as a vicar's son and you being elevated from your life as a cunning woman's daughter."

Sybil schooled her features to keep from reflecting her shock.

He knew more of her than she would have liked.

Mother never called herself a cunning woman, or a wise woman, or anything of that nature. She was a daughter of the earth, a nurse who tended to the ill and the wounded. To others, she was simply a friend.

Matthew Hopkins leaned forward on his elbows, his hands clasped and resting on the desk's surface before him. "You are surprised that I know as much about you. Sybil Brantham. I assure you, I know much more."

Sybil kept her expression impassive and he plunged on, "I know your mother had knowledge of herbs and many sought her skills. I know they seek you now for such purpose, though you offer aid without charge. You need no additional coin. Henry Brantham was flush with the wealth of his wool merchant's legacy when he took an interest in your mother's learning. And then she became ill."

He offered a small pout, more condescending than earnest. "She died, leaving you and your sister to fend for yourselves. And you did for some time, before Henry took pity on you and married you, sweeping you from that pathetic little cottage into a great manor. How high you rose." His lips quirked at his crude statement.

Sybil did not deign to reply.

"You both had what you wanted," Hopkins continued. "He had a young new wife that was far comelier and more fertile than the nag who failed at her role to deliver him a child. And you and your sister—well, you had anything you could ever want." He spread his hands out. "Is that the whole of it?"

He was certainly missing some chapters in her life's story.

Which was for the best.

And most men only saw what they wished to see.

If he wanted to see her as a vapid girl who used her youth and looks to secure a rich husband, so be it. She would allow him to underestimate her.

"Yet that new life wasn't enough for you." Hopkins tilted his head and a lock of curled hair rolled over his shoulder. "I understand, Mrs. Brantham. I am a man who appreciates finery myself. A man who always wants more."

He offered a self-indulgent smile and glanced down at his stately attire, clearly new by his jacket's crisp appearance.

"Except you killed your husband for your wealth." He tsked.

"I did not, but you clearly killed innocent women for yours." She spoke with a calmness belied only by her frantic pulse.

Color flooded his cheeks. "Mind yourself, Mrs. Brantham." The playfulness of his tone held an edge.

She would not be so easily put off. "The clothing upon your person was paid for with the blood of the four women you murdered in Manningtree."

"They spoke of witchcraft." Hopkins exploded to his feet, his fist slamming upon the wood in a sharp, hollow thud. "As God as my witness, I heard them with my own ears. I purged the earth of their condemned souls."

His hat tumbled from his head and those careful curls were a wild riot about his shoulders. He paused, drew in a deep breath and tugged his doublet over his paunch where the fabric had bunched. With great care, he retrieved his hat and sank into his seat, once more composed, cheeks still florid with his fury.

In that moment, she had seen the man he was, beyond the genteel clothes and nature, beyond his affected manner.

He was a man plagued by guilt.

And paid handsomely for his unforgivable transgressions.

"Tell me of how your lover bade you kill your husband." Gone was his genial tone. In its place was the flatness of unfeeling apathy.

She understood then. In his mind, he had shown her kindness, he had offered a part of himself which she had exploited. For that one brief moment, when he'd lost himself to his rage as she'd remained stoic and composed, she had possessed the power.

He would not make such a mistake again. She was equally as certain that he would no longer see her as similar to himself.

No, he would regard her as he did the others—inhuman. Incapable of feeling.

Unworthy of mercy.

"Did your lover also have you turn the milk at the Bryon's farm?" he asked when she did not answer. "Was it also your lover who made the Andersons' horse go lame?"

"No," Sybil replied firmly.

Hopkins raised his brows so they disappeared beneath the over-wide brim of his ridiculous hat. "No, it was not your lover? You must speak plainly."

"What lover?" Sybil demanded.

"Why, the Devil, of course. You have taken him as your lover, have you not?"

"Of course I have not," Sybil cried, incredulous.

Was this what the other prisoners endured?

Hopkins turned his attention to the parchment in front of him and began to write, the scratch of his quill overly loud in the quiet room.

"So, you have not lain with the Devil?" He asked the preposterous question with such sincerity, she might have burst into laughter under other circumstances.

"I have not," Sybil repeated sternly.

"Have you met Mother Cornell?"

She shook her head, brow pinching in confusion. "No."

"Has the Devil come to you in the form of a small boy?"

"No," Sybil said again, tamping down her exasperation.

Clearly, Hopkins wanted to inspire a passionate reply, to pique her ire that she might have a slip of the tongue he could twist into condemnation.

Every word she spoke was measured, every action carefully weighed. "I have neither met nor known the Devil in his form or any form."

"Did you attend the sabbath with the Devil?"

"I could not when I have never met him." She tried to keep the cynicism from her tone.

"Then you must have familiars." Matthew Hopkins looked up from his writing, mustache glistening in the candlelight.

"Familiars?"

"Animals that are connected to you."

This, she understood.

Daughters of the earth had animals they befriended with their hearts and souls. After all, those with gifts often lived in solitude. Like Edith.

The affinity between a woman of the earth and the animals they connected to was precious, akin to the bond between a mother and child.

Animals offered comfort and companionship, two lost pieces that fit together in the great world. Like Sybil's own steadfast Brixton, and Jacinda's kestrel, who never let a human lay hand upon him until Jacinda. Like Kat's squirrel that never ceased moving, and Edith's plain woodlark, whose song was lovelier than all the others.

The attachment between them was beautiful, forged by similar features possessed by woman and animal alike, a connection broken only by death.

But then Hopkins continued. "These familiars suckle blood from teats upon your person, and act as conduits to the Devil himself."

Sybil could not stop the look of horror that crossed her face. These witch hunters had taken even the wondrous nature of the friendship between woman and animal and wrenched it into the prurient and vulgar.

"Absolutely not," she replied, unable to keep the vehement denial from her tone.

"Do you testify you have spoken the truth?" Hopkins asked, quill poised over the parchment.

A drop of black ink slid from the tip and blotted the page like a spatter of blood.

"I do," Sybil replied. "I will sign my own name stating as much."

"That is not necessary." Hopkins scribbled with flourish. "Think on your words," he cautioned. "When you return next, I hope you shall speak the truth."

"I have spoken the truth."

Ignoring her words, the guards grabbed her shoulders and roughly hauled her to her feet. The chains at her wrists rattled, the heavy manacles cutting into her skin.

"And remember," Hopkins said as she was led toward the exit, "your sister has your mother's cunning blood as well."

He looked up, watching as she was dragged away, the threat apparent in the gleam in his eyes. A man like him would not be happy with only Sybil.

Jacinda was in danger, too.

CHAPTER TWENTY-ONE

Lilith

Lilith carried a cup of chamomile tea into the living room, where Aunt Jacqueline lounged in her recliner, now cleaned up in pleated pants and a blue-striped blouse.

Thankfully, she'd shaken whatever trance had brought her to the manor.

Lilith set the mug on the table beside Aunt Jacqueline, the sweet herbal fragrance scenting the air.

Aunt Jacqueline startled at the tap of the mug on the table and looked at Lilith in surprise. "I didn't see you there." She smiled. "Thank you, dear."

Outside, the crunch of gravel under tires told Lilith Asher had arrived.

Anxious excitement tightened in her chest. She was desperate to return to the manor, to see if she could find Jacinda again. Perhaps locate…whatever it was she was supposed to find.

And yet, she needed to press Aunt Jacqueline again, to understand what the older woman had meant, not only about the peppermint tea, but also her cryptic claim that the house had been waiting.

Had she meant the house had been waiting for Lilith? Or for something else?

All Lilith knew was that she might not get another chance.

Licking suddenly dry lips, she addressed the older woman. "When you brought the peppermint tea, you said it would open my eyes, and that the house had been waiting. Do you remember?"

Aunt Jacqueline looked blankly at her, as she had done before.

"Did you mean Brackenmere Manor has been waiting for me?" Lilith asked.

This time, Aunt Jacqueline settled her hand over Lilith's, cool and dry and threaded with ropy blue veins beneath her thin skin. "Yes, dear. The house has been waiting a long time. Since even before Asher—"

The front door opened and Asher rushed in with Toby at his side. "Aunt Jacqueline, thank God you're safe."

She shot her nephew an indignant look. "Why in heaven would I not be?"

Asher's shoulders lowered, with relief or resignation, Lilith couldn't tell which. "Because Lilith found you wandering around outside by the manor and you collapsed."

It was the story Lilith spun for him when she'd called him at work. She said Aunt Jacqueline had been outside the manor rather than inside, which absolved them both of guilt since Aunt Jacqueline gave her the key.

Aunt Jacqueline scoffed and rolled her eyes. "I had important business to tend to. I assure you, I'm fine."

His lips thinned at her words and he turned to Lilith, his gaze softening with gratitude. "Thank you for helping her."

Lilith waved off his apology. "Happy to."

Toby growled suddenly, drawing their attention to the doorway, where a stout skunk waddled over the threshold.

"No," Asher said firmly.

"Just for a few moments," Aunt Jacqueline pleaded, her voice suddenly frail in a clear tactic of manipulation.

"Absolutely not."

Toby snarled louder, echoing his master's sentiments.

Aunt Jacqueline huffed, exasperated. "Oh, he won't spray."

Lilith looked between the two, who appeared to be locked in an argument they'd had many times before. "Is this…her…pet?"

Asher heaved a beleaguered sigh, and Aunt Jacqueline spoke up, "Allow me to introduce you to Lord Wimbleton the third."

"There's been three of them?" Lilith asked in surprise.

"No, there hasn't," Asher replied dryly. "And he's not coming inside." He looked pointedly at his aunt, who sank back into her chair with a pout, like a sulking child.

"You're the one who gave him to me," she said in a petulant tone.

Lilith looked at Asher in confusion. "You gave her…a skunk?"

"As you know, skunks aren't native to England."

"Oh…right." She hoped she sounded convincing because she, in fact, did not know skunks weren't native to England.

Asher nodded to the creature. "The skunk—"

"Lord Wimbleton the third," Aunt Jacqueline corrected.

"Yes," Asher said tiredly. "Lord Wimbleton the third was part of an exotic animal menagerie owned by an eccentric millionaire. When he passed, many were taken to zoos, but no one wanted a skunk."

"And so, we took him in to love him," Aunt Jacqueline said with a coo of affection.

"Under the promise that he remain outside." Asher gave a pointed look at his aunt.

In the doorway, the skunk—Lord Wimbleton the third—was slowly backing away from Toby's glare.

"I can take it from here." Asher gave Lilith a grin that hit her right in the solar plexus. "Thanks again. I genuinely appreciate your kindness."

She nodded in reply, her cheeks warming. How embarrassing that one little compliment could undo her. Self-consciously, she tucked a strand of hair behind her ear and gave him a shy smile.

The corners of his eyes crinkled and he turned back to his aunt to see to her.

Now that she was being tended to, the afternoon opened up for Lilith. The manor called to her, tugging the thread of curiosity about what Jacinda had asked her to find. Lilith wanted to see Jacinda again, to talk to her again.

Because as much as Lilith tried to rationalize away the idea that she was just seeing things, she knew that conversation had happened. She *had* seen and spoken to Jacinda.

But she certainly wasn't so unfeeling as to ask Asher to take her to the manor after he'd left work early to tend to his aunt.

Instead, Lilith hovered there in her own awkwardness, not sure what to do with her arms or the rest of her body before finally slinking to her room. A wave of unexpected homesickness slammed into her.

At least in Savannah, she had a whole house to disappear into. Here in someone's home with one rented room, there was the sense of being contained, judged.

She picked up her phone and tapped out a message to Essie: I miss home.

Essie: No, you don't.

Lilith gave an incredulous scoff. You're right about a lot of things, but I'm pretty sure I'm right about how I'm feeling.

Essie: And I'm pretty sure you need this adventure in your life. Lil, you were so excited about this trip, talking about the manor and finding a connection to your past.

Lilith: Except Mr. Darcy won't let me go to the manor without him.

The dots appeared, then disappeared. Then appeared.

Lilith smirked and tapped out a reply: Do not tell me you're trying to find a way to lawyer-talk me into permission to break in.

Essie: I was trying, but really can't justify breaking and entering, especially in a country where you're a foreign national. Sorry.

Lilith decided not to mention that she had already disobeyed Asher's wishes using Aunt Jacqueline's key, since it might technically be considered breaking and entering.

Essie: This is the first time in years that you've been so enthusiastic about something. Don't let Mr. Darcy take that away from you. And don't let missing home get you down either. If it helps, Savannah is ridiculously hot right now. Like I had to change my bra cuz of all the boob sweat after a client wanted to eat outside at lunch kind of hot.

Lilith laughed and replied back: Boob sweat is the worst.

Essie started typing again: What about that museum? Moblys?

Lilith: Moyse's Hall

Essie: Have you been yet?

The birthmark on Lilith's arm tingled, echoing Essie's sentiments.

Essie replied again: I take your silence for a no, which means you can go there today.

Lilith: It's unfair how right you always are.

Essie: I'd say it's a blessing and a curse, but it's really just a blessing.

Lilith: Lucky for me you share that blessing with me.

Essie: Can I remind you of that in the future?

Lilith: You're going to anyway.

Essie replied back with a grinning emoji face and a red heart emoji. Good luck!

Lilith needed all the luck she could get.

Heat pulsed beneath her birthmark, causing her to flinch in surprise. This time, the certainty of the sensation echoed in the twist in her gut.

Whatever waited in Moyes's Hall, she knew it was something she needed to see.

CHAPTER TWENTY-TWO

Lilith

Bury St. Edmunds blurred past as Lilith rushed up Abbeygate Street toward Moyse's Hall. Even in her haste, she couldn't help but notice the abundance of Tudor era homes leaning on their centuries-old frames with the telltale second floor jutting above the first. All far older than what she was used to in Savannah.

And yet, the medieval grid street tugged at her with the same eerie familiarity as the land around Brackenmere Manor.

She passed quaint shops and restaurants as people wove around with shopping bags and strollers.

Suddenly, a surge of dread slammed into her. Her breath came short and fast, her head spinning with the same sensation she'd experienced at Brackenmere Manor.

She did not want to faint again. Not here.

Desperate to stay upright, she pressed her palms to the gritty bricks, grounding herself.

Her heart rate slowed. Breathing came easier.

Please let this be jet lag. Or dehydration. Or something normal.

Still recovering, she pushed forward on shaky legs. But even as she continued the upward climb of Abbeygate's sloping street, ice threaded through her veins.

Fear.

Horror.

Death.

A little girl skipped by with a bear dangling from her fingertips and two women passed, laughing.

Clearly, Lilith was alone in her terror while the rest of the world moved on, oblivious. She turned right onto Skinner Street and the awful sensations abated.

Pausing to recover fully, she tilted her face toward the sun, letting its warmth and strength wash over her. Tension bled from her body and whatever gripped her finally let go completely.

What had she been walking toward that affected her so deeply?

No sooner had she asked herself the question than a vision flashed in her mind's eye. A prison, crumbling with age, murky with darkness, the air wet and dank, the fetid odor of people crammed into cages meant for a fraction of the number of prisoners.

The thought was visceral, more like a memory than something imagined.

If she had continued up Abbeygate Street, she would have come to that prison.

If it even still existed.

She hoped it did not.

A tall sandstone brick manor house at the end of Skinner Street caught her attention.

Moyse's Hall.

An older gentleman with a thick head of white hair spoke

to a group outside the museum. His blue vest indicated he was one of the Bury St. Edmunds tour guides, which she'd noticed when picking up a town map.

"If you're looking for history, it doesn't get much older than this." He nodded up at the building. "Moyse's Hall is almost nine hundred years old."

Lilith gazed up at the building with renewed appreciation. Nine hundred years was such a wealth of history. The sum of countless lives, layered upon one another like sediment. The births and burials, love affairs and celebrations, nights swollen with worry that felt so important at the time—all moments bright with life now reduced to the embers of time.

The tour group funneled inside. Lilith stepped forward to join them when the door slammed in her face.

She jerked back with a start and pushed inside.

The museum employee blinked at her, as if in surprise. "Oh, I'm sorry, I didn't see you there."

A chill tingled over her skin.

You will cease to exist.

The warning rose unbidden in her mind.

She was being paranoid. It was just an accident.

Still, Lilith's hand trembled as she accepted a glossy brochure of recent exhibits and beelined toward the witch trials.

Chipped clay pots mottled with age were displayed in glass cases, charms once used to discourage witches from entering one's home. There were more artifacts on display, including an armoire with deep burns and daisy-shaped carvings, also meant to keep witches away.

There was an irony to the fact that every charm on display was used not *by* witches, but to repel them.

Another glass case prominently displayed the pamphlet of a trial dating back to 1664. Lilith hesitated, running her fingertips over her birthmark.

It remained cool and unfeeling under her touch.

No, that wasn't what she needed.

A digital archive drew her over. She scrolled through the options, stopping instinctively on a trial set during 1645.

The year nudged at something in her mind.

Yes. This.

The largest execution of witches in England, where eighteen victims were convicted of witchcraft and hung, with an additional one who had been burned alive.

The hair stood on Lilith's arms.

The names were listed—so many Annes and Marys and Margarets.

Almost all were women, convicted by men. Lilith recalled the line she'd once read in *The Scarlet Letter* by a male character casting his judgment on Hester Prynne. "Is there no virtue in woman, save what springs from a wholesome fear of the gallows?"

Likely the jury of men who condemned these women ascribed to the same thought.

There was one final name, the victim who had been burned alive.

Sybil Brantham.

The name shot through Lilith like a jolt of lightning, making her birthmark burn.

Breathless, she scrolled down on the screen.

All nineteen victims were put to death on Thingoe Hill on August 27, 1645.

Lilith's birthmark blazed.

A warning.

This date was of great importance.

She searched the remainder of the exhibit and though her birthmark remained hot to the touch, it did not flare with the same spark as before.

Moyse's had given her a key, now she had to figure out how to unlock the mystery. Likely the rest of what she needed was at Brackenmere Manor.

A knot of unease curled in her stomach.

She couldn't keep sneaking around behind Asher's back. The man might be grumpy as all get out, but he'd shown her kindness. He didn't deserve to be lied to. And if she was being entirely honest with herself, she hated the idea of disappointing him.

Lord help her.

Much as she was dreading it, she had to ask Asher to let her back in the manor. After all, it was the whole reason she'd come to England.

And the reason suddenly seemed more important now than ever before.

CHAPTER TWENTY-THREE

Lilith

The dream was unlike any Lilith had before.

The floor was cold as ice under her bare soles. She wrapped her arms around herself and gazed down the hallway of mirrors stretching into forever.

Whispers echoed through the air, muffled and distorted, like the apparitions at Brackenmere Manor.

"Hello?" The volume of her voice came out small, her words swallowed by the vastness of the place.

Where was she?

The speed of the murmuring voices intensified, making her flesh crawl. She surveyed her strange surroundings, the world dark beyond the hallway of gold rococo-style mirrors, as if floating in space.

"Hello?" she called uselessly once more, walking forward.

That's when she noticed she had no reflection.

The mirrors faced one another, a long line of gleaming panes of glass, like a snake with no tail. No matter which way she turned, there was only the image of infinity. One without her.

Her breath caught, stomach clenching in fear.

She checked the next mirror. Then another and another.

On and on down the line, turning from one side of the hall to the other until the truth punched her in the chest.

Not one reflected her image.

As if she had ceased to exist.

Panic jabbed the back of her brain, and her breathing came in ragged gulps.

Run.

The cry was more base instinct than thought, and her legs pumped under her, propelling her down the hall at breakneck speed.

The icy ground blazed with heat, singeing her soles, and the whispers began to crackle, like firewood burning and popping. Thick plumes of smoke curled around the mirrors to form a disorienting nebulous haze.

The fumes sucked into her lungs, and she choked, coughing.

A mirror appeared in front of her, and she began to slow.

The smoke cleared, the floor now cool enough to stand on.

Lilith gasped a breath.

Finally, the end had come.

A figure materialized in the mirror, dressed in a white shift, a cap on her head.

Sybil.

The woman clutched the inside of her right arm as if in pain, and an answering ache lanced through Lilith's birthmark.

In the mirror, Sybil's lips moved.

The fire was roaring now, making hearing impossible.

Lilith shook her head. "What?"

Sybil's face contorted in agony, and she shouted, "You're running out of time."

Then, she disappeared, leaving Lilith standing in front of an empty looking glass, her reflection missing once more.

Lilith jerked awake with a cry.

Her heartbeat slammed against her ribs, as if trying to escape from her chest. The odor of smoke still lingered, leaving grit in her mouth.

She peeled herself out of bed. The floor was cold, bringing back the recollection of the dream. Suppressing the urge to shudder, she padded toward the bathroom, the stink of smoke redolent in her hair.

The door to her bathroom was almost completely closed. She paused, a sudden spike of fear nailing her in place.

But she scoffed at herself. She was being ridiculous. With a roll of her eyes, she pushed into the bathroom, clicked on the light, looked into the mirror.

And screamed.

She had no reflection.

Lilith jerked awake with a cry.

What the hell was that?

She lay in the dark, gasping in fear. The crescent moon birthmark still ached.

August 27.

The date echoed in Lilith's mind, prodding the wound of her legacy.

Her heart stuttered in a hard, painful beat.

Did that mean she had until August 27?

If so, she only had…

She reached for her phone and glanced at the screen, reflecting a few minutes past midnight.

The white numbers displayed over her background picture of Amara: Saturday, August 24.

Three days.

Three days to save Sybil—if the dream was indeed a warning.

You must help her.

Or you will cease to exist.

Chills skittered over Lilith's flesh.

Three days to save Sybil.

And three days to save herself.

CHAPTER TWENTY-FOUR

Sybil

A moldy piece of bread landed in the rushes. Sybil snatched up the chunk before a lump of brown fur could fall upon it.

Man and beast alike starved in this prison.

The women in the next cell had been given their daily ration of stale bread.

Sybil had not appreciated that meager allowance until she was deprived.

The women had been separated into several cages. Hers was specifically for those who had not confessed, an attempt to lure them into admission through starvation.

This was Sybil's fourth day with no food, and Edith's fifth. The only sustenance allowed was a small cup of ale once a day, sour and teetering on rancid. Still, they gulped greedily with a thirst they feared would never be quenched.

They had not yet received their cup that day, and the burn

in Sybil's throat was more visceral than even the gnawing ache in her stomach.

The crust trembled in her hand. A gift from a stranger in another cell, a fraction of an already pitiful ration, tossed behind a guard's turned back.

Sybil faced the rear of the cell and shoved the food into her mouth.

The bread was stale and sharp against her gums as she tried valiantly to chew. Her teeth gnashed in vain while the bread absorbed the scant moisture in her body, turning into a wad of thick paste that stuck to the roof of her mouth.

Bit by bit, she managed to swallow the lump where it lodged midway down in her chest.

"Oy," a guard shouted.

Another crust of bread landed in Sybil's cage, tossed by one of the imprisoned men.

"Who did this?" The guard reached for the bread, but a rat seized it out from under his hand. The guard screamed with a shrillness that set a few of the men chuffing with mirth.

He glowered at them, assuming himself mocked, face purpling with humiliation beneath his gray hair. A scar bisected his right eyebrow from some long-ago fight likely fueled by his short temper.

"Do you find me amusing?" He unlocked the cell and whipped his cudgel about, catching an old man on the back of the head. The man cried out and held the injury as he scuttled into the shadows.

The other prisoners lurched away, too. All but Edward Morris, who sat against the wall, his stare fixed in a different time.

"Was it you?" the guard bellowed.

Edward Morris did not so much as lift his gaze.

The guard kicked Edward's leg, but managed to slip in refuse on the floor, hitting the ground with an undignified *oof*.

This time, no one laughed.

Silence descended over the prison, heavy with fear.

The guard leaped up like a beast and set upon the young man, the war hero who had been rumored to have slain at least twenty at the Battle of Marston Moor.

With grunting effort, the guard kicked and punched and pummeled.

The soldier did not fight back.

When, at last, the guard straightened and came away, short of breath from his efforts, Edward Morris lay on the floor in a growing pool of blood. His stare was vacant still, only this time, his eyes saw nothing.

Edward Morris's body remained on the floor for two days before he was removed at the behest of the guard who beat him to death and now complained of the smell.

There was no further generosity among the prisoners in sharing food.

The little girl was now in the cell with those being starved and Sybil sat beside her. If Sybil had to guess, she would assume the child was perhaps ten. Still mute, the girl pressed her back to the wall, legs tucked to her chest, arms folded protectively around her knees.

Edith had finally been relocated to the other cage, not for confessing, but to keep her alive—building her strength, so they might starve her again. Or enact some new form of torture under the guise of encouraging an admission of guilt.

At night, those who had confessed to spare themselves cried out for God to forgive them, wailing their innocence to anyone who would listen.

And confessed or not, they all wondered when they might die.

It was a question no one could answer. Not when the court remained on hold while both sides of England fought on the battlefield of their own country. Certainly, the assizes were not traveling to see to legal matters in small towns amid a landscape of such danger.

But what was to become of the prisoners? Left to starve to death in jail, or be beaten like Edward Morris.

Though Sybil knew the earth could not hear her with the iron manacles severing her connection from her gifts, she whispered for the soil to receive Edward Morris with love, that he might find peace with his deceased wife and daughter.

A pang resonated in Sybil's chest with a hurt she could scarcely stand.

Her soul longed for the hum of the earth's energy, for the energy that once coursed through her body with love and light. She tried to turn her thoughts from such yearning for the idea of never feeling that connection again was far too bleak.

Thoughts of her gifts always led to those of Jacinda. That is when the true agony began. Raw and sharp and insistent.

What might become of Jacinda with no one to warn her away from her powers? Would she be discovered if she used them without care? How long until she, too, was dragged into the prison?

Sybil had thought herself helpless as a woman her entire life, bound to silence for being born the weaker sex, limited in her learning and aspirations. In her marriage to Henry, she'd had a modicum of power, a thread of a voice. That had weakened with his death and was now nonexistent.

Once more, she was rendered mute, powerless. Helpless even to protect Jacinda.

The cage beside Sybil's opened and a new woman was shoved into the pen, her eyes wild, hair streaked with mud. A new prisoner.

One Sybil did not know.

This time, at least.

Still, the danger felt too near. Too real.

A wild rage tore through her, a revival of spirit in her determination to do something—*anything*—to keep Jacinda safe.

Sybil's fingers wandered over the crumbling stone behind her as she sat by the girl, seeking out weakness in the seams between the rocks, where a stone might be loosened to create a gap wide enough for someone to squeeze through.

The iron was impenetrable. But perhaps stone…

"Sybil Brantham," the barrel-chested guard bellowed.

Her hands dropped from the damp wall, her insides shrinking against themselves.

There was only one reason her name would be called.

The time had come for her to speak with Matthew Hopkins once more.

CHAPTER TWENTY-FIVE

Lilith

Though exhausted, there was no more sleep for Lilith. Not when doing so might drag her back down that hallway of mirrors where she did not have a reflection.

Not when her birthmark continued to ache with warning.

Not when she only had three days left.

The clink of dishes sounded from the kitchen, evidence that Asher was awake and moving about. Then she remembered she had to talk to him, to ask—beg—to be allowed into the manor.

With a sigh, she pushed from bed and readied herself for the day, telling herself the extra care she took with her mascara had everything to do with convincing Asher and nothing to do with the man himself.

The iron table was waiting for her again with a fresh carafe of coffee. She sat down, shuddering at the effect of iron against her, and poured a cup of coffee as Asher entered the room. "English breakfast all right?"

It didn't escape her notice that he was wearing his vet scrubs even though it was Saturday.

"Yes, thank you." She sipped her coffee, pretending to be casual. "Are you going into work today?"

"For a few hours."

"I hate to put you out, but..." Lilith winced, letting him know exactly how painful this question was for her. "Do you think I might could borrow the key for the manor to check it out on my own?"

"By yourself?" A small line showed between his brows. "Did Aunt Jacqueline put you up to this?"

Lilith hesitated. Was there an Aunt Jacqueline conspiracy underway that she wasn't privy to?

He gave a slow nod, saving Lilith from having to answer. "Actually, yes. You can. It's the least I can do for your help yesterday."

Lilith gave him her best debutante smile. Not that she had ever been a debutante—much to Mama's dismay.

The smile he returned could have melted butter, all hotness and not a lick of grump to him. "Be right back."

Her foot jogged under the table, her entire body alight with the need to hurry through breakfast and get to the manor.

True to his word, he returned with the heavy iron key and a pitcher of tea. "Aunt Jacqueline said you wanted some peppermint tea this morning as well. In addition to your, erm, coffee?" There was a slight question in his tone. Because *how odd*.

But something in Lilith's gut told her Aunt Jacqueline was on about the tea for good reason.

"Yes, thank you," Lilith replied without explanation. Not like she had one to give...

A plate of hurriedly eaten fried eggs and baked beans, plus a cup of peppermint tea later, Asher left with a wave that made more warm fuzzies in Lilith's chest than she cared to admit.

Just like his trust in giving her that key mattered more than it should.

After ensuring Aunt Jacqueline was still peacefully sleeping, Lilith slipped out of the bed and breakfast and rushed to the manor.

Entering the old building was less disorienting this time, the seam between past and present more normal—if such a thing could ever be called "normal." The ethereal form of a maid swept from the Great Hall into the kitchen.

The layer of the past over the present seemed clearer now. Stronger.

Maybe due to the peppermint tea?

A glance at Lilith's watch indicated nine in the morning. But she'd seen Jacinda in the afternoon previously.

A look around the bottom floor confirmed Jacinda was not in the vicinity.

Lilith climbed the stairs and her birthmark tingled. A certainty settled into her gut.

She was on the right path.

The figure of a maid moved from one doorway to another, an amorphous white bundle in her arms. Lilith avoided the figure, contemplating which bedroom was Jacinda's when a flash of heat burned over her birthmark. She turned to find the entrance to the library and a familiar figure within.

Lilith could make out Sybil's face a little better now. One very similar to her own, with high cheekbones, a broad mouth, and hazel eyes.

"Sybil?" Lilith said softly.

Sybil moved to the desk, not seeming to hear. She wore the same green silk dress as before.

The realization came with the reminder of how Lilith had heard the clattering pan and breaking glass two days in a row.

Was this one day in history happening over and over again?

"Sybil." Lilith spoke louder this time, desperate for answers.

The woman picked up a book from the desk and walked toward Lilith.

Not seeing her at all. Not the way Jacinda had.

Was Jacinda the only one who could see Lilith?

Sybil exited the library, and Lilith sighed in defeat.

None of this made a lick of sense.

She approached the bookshelf instead, seeing through texts that were no longer there, and shuffling about mouldering books that appeared to be decades old, with yellowed pages and curling paperback covers.

When her fingers skimmed the shelf to the left of the hearth, her birthmark prickled.

If nothing else, her birthmark was handy.

A number of books remained on the shelf, sagging against one another like a line of dominoes with nowhere to go. Their spines were cracked and faded, reflecting an array of publications likely from the twentieth century. As if occupants had resided in the house for quite some time during the last hundred years or so.

She recalled how Asher ignored her questions about the most recent occupants. Had *he* lived there?

The book lover in her wanted to find out what each book title was, to open them one by one and breathe in that precious, ineffable smell of old books. But she was on a mission.

Her fingers skimmed the row Sybil had paused by yesterday, recognizing some of her own favorite reads. *Jane Eyre*, *Emma*, *The Scarlet Letter*… Whoever curated this library had great taste. A hint of the books existing during Sybil's time was visible, but the titles were too transparent to read.

The old copy of *Jane Eyre* looked like the ancient 1980s paperback from Mrs. Bayard's English class. Lilith set it aside to bring back with her. Classics needed a good rereading from time to time.

A resounding thwack made Lilith jump. The book beside *Jane Eyre* had flopped forward, falling into the newly empty space.

She removed the book from the shelf when a shadow against the end of the shelf caught her attention. Her fingertips skimmed the area, finding something hollow along the side.

Frowning, she leaned forward, straining to peer into the shadows amid a dingy stream of morning sunlight. Still unable to see properly, she felt around the space again. Yes, there was a distinct gap at the front of the bookshelf there.

She stuck her head into the shelf to study the unusual construction. Where the decorative trim connected, there appeared to be a gap, about an inch wide and five inches high, easily covered by a book. And entirely undetectable, unless…well, unless someone decided to stick their head into the bookshelf.

Without thought, she reached for the hole, pushing her fingers into the darkness.

It was a dumb thing to do in an abandoned building, where a random hole in the wall could very easily contain any number of spiders or snakes or who knew what else.

But even as she chastised herself, her fingertip met with something hard and cold. The abrupt quiet around her suggested the metal was iron.

A lever?

She curled her fingertips around it and wiggled, to no avail.

Pull.

She didn't know where the thought came from, but she obeyed, tugging the lever toward the wall in a firm yank.

A groan sounded beside her and the thick wooden frame of

the hearth slid to the side, like a board loosely nailed into the wall, revealing a dark passageway.

She couldn't see where the hall ended, but the empty black held a chill that told her entering the creepy mysterious secret room was probably stupid.

And stupid or not, she'd already made her choice. She was going in.

CHAPTER TWENTY-SIX

Lilith

Lilith stepped into the passage, the darkness so absolute her eyes ached.

Without thinking, she pulled her phone from her back pocket and clicked the flashlight on. Light washed over what appeared to be an L-shaped room at the end of a short hall, set safely behind the hearth.

Lilith turned the corner and stopped short.

Shelves were embedded into the wall, filled with glass bottles layered in dust. The contents within bore signs of extreme age—oils long since soured to yellow, desiccated organic matter that was indistinguishable. Herbs dangled from the rafters, swaying at her disturbance, their brittle leaves rustling like whispered secrets.

But the herbs and bottles were not what captured her attention.

The table at the far end drew her with an undeniable lure,

its length taking up the entire back wall, littered with various stones and flowers long since withered to a shade of brown that gave no hint as to their original color.

Three candlesticks bracketed the sides and back of the table, the wicks blackened from previous use.

At the center was a book, the pages spread wide, as if someone abandoned the room while in the middle of reading.

A feather lay on the table amid the dusty debris, the tip sharp and black.

A quill most likely.

Lilith bent over the handwritten script, the ink faded to almost nothing. Even squinting, she could barely make out a word or two. Without thinking, she reached out to brush the top of the page. Dust came away on her fingertips, the vellum beneath strangely warm to the touch.

Like something alive.

She hesitated, her palm hovering over the book. Her birthmark seemed to hum, heeding a soundless call.

As if she had been waiting for this moment her entire life.

With a shaking breath, she pressed the flat of her hand against the page.

The writing shimmered and fresh air swept through the room, bringing the crisp, verdant notes of herbs: rosemary, lavender, sage, nettle, and so many more. Each identifiable in some memory she'd never created.

The candles flickered to life, sprouting flames that bathed the room in a golden light so bright, she no longer needed her phone.

Maybe she should be afraid.

But a deeper, innate part of herself felt more right about this than anything in her life ever had.

The jars on the shelves shone as if new, their contents rich with ingredients necessary for anything Lilith might need.

But for what?

To heal? To save? To protect?

To make herself exist?

Was that even a thing?

She hoped it was…

Returning her focus to the book, she discovered the writing was no longer faded, but dark, as if freshly written. Even the ink on the quill glistened. She touched the sharpened point and her fingertip came away black. Still wet.

The flowers on the table plumped into marigolds, their heads brilliant shades of gold and yellow. Among them, various stones and crystals gleamed in the candlelight, power glinting from within.

A smooth purple one caught her attention. Amethyst?

She lifted the stone and the cool surface pulsed against her palm, imbuing her with strength. With certainty.

Her mind sharpened and she returned her focus to the book.

Grimoire.

The handwriting inside was some old-world jumbled mess of ornate letters with elongated *s*'s and *f*'s and sweeping tails on the *p*'s and *y*'s. Despite the unique writing, Lilith could still read the archaic script as easily as one of Essie's texts.

Jacinda,

Read this from the beginning and you will understand.

Love eternally,
Sybil

Lilith's breath caught, with disbelief and excitement entwined with everything she'd hoped for when she set out on this trip for England.

She'd just won the creepy old house lottery.

Perhaps this book would tell her more about both women. And hopefully more about what was expected of her.

Lilith flipped to the front of the book—the grimoire—eager to read more, as Sybil encouraged.

For the answers she would find, for the path she must forge ahead with. There was no going back now.

CHAPTER TWENTY-SEVEN

Sybil

The aroma of roasted meat lingered in the hallway of the prison. The savory fragrance carried toward Sybil like a dream. Like a nightmare.

Matthew Hopkins awaited her, knowing she hadn't eaten in almost a week.

Her stomach twisted, her need savage. The focus of her existence narrowed as she imagined gripping the greasy flesh in her hand, sinking her teeth into the crisp skin to the tenderness beneath, savoring the salty, herbed juices exploding in her mouth.

She was practically panting with desperation when the guards deposited her into the room for a second interrogation.

A massive platter sat before Hopkins, featuring a goose roasted to golden perfection and glistening in the candlelight. An assortment of vegetables framed the bird: potatoes, carrots, parsnips, and string beans.

Sybil hadn't thought there was moisture left in her body, but now, thick saliva flooded her mouth, and a sharp ache fisted her stomach.

"Have you had time to think?" Hopkins asked by way of greeting.

Sybil scarcely heard him over the vision of that roasted goose. A tremor rippled through her, an uncontrollable shudder of need.

"Have you had time to think?" This time when he asked the question, he lifted a pewter mug. The liquid inside sloshed wetly.

The primitive part of Sybil redirected her focus to the contents of that mug. He brought it to his lips, drinking noisily, the muscles of his neck squeezing as he swallowed.

Without realizing what she was doing, Sybil's mouth parted, and her empty throat worked with each of his greedy gulps.

Ale.

It was ale.

The yeasty scent, the hint of sweetness from the malt, the smell unmistakable.

Hopkins set the mug down, and some of the contents splashed out over the desk in beaded droplets. "Do you have anything to tell me?"

Sybil stared at those droplets, desperate enough to lap them up from the wooden surface.

She tried to swallow, but her parched throat clicked in protest. "I have nothing to say." The laconic reply had to be forced out. Her thoughts were thick as mud, her voice hoarse, her lips dry and splitting. The stink of her own breath was both evident and appalling.

No doubt he could smell her, too. Not only the halitosis of starvation, but the filth of her unwashed body, her snarled, oily hair.

"No confession then?" Hopkins took up an eating dagger

and sliced into the goose. Rivulets of clear juice streamed from the incision and the golden skin peeled back to reveal tender white flesh.

A soft whimper rose unbidden from Sybil's throat.

Hopkins paused in his task and looked at her, his brow quirking slightly. The corners of his mouth twitched.

He had heard.

Sybil hated how easily he'd witnessed her weakness.

"I imagine you are hungry." He plucked the slice of meat with the tip of his dagger. "I would share my meal with you, if you would have it."

Her heart smacked against her ribs, throbbing with anticipation.

Hopkins tilted his head, his expression one of sympathy. "But first, you would have to confess."

A twisting pain knifed through her stomach. Sybil shook her head rather than speak.

With a casual lift of his shoulders, he brought the goose to his mouth and peeled his lips back so she could watch his teeth sink into the meat. He chewed noisily and tilted his head back, eyes closing in pleasure as he moaned.

"This might be the best goose I've ever tasted." He licked his lips, leaving them wet, a smear of grease slick on his chin. "I can't say much for this town, but you do have fine cooks." He sliced off another morsel, this time extending a hunk of quivering meat to Sybil.

How she longed to snatch it, not caring if the dagger cut her fingers in the process. She wanted to shove the chunk in her mouth and lean her head back in pleasure as he had done, groaning around the meat as it slid down her throat.

"Speak your confession." He waggled the goose flesh, dripping flecks of juice upon the desk, where they puddled with an iridescent sheen. "Say you're a witch. Admit you took the

Devil as your lover. Admit you danced around the fire with him at the Sabbath, that you suckled familiars." Hopkins's voice became louder with each declaration as he bade her speak. "Admit you killed your husband with the powers the Devil gave you. Admit your sister is of the same pact with the Devil as you."

Sybil's focus snapped from the knife and the offering extended toward her. No longer did she think of food or drink, but of protecting Jacinda.

And of justice.

Over any food in the world, she would choose her grimoire, that old text bequeathed to her by her mother. The one she had left for Jacinda with a small spell that it should find its way to her should she have need of it.

In that moment, Sybil would employ any enchantment, sacrifice the last bit of her gifts, to see this man destroyed. To ensure women remained safe.

But she could not have her grimoire.

She did not even have a whisper of the earth's power.

All she had was the fortitude of a woman protecting what she loved.

And a vow to live long enough to see this man fall.

"No." Her protest came out with finality. "I admit to nothing as I've done none of those things."

Hopkins got to his feet and lifted the mug, carrying it as he approached. "I've had a witness say they hear you speaking with the Devil at night, that he bids you harm others." He stopped before her and drank deeply again, every gulp making her throat scorch with a yearning unlike she'd ever known.

When he lowered the mug, his mouth wet, ale trickling down his chin. He held the cup to her, the scent sweet with raw temptation.

"No," she said again.

His nose wrinkled, and he pulled back. "I would let you bathe as well." He sneered down at her once fine gown, now stained and rumpled.

Through his eyes, she saw herself reduced to the inhuman prisoner he wanted her to be.

"I am no witch," she said firmly.

He sighed, as if she were a recalcitrant child. "Very well."

At his nod, rough hands snatched her up, dragging her backward.

That iron grip upon her body reminded her of the magistrate, of the assault.

Her body stiffened in preparation to fight, but the strength sapped away as soon as it had flared, weakened by her state of extreme deprivation. They carried her to the prison, her feet bumping over uneven cobblestones, and deposited her in an unceremonious heap on the filthy rushes.

She did not know how long she lay there. Edith reached through the bars between their cages, straining to comfort Sybil and receiving a kick from the guards for her kindness.

Eventually, Sybil would be relocated as well, though she did not know when she would be moved. Or when she might eat again.

She let her head fall to her bent arms, made wholly feeble from the encounter.

Though she may be weak of body, she was determined to remain strong in spirit. In her helpless state, her fortitude was the only power she possessed to keep Jacinda safe.

CHAPTER TWENTY-EIGHT

Lilith

Lilith leaned over the text of the ancient book, heart racing at the discovery of something so extraordinary. Maybe even something…magical.

Breathing in the musky scent of the marigolds scattered over the table, she turned to the first page. Amid the pulsing warmth of her birthmark, she began to read.

There is danger in putting these words to parchment. Yet there is even more danger in not.

My dearest Sybil, I hope you read this book someday when you embrace the power of the world around us. We are but flesh and bone in a cycle of life that will not cease for our whims. When interest in your gifts is aroused, I may no longer be of this earth.

And so I gift this text to you, to share all I have learned, all that has been passed down to me through generations of women.

There are those who would seek to persecute us for our power. Out of fear. Out of envy. Out of ignorance.

Emotions that are not only vicious, but also dangerous.

We were not always so strong.

Our ancestors were bent into submission, abused for their supposed weakness. But there was one who the earth beckoned, offering her the promise of protection and strength.

This ancestor learned the language of the sun's path and all the phases of the moon. She witnessed the power in the changing seasons, in the elements around us. She honed her mind to understand the earth's gifts—how dragon's glass can sweep away time to expose what will come to be, how tin stone can bring great silence, how even a simple sprig of mugwort can enhance dreams.

The earth can aid in all areas of life. But what can heal can also kill.

You are forewarned if you do not stay on the chosen path, your gifts will fall silent. It is for that reason I implore you to enlist caution when creating your charms and enchantments, daughter. Work with a pure heart lest your harm to others befall you threefold.

If you read this to learn, do so under a waxing moon to sharpen your understanding.

If there is no time to spare for such measures, trust the earth to guide you.

First, open your heart and center your mind on the world. From the dirt beneath your feet, to the leaves in the trees, the chattering rush of a stream, the song of the wind, the life-giving warmth of the sun, the power of the moon's silver gleam.

There is power all around us. It will call. You need only answer.

Do not allow your frustration and impatience to sway you. You are a chalice to be filled with the potency of this world. Clearing your mind will ease your struggles.

Here is a simple charm to enhance your gifts.

Place into a satchel to wear upon your person:

- *Crystal to amplify intentions*
- *Amethyst to elicit power*
- *Rosemary to heighten your senses*
- *Heads of snakeroot to amplify your need*
- *Laurel for success*

Bring these together by the light of three candles with focus and intention.

This bears repeating: Only use the earth's energy for good, no matter the harms you face in life.

May the earth and my love guide you.

CHAPTER TWENTY-NINE

Sybil

Sybil finally received her meager ration of bread and ale the following day and was relocated into the cell with Edith.

Despite the desperate gnaw of hunger and risk to herself, Sybil tossed a bit of her bread to the little girl who still remained in the cell of starving women. Hopkins would likely call for her later that day.

The guards mocked the girl often, laughing at her inability to speak or even nod or shake her head.

How was a child with such limited ability to communicate supposed to confess to witchcraft?

She caught the bread with a quiet look of gratitude.

During the days spent starving together, Sybil had come to learn more of her. Not through speech, but through the nights when the child slept, tucked into herself like a babe pulled too soon from the womb. In the whimpers she issued forth, the soft cries for her mother.

A mother who never answered. A mother who never sought her child locked within the prison.

That was all Sybil needed to know.

A commotion of shouts came from the door and the prisoners stirred into action. Some ran to the bars, peering out to see who had arrived. Others cowered back against the wall, out of the way of a cudgel swing.

The guards staggered forward, dragging a woman between them, flame red hair spilling down her back.

Sybil's heart snared in her throat.

Kat.

The guard with the scarred eyebrow gave an outraged howl and abruptly struck Kat across the face, the sound solid and meaty.

"For shame to strike a woman thus." The old vicar pressed against the cage, his feeble body severely deteriorated through his incarceration. Even when holding himself upright on the bars, his head wobbled as if his neck could scarcely keep it perched atop his stick-thin body.

"Leave off, old man," the barrel-chested jailer groused. He glared at the guard with the scar. "Let's on with it."

"The trollop bit me," the scarred man complained.

"I've seven children at home needing their mam." Kat lifted her head defiantly. "Ye're lucky that was all I did. And I won't promise not to do more." She bared her teeth and nipped at the air over his arm.

The man jerked back, sending them all stumbling. The barrel-chested guard pulled out the key, clattering it in the lock to Sybil's cage. Once the door swung open, the jailers threw Kat inside. She landed in a heap of green and black linen before jumping up like the ground was on fire.

"Ye'll be hearing from my husband," she vowed to their turned backs.

With a huff, she wiped her hair back from her face with the

flat of her hand and surveyed the room. Her dress was not as filthy as the others who had been walked through the streets of Bury St. Edmunds. Perhaps her husband's elevated status had spared her such brutality.

"Kat." Sybil approached with Edith.

Kat caught sight of them and tsked. "Oh, ye both look awful." She laughed at her own critical greeting, her eyes bright with tears as she pulled them in for an embrace. "And ye smell like a chamber pot."

"If you keep up this flattery, we're going to see you out," Sybil offered wryly.

"Is that all there is to being free of this place?" Kat winked, and Sybil felt herself smile for the first time in days.

She had forgotten how Kat could make light of the darkest times. Likewise, she hadn't realized how sorely she had needed that levity against the oppressive force of her predicament.

Ah, what love could do in a place filled with hate.

"What happened?" Edith asked. "How are you come to be in here?"

"My fool of a neighbor said having seven well-behaved bairns under the age of ten was unnatural." Kat rolled her eyes. "Quite rude of her, the jealous old sow. Then they arrested me."

She folded her arms over her chest. "And here I am in prison. How do they know I'm not with child?"

"Are you?" Sybil glanced at her friend's flat stomach.

Kat shrugged in her unaffected way. "Probably. Ye ken I can't hang my nightdress next to Tom's trousers without coming away with a babe in my belly."

Even Edith gave a little smile at the reply.

Kat lowered her voice, "My Tom will have me out of here before that Matthew Hopkins can pat himself on the back for my arrest."

Likely Kat was correct.

Tom worked at the Guildhall Feoffees, dealing with property ownership. What weight he did not carry in wealth, he made up for with influence. Especially after taking on several roles for officials who refused to travel during the war. And a man on his own with seven children would not be able to apply himself sufficiently at his trade.

"Jacinda." The name caught in Sybil's throat. "Pray, tell me news of her."

The fire cooled from Kat's gaze. "She is well, Sybil. Yer servants have been loyal, seeing to her and ensuring the estate is secure. There have been many who circle it, the vultures. Anne and Bess have tried to see ye, to bring food and ale and fresh clothes, but they're always turned away."

Sybil's tense body relaxed somewhat. Yes, the food, ale, and clothing might have been a wonderful luxury, but the disappointment at their denial was outweighed by the relief that Jacinda was safe.

"Have there been any rumors about Jacinda?" Sybil asked in an almost imperceptible whisper. "That she might be sent here next?"

Kat shook her head. "I've kept my ear keen to the ground for such news and there's naught a word of it."

Sybil put her hand over her heart where a knot of tension loosened for the first time in days. "I never told Jacinda," she admitted, face hot with shame. "I never told her…well, anything. I should have, but I worried about the danger."

Kat nodded. "I figured as much when I saw that bracelet on her."

"If you're freed…" Sybil didn't want to put any damning words to voice where too many ears could listen.

"I'll see to her," Kat promised, understanding the unspoken request.

Because Jacinda did need to be told what she could do. That

using her gifts in such uncertain times might be seen by the wrong person. Only one denouncement could result in an arrest.

"There are ways to get ye out," Kat said with that look in her eyes—the one that gleamed with the opportunity to bend and break the rules.

"No." Sybil shook her head. "Please just see to Jacinda."

Kat nodded in understanding. Her thumb worked under the manacle with a frown. "It's so silent."

Sybil knew she didn't mean the prison, which was filled with the shuffles and moans and murmurs of scores of people.

Even in the din, the silence of the earth's hum was stifling. A pang radiated through Sybil, mourning and longing all at once.

A clatter rattled over the bars and Sybil's stomach tightened in anticipation. They were to be fed. Sybil and Edith snapped to attention along with the rest of the prison, like animals alert at the notion of food.

There was a shift in Kat's expression, dulling the playful part of her as she truly took in the surroundings.

Sybil saw everything freshly through her friend's eyes—near-skeletal bodies, the misery, the soiled rushes that contained more life beneath than above.

"Oh, Edith... Sybil...how...?" Kat pressed a hand to her chest, emblazoned with a decorative filigree she'd likely hand stitched.

"Don't." Sybil handed Kat a piece of bread. "We need your fire more than your empathy."

"The fare is hardly edible," Edith said, almost apologetically. "But when you're hungry enough..."

Even as she spoke of hunger, she tore her bread in half and gave the larger portion to a woman who had been ill the night before.

"It's not about hunger." Kat smirked. "It's about letting your fancy take over." She lifted the crust. "This is not, in fact, a piece of stale rock-hard bread."

The little girl watched, large eyes fixed on Kat and the bit of bread pinched in her fingertips.

So, too, did the beautiful young woman who kept mostly to herself. Matthew Hopkins had seen her three times already, and each time, she returned weeping. The last time, her breath had smelled of ale and roasted meat.

"Imagine the greatest cook ye know," Kat instructed. "And they've created yer favorite meal. Hold that in yer head and eat." She studied the gray lump in her hand. "This is my mam's apple pastries." Her eyes scrunched shut. "The best pastry to ever grace England."

She popped the morsel into her mouth, and everyone watched as she chewed. Finally, she swallowed and opened her eyes. Sybil practically leaned forward at the display, eager to see if one's thoughts truly had the power to create a feast where there was simply moldy bread.

Perhaps *that* was true sorcery.

"Well?" the pretty young woman asked.

Kat pursed her lips. "I think the apples turned. It tasted like moldy bread."

Regardless, every woman considered their bread a moment longer than usual.

If Sybil could consume any one thing again, it wouldn't be a meal, but tea.

She ate her bread and saved her small ale, letting the memory wash her away.

Those nights she returned from the pesthouse in St. Peter's, weary in body and wearier still in soul. As she splashed vinegar upon her hands at the plague stone and Bess boiled her clothing to kill any plague seeds, Henry would come to her with a tea of his own making. The recipe was one derived from the knowledge he'd acquired from Sybil's mother.

Chamomile and lavender for relaxation after a long day, valerian root to calm her mind of the horrors she'd witnessed in the plague house, and nettles to keep her body healthy. All this with a bit of honey to sweeten the bitterness of life that she witnessed day after day.

Though she'd begged him to stay on the outskirts of town at Brackenmere Manor, he had come with her to their townhouse in Bury St. Edmunds, at her side in her darkest hours despite the great risk to himself. For by then, he was nigh on five and fifty and his body was frail from the passing of time.

She thought of how he lovingly passed the mug into her hands, leaving the air awash with the pungent fragrance of steeping herbs. In her mind, she savored how his hands moved over hers, the heat of his palms chasing away the chill from the vinegar wash.

For in that moment, she was cared for. Cherished.

Safe.

Then she closed her eyes and drank the cup of rancid ale and swore she caught the sweetness of honey.

A guard's voice broke through the memory. "Kat Calver."

Sybil's eyes flew open, fear for her friend flaring like a stoked flame.

Kat stomped toward the prison door. "I'll have ye know that I'm with child…"

In an instant, she was gone, but in her wake, she had left something Sybil hadn't possessed in far too long. A trailing glimmer of hope. For herself, but also for Jacinda.

CHAPTER THIRTY

Lilith

Eager to implement what she'd read in the grimoire, Lilith rushed back to the bed and breakfast to pull together the ingredients. The home was quiet within, Aunt Jacqueline's door closed with the sound of a running shower inside.

Meaning Lilith had some time to herself.

The first thing she did now that she was connected to Wi-Fi was google the daunting items mentioned in the old book.

Crystal was simply clear quartz.

Tin stone was cassiterite.

Laurel leaves were bay leaves.

Dragon's glass was obsidian.

And snakeroot was echinacea, the heads being flowers.

Those weren't nearly as terrifying or impossible to acquire as anticipated and were almost laughably boring. She thought back to the stones and crystals still scattered around the grimoire. One appeared to be amethyst and another quartz. If she was correct, she had nearly half the ingredients for the charm.

The rest she could likely locate in the house. The kitchen was her first stop, where she found some dried bay leaves conveniently stored inside a plastic spice jar.

She tucked the stiff, fragrant leaves into a necklace pouch she found in her luggage, fortunately absent any florals despite having belonged to Mama.

Outside, the sun gilded the world in brilliant light, its warmth enhancing the fragrance of grass and the various blossoms.

Lilith was spared foraging in the forest by Aunt Jacqueline's garden.

The colorful rows were not just flowers as initially anticipated, but various herbs: lavender, chamomile, and the wonderfully recognizable pink of echinacea blossoms.

Lilith plucked a couple of the latter and secured them in the necklace pouch alongside the bay leaves.

Rosemary was just as easy to identify with its spiky stalks and sharp, medicinal scent.

She carried her findings to her room. This enchantment that had seemed impossible over an hour before now felt entirely doable.

And she'd accomplished it all by herself.

A warm sense of pride unfurled in her chest.

She slid her small, precious harvest into her back pocket, ready to return to the manor to retrieve the crystals. But as soon as she stepped outside, Asher's black Mercedes pulled into the driveway.

Essie would be tickled to death when she found out he drove a Mercedes—Lilith would never hear the end of it.

He nodded to her in greeting and her heart tripped over itself. As he exited the car, he pulled a pet carrier with him. Toby bounded out behind him, trying to peer through the grate of the carrier. Tutting, Asher drew the carrier higher, out of Toby's reach.

Lilith crossed her arms over her chest. "If you're planning on taking Lord Wimbleton the third away, Aunt Jacqueline will never forgive you."

Asher lifted a sardonic brow. "Don't tempt me." He tilted his head to the carrier. "But I don't think this chap would appreciate having a skunk in here with him."

Lilith moved forward, lured by what could possibly fit in the small crate. "Can I see?"

Toby snuffled and snorted in his eagerness to get to whatever was inside.

"Let's go in the house first." Asher closed the car door with such care it made barely a sound. As if he were trying to keep from startling the animal.

Once inside, Asher pinched the lock together and opened the cage-like door. Toby perched on the couch with his stubby front legs, trying to peer in, but Asher gently nudged the dog away.

Lilith leaned closer, craning her head toward the opening.

At first, she saw nothing, but then a shape appeared in the shadows—a black cat pressed against the rear of the crate, his tail spiraled in front of his body like a shield.

"He hasn't left the carrier, poor chap." Asher rested his elbows on his knees and lowered his head near Lilith's. His scrubs smelled like fresh laundry and Lilith hated how much that made her want to curl up against him and breathe him in.

Oblivious, Asher continued, "His owner wasn't caring for him properly, so the RSPCA removed him from the home. When they found him, he didn't have any food or water and had been so hungry, he'd torn into a bag of bread on the counter."

"Bless his little heart." Lilith shook her head. "I'll never understand people who neglect their animals."

Asher fisted his hands, and the veins in his forearms stood out against his skin. "Me neither." His voice softened. "The mite is malnourished and stressed. I thought he might do better here…as long as Toby minds himself." He looked over his shoulder to where Toby was edging closer to the cat carrier.

The dog gave an indignant grumble and slunk back to his bed in the corner.

They shared a smile and turned back to the carrier to find a small black head emerging curiously from the crate. Lilith turned her hand palm up, trying to appear as nonthreatening as possible.

The cat sniffed carefully at her thumb, his jerky exhalations tickling against her skin. Then he turned his large green eyes up at her, wide with a trust that tugged at her heart.

As if sensing her reaction, the little cat stepped forward, revealing bald patches on the backs of his front legs.

"He's been licking to self-soothe." Asher nodded to the bald spots.

The tug at her heart became a visceral wrench.

The cat crept closer—first onto her knee, weighing scarcely anything—then her thigh, revealing his slender frame, hip bones jutting from beneath his black fur.

He perched in her lap, curled into a ball, and settled against her like Amara did with Essie, yielding to an embrace filled with love and complete trust.

Asher looked at the cat and smiled up at Lilith. "Everyone at the office has been trying for two days to lure him out. Looks like he just needed the right person."

Lilith stared down at the ball of warm black fur nestled against her. The small cat had chosen her. As if he could sense the pain inside her the way she sensed it in him. Two wounded souls bound together.

She wanted to heal his hurt, to make him forget everything

he'd endured. To ensure he would never be vulnerable and ill-treated again.

Even after Mama had died, Lilith hadn't gotten a pet. The idea of something else depending on her was more than she could bear.

But the need in this tiny, misused creature was pure and tender. What brought him to Lilith wasn't about taking and hurting but trusting and healing.

She stroked a hand over his slender body, noting every prominent rib her fingers skimmed. A steady purr revved in the cat's throat, trusting and eager for affection.

Her chest swelled with more love than she'd ever imagined possible.

Unexpected emotion knotted in her throat. "What's his name?"

Asher's gaze was soft as he considered the cat. "Sometimes it's best to rename animals when they haven't lived in a good home." He looked up at her and his knee brushed hers. "Care to do the honors?"

Heat rushed up her neck and she lowered her head, the flush likely creeping over her face. She continued stroking the cat's silky fur, dark as obsidian. Like dragon's glass. "I think…Dragon."

The cat cast a side glance up at her, the expression sly, as if sharing their own little secret.

At least this secret was one she understood, especially when there were still so many to unearth.

CHAPTER THIRTY-ONE

Sybil

"I'm leaving today."

A moment passed before Sybil registered Kat's whisper.

"Are you certain?" Sybil asked, wishing Edith was with them to hear the wonderful news of Kat's freedom. But she'd been pulled away that morning to see Matthew Hopkins.

"As certain as a Puritan loves Sunday," Kat muttered.

Sybil leveled a look at her friend, a silent caution to watch her tongue. But Kat was never one to safeguard her words.

"With the war on, there are too few men who can sort out the property issues," she said. "Tom is the only one to see to it, and after bringing the bairns to Guildhall Feoffees for half a sennight, the Commission banded together and petitioned Matthew Hopkins to acknowledge my innocence."

Few could rally such support. Fewer still kept that kind of powerful demand for a release quiet. Most of the men who protested the arrests of their wives ended up imprisoned as well, like Mr. and Mrs. Everard.

Sybil glanced at the white-haired woman standing on the side of the cage closest to where the men were kept. Where her husband was imprisoned after fighting to help her.

Mrs. Everard had been accused of entering a covenant with the Devil to kill their grandchildren. Mr. Everard, a popular cooper in Halesworth had sworn that his wife was no more in league with the Devil than he was, which they took as a statement of guilt. The pair had been brought in together.

If rumors could be believed, her hair had been brown when she arrived.

Meanwhile, Mary Bacon wept daily over her own husband, a former soldier, the kind who didn't back down from a fight. He continued to publicly lash out at Hopkins for the arrests.

Her fear that her husband might soon join her was not unfounded.

But then Henry would have fought as passionately for Sybil. In her heart, she knew he would. It almost made her glad he was gone, to spare him such pain.

She yanked her thoughts from Henry.

"Before I go," Kat said softly. "I need some of yer hair."

One never knew when strands of hair were necessary for a charm.

Sybil plucked a few strands, embarrassed at her own filth. Not having a mirror was likely a small mercy. Worry over the state of her appearance seemed a waste of her limited energy, but her hair had always been her one vanity.

"I must beg another favor," Sybil said apologetically as she offered the strands to her friend.

Kat tucked them into her sleeve and nodded.

"Do you remember John Griffin?" The name came easy

on Sybil's tongue despite having not spoken it in over a decade.

Kat's brows flinched. "I could never forget him, what he was to ye."

Despite the damp chill of the prison, Sybil's cheeks warmed.

She had never stopped loving him. Four years ago, she saw him on the street once and thought she would perish then and there at the pain of seeing him.

He'd worn the dark slim-fitting cassock of a vicar. She could not bring herself to ask around to see if he had a wife. Her heart could not stand the idea of him being with a woman who was not her, a woman his father would deem worthy.

"I think he may be able to help," Sybil said. "With his sermons, not with vengeance, but with love from someone who guides them with wisdom, so they might see the wrong happening through their own beliefs."

"I can speak for ye." But even as she agreed, Kat's gaze slid toward the old vicar who'd broken after the swimming test, the ancient man who had condemned himself decades earlier when he'd helped a woman accused of witchcraft. She had died in the end, and now, all these years later, when charges resurfaced, so too would he.

"If nothing else, mayhap the church can help see to Jacinda's care," Sybil hedged, suddenly unsure of the plan that felt certain in her mind only moments before.

Kat nodded soberly, understanding the danger. "And if his parish cannot offer aid, I will take Jacinda in as mine own."

They held hands, palm to palm, a fleeting moment of sisterhood, a reminder that life could still hold something beautiful.

Once the earth had pulsed between their fingers, an energy that resonated in their souls. The flat silence landed hard in Sybil's heart and the longing for her gifts returned tenfold.

And then Kat was freed, much to the dismay of the guard she'd bitten.

Edith had not returned. Each hour that passed sent a warning creeping up Sybil's spine.

In the absence of her friends, at the loss of Kat's good humor and light, the darkness of the prison pressed in on Sybil, aggressive and entirely without mercy.

She did not know how much time passed, only that day faded to night and then to day once more, and still, Edith had not been returned.

Finally, that third night, Sybil was startled awake by the familiar shrieking groan of the rusted prison door scraping open.

A shadow of a woman was dragged between two guards and thrown into the cell. Though their victim issued only a grunt, Sybil knew the woman to be Edith.

Sybil leaped to her feet and crouched beside her friend.

"They wouldn't let me stop walking," Edith gasped. "On and on. My feet. My feet." She whimpered, her breath coming in great huffs like a woman in childbed. "Oh, my feet."

The little girl roused and cautiously approached, her face creased with worry while poor Edith continued to murmur, her words blurring together in an exhausted rant.

"They walked her." The pretty young woman appeared at Sybil's side, almost unseen in the darkness. "To make her confess. They will do anything to obtain a confession." There was something flat to her voice when she said this, a note devoid of life. "None of us are safe."

"We must tend to her." Sybil looked around their cell, heartily missing her assortments of salves and tinctures and teas. "Perhaps we might find some water?" She voiced the impossibility aloud.

The girl slipped away and eased her slight frame between the bars. Sybil's eyes widened. The child could have been freed from their cage long before.

As silently as she'd left, the girl returned, a cup of dank water in hand. By the light of the moon, they cleaned Edith's wounds as well as could be managed. They would have to wait until dawn to make out the true damage. Edith trembled in her sleep, body twitching with pain and trauma.

Sybil lay at her back and wrapped her arms around her friend to soothe her suffering. The girl observed this and tucked herself against Edith as well, sharing her body heat.

Edith slept deeply with an unnatural slumber, brought on by extreme fatigue and agony. Even when the sun peeked through the narrow windows, she did not rouse. Such sleep was a mercy.

Sybil examined her friend's feet and sucked in a breath. The heel and ball of each foot revealed open wounds where she had worn through leather and flesh alike.

Lacking any other means of a bandage, Sybil tore at her petticoat where the linen had remained clean enough to still appear white. These strips were bound carefully around Edith's feet.

A fiery rage simmered in Sybil as she tended to her dear friend.

Their numbers in the prison had risen to seven score. All women save less than a dozen men. The few men who had been arrested were those who spoke out to save their wives, or were the old or addled. Pariahs of society, ones who did not adhere to the strict rules of a Puritan life.

"Sybil Brantham." The guard's voice rang out and fear doused Sybil in ice-cold dread.

She hesitated, wishing she had the time to tear up several more strips of her petticoat to layer the soles of her shoes with. For she knew exactly why her name had been called.

And she suspected the pretty young woman was right—they would all have their breaking point.

Sybil could not help but wonder what hers would be.

And exactly what breaking might cost her.

CHAPTER THIRTY-TWO

Lilith

A delicious scent lured Lilith into the kitchen with Dragon at her heels like a little shadow.

"Smells amazing," she commented.

Asher waved a hand at the pan with gravy-laden beef atop a bed of potatoes and carrots. "Roast and veg. Proper comfort food."

A flush of pleasure warmed through her chest. "You didn't have to cook for me."

"It's the least I can do." Asher gave her that lopsided half smile that was far too appealing. "After helping with Aunt Jacqueline and Dragon."

Hearing his name, Dragon propped his front paws on the cabinet doors.

Lilith brushed off the compliment even as she flushed with pleasure. "It was really no trouble at all."

Asher popped open two cans of food and set the bowls to

the ground, which Dragon and Toby fell upon with indecent enthusiasm.

"Aunt Jacqueline ate a little earlier." Asher pulled two plates from the cupboard. "I think she's still quite exhausted from yesterday, though she won't admit it. She's been more active than usual lately."

"That might be my fault," Lilith said slowly. "Aunt Jacqueline seems to think there's a reason I'm here."

"Dragon would agree with her there." He winked.

Lilith's stomach fluttered with a whole mess of butterflies.

She bit her lip, hating her next statement before it was out of her mouth. "She says the house has been waiting for me…"

Asher stilled, his expression tense. A beat passed. Two.

Then he smiled in a way that was too quick, too easy, and passed her a plate.

Lilith took her food with thanks and they settled at a round wooden table in the kitchen with heaping servings and a bottle of wine.

Rather than press him for more information, she let an easy conversation fall between them, about his vet practice he'd started ten years ago, how Savannah compared to England.

Though she'd only been in England a few days, there was something comforting that felt more like home while Savannah somehow seemed foreign.

As the wine disappeared from the bottle and their questions flowed smoothly, an urgent nudge remained in the back of her mind.

The manor.

August 27.

How quickly time was running out.

A shuffle sounded behind Lilith. Aunt Jacqueline entered the kitchen in her nightgown, her hair like loose cotton around her shoulders.

She extended a small burlap pouch toward Lilith. "Dried hops for you. For a restful sleep."

Asher quickly leaped to his feet. "Do you need something, Aunt Jacqueline?"

"Just delivering a gift." Her eyes sparkled as they met Lilith's, like they were in on the same secret.

Aunt Jacqueline exited the kitchen and Asher shook his head. "Sorry. You can just toss that in the rubbish bin if you'd like."

"It was sweet of her to think of me." Lilith set the small bag aside and the dried flowers within crackled at her touch. "Something tells me she always keeps you guessing."

"That's one way to put it." He cleared away the plates and indicated a bottle of wine on the counter. "Shall we open another?"

Before Lilith could reply, Dragon hopped into her lap, his belly round and full as he fell instantly asleep, purring in contentment. "It appears I'm not going anywhere for a while."

"Ah, yes, the cat on the lap excuse." He chuckled.

She liked the timbre to his warm laugh and the way it made her want to tease more out of him.

Asher popped the cork from the bottle with a hollow *plonk* sound. "I suppose I'll have to join you. After all, it's been nice to have company." He filled their glasses with a rich red cabernet. "For the record, I was talking to Dragon, not you. You know I'm better with pets than people."

He winked.

Oh, he was definitely flirting. And the low chuckle rising in her throat betrayed that she was not indifferent.

And how could she be?

He cared for his aunt with kindness, saved animals, and still found time to cook.

"Well, thanks for putting up with me." Lilith stroked a hand over Dragon's vibrating form.

"It's amazing how quickly he's latched onto you." Asher smiled at the little cat sleeping in her lap. There was a gentleness to his tone when he spoke, a warmth to his expression. "I think he suspects you've never had a pet before and wants to set the standard."

"He's set the bar pretty high." She scratched under Dragon's chin, and he lifted his face, eyes closed in pleasure as his throat vibrated under her fingertips. "I'm in love already."

"Do you typically fall in love that quickly?" The corner of Asher's lips lifted, and Lilith suspected he'd had a bit too much to drink.

But, then, she had too. "No, actually."

The statement hadn't meant to be so sobering, but the smile fell away from Asher's face. "Why?"

She frowned in thought. "Why?"

"I'd say it's as easy as not having found the right chap..." His eyes narrowed in a way that suddenly felt overly perceptive. "But you're not a simple woman. I imagine your reasoning is complicated. Deep."

Lilith swallowed, hating that he saw her so easily. But also grateful.

No one had cared to see her in far too long. Essie was the only one who even really knew her. Well, her and Daddy. But Essie was so busy these days and Daddy was gone...

Lilith chose her words carefully. "I didn't have a great example of love growing up."

"That can be hard." Something flashed in Asher's eyes. Pain. Understanding.

Lilith considered that look, dissected it to unearth its meaning. "My Mama," she said slowly, her tongue loosened by the hope that he actually did get her.

She took the first sip of her third glass, letting the heady taste of wine sit on her tongue before sliding down her throat. "Mama wanted a better life than she was dealt. Daddy was a lawyer and she thought she hit pay dirt. But then…"

Lilith set her glass down and lifted her hands in a helpless little ta-da. "Surprise! I showed up and ruined everything."

"What about your father?" Asher asked.

"Daddy chose me." A twinge pinched inside Lilith's chest. "He stopped trying to climb the corporate ladder so he could spend more time with me."

Asher tapped a finger on his wineglass. "I wager your mother didn't take too kindly to that."

Lilith took a hearty swallow of wine, letting what she once savored burn a path down her throat. "Mama never forgave me."

The recollection of the journal floated into Lilith's mind. The way Mama confessed to never feeling complete. How she envied Lilith's interest in the supernatural, how she resented it.

With the trip to England and impending doom, Lilith had scarcely thought about the journal.

"I'm sorry," Asher said quietly, breaking into Lilith's thoughts.

She lifted a shoulder. "Mama grew up poor. Like, real poor." A Southern lilt bled through Lilith's words, the crisp edges of her speech softening with the wine. "Sometimes a hard life makes people better, sometimes it makes them bitter. And Mama was a real lemon."

She smiled as if she'd cracked a joke, but neither of them laughed.

And maybe there was more to Mama than that bitterness.

The corner of Asher's lip tucked down. "Difficult families can be…"

"Difficult," Lilith finished for him.

They both chuckled, the kind of laugh you give because it's easier than embracing the pain.

Lilith took another sip of wine. "Was your family…?"

"Difficult?" Asher finished with a sardonic grin.

"Yeah. Because you're pretty complicated yourself, sir."

"Complicated?" Asher arched his brow, making him look more debonair than skeptical.

"Do you fall in love quickly?" she asked with a grin, firing his question back at him on a slingshot of flirtation.

"With animals, always." He reached down and rubbed a hand over Toby's belly, earning him a grunt of happiness from the slumbering dog. "With people…I didn't have the best example either."

Lilith sat forward. Maybe she would finally get some answers from Asher.

And as much as she wanted—needed—to find out more about the manor, she realized she wanted just as badly to find out about the man.

CHAPTER THIRTY-THREE

Lilith

"Was it your mama or your daddy?" Lilith asked. Because a complicated childhood was always the fault of one or the other, wasn't it?

"My father." Asher's fingertips lingered on his wineglass. "He spent his whole life trying to reclaim the greatness our family once had, never accepting that his father squandered the last of the inheritance. All Father had left was that house. It was everything to him. And for a while it was everything to m—"

He cut off abruptly and shook his head, jaw clenching.

Had he meant to say it was everything to his mother?

"How did your mama cope?" Lilith nudged.

"She didn't." He scoffed, the sound harsh with pain. "She was lonely and soothed herself with the bottle until it wasn't company enough, then she left."

"I imagine you were lonely too," Lilith said softly. "Even before she left."

Asher's gaze slid away from hers.

Lilith stretched a hand toward him without thinking. Not until her fingers brushed his forearm. He lifted his eyes to hers, securing the connection between them in a way that made Lilith's heartbeat stutter.

"How old were you?" she asked gently.

"Ten." Asher took a drink and continued, "My father took to the bottle after she left. One night, he went out and never came home. Drowned in the neighbor's pond."

Lilith hurt for the little boy Asher had been, orphaned and entirely alone.

"Oh, Asher..."

"Aunt Jacqueline dropped everything to come here and care for me." Asher glanced at the kitchen exit where Aunt Jacqueline had stood earlier, his gaze earnest. "I can't imagine my life without her."

Lilith wrapped her hand around his forearm and squeezed, letting it stand in for the soul-deep hug she longed to give him. "I'm so sorry."

"That's life sometimes." He lifted his wine in a mock toast. "I like to think it made me better rather than bitter."

"I believe it did." She patted his arm and released him to pick up her wineglass. "To being better." They clinked glasses and drank together, smiles teasing their lips.

"Is that why you hate it?" she asked abruptly.

He blinked at her and set down his glass.

"The manor," she specified. "Is that why you never want to talk about it...because of your daddy?"

Asher was silent for a long moment, his expression impassive. Finally, he settled back in his chair and released a long breath. "Well." He reached for his wine again. "That is astute."

The openness of his expression shuttered.

She'd done that with her abrupt questioning.

And while she could kick herself, she still had so many questions. About the manor, about the secret room, about the grimoire and whether he knew of its existence.

And she needed answers like a drowning woman needed a life raft.

"Legacies…" Asher spoke with apparent care. "Are not always wanted."

That was absolutely something Lilith could understand.

Her phone buzzed next to her and Essie's name flashed with a text. "Sorry," Lilith apologized, flipping her phone over.

Asher swallowed the last of his wine. "Honestly, it's getting late, and Toby will remind me we have an early day tomorrow morning." Toby gave a broad underbite smile and wagged his nub of a tail.

Asher put their glasses in the dishwasher and Lilith snuck a glance at her phone.

Essie: How's Mr. Darcy? 😉

Lilith replied with a blush face, to which Essie immediately replied with a heart eyes emoji.

When you knew someone well enough, you could have an entire conversation in emojis.

Lilith scooped Dragon from her lap and stood, tucking the cell phone into her back pocket. "Thank you again for dinner—and for the chat."

Asher walked with her toward the rear of the house where the guest rooms were, clicking off the lights as they went. "My pleasure. I enjoyed getting to know more about you."

"Likewise," Lilith replied.

They reached the hallway where her room split off to the left with his to the right. She looked up at him, suddenly feeling unsure of what to say or do. There was a new intimacy between them, one borne of vulnerability and confessions of past hurts.

Certainly, it was the most intimate conversation she'd had with anyone in far, far too long. And he understood her. Like, *really* understood her.

He made her feel seen.

As if hearing her thoughts, he gazed down at her, the soft look in his eyes confirming the quiet affection heating between them. The light scent of his laundry detergent filled her senses, but beneath that was a spicy, masculine scent.

Her pulse fizzed like a shaken can of Coke.

She was just a girl with a cat in her arms, standing before a boy with a dog at his side.

And this suddenly felt so right.

Exactly where she was supposed to be.

He glanced down to her mouth and her heart caught in her chest where it remained, stuck like gum. Waiting for him to make the first move.

Desperate for him to make the first move.

He smiled and looked down at the ground. "Good night, Lilith."

Disappointment washed over her, raw and tangible. "Good night, Asher."

They turned in opposite directions, Lilith suddenly eager for the solitude of her room, where she breathed out a long exhale. She set Dragon on the bed. He yawned, revealing sharp white teeth and a curl of pink tongue.

Do you think it's OK to have a relationship with one's bed and breakfast owner? Lilith texted.

Essie replied immediately: It is absolutely encouraged, and I want all the details!

Lilith bit her lip. But what if I ruin it like everything else? This trip is so important.

Essie: You're killing me. Embody Elizabeth Bennet and go for Mr. Darcy.

Lilith: She turned him down the first time, remember?

This time Essie's reply came in all caps: KILLING ME! 💀

Lilith laughed, but her mirth dimmed as she prepared for bed—as chilling memories of the dream from the night before replaced the pleasant heat from her flirtations with Asher.

Because she wasn't here to have some rom-com detour. She wasn't even here to explore her family tree, like she'd let Essie believe. Though that was only partially true.

Her life was in danger, and somehow she might could get wiped clean away from the world.

August 27…

And though she had the ingredients for a charm written in some old magical book—which admittedly was simultaneously cool and ominous—she would only have two days left when she woke up.

She didn't know what was on the other side of those two days, but she was terrified to find out.

Before going to sleep, she took the small pouch from Aunt Jacqueline and placed it under her pillow, hoping it might be as effective as the peppermint tea had seemed.

And if those simple herbs made a difference, what might the combined effects of them in an actual charm do?

Because at this point, she needed all the help she could get.

CHAPTER THIRTY-FOUR

Sybil

The wood-paneled room still reeked of temptation for Sybil, the savory aroma of roasted goose and the stale tang of ale. How many times a day did Hopkins torment his prisoners with the allure of a full meal?

How many prisoners just below their feet had stomachs gnarled with hunger and throats burning with thirst?

She was forced to stand before the desk once more.

Hopkins steepled his long fingers in front of his face. "You have been difficult, Mrs. Brantham."

Last time she had been weakened by starvation and thirst. Now she kept her back straight, her stance proud despite her deplorable appearance. "You mean, I am innocent."

"No." His lips thinned with apparent disapproval. "That is not what I mean. I have a signed declaration from someone in your household saying you whisper with the Devil at night. That you made a poppet for tormenting your neighbors."

The accusation struck like a slap.

Her household?

"Who denounced me?" she asked, despite herself.

Who?

Who would send her to a place such as this?

Who would endanger Jacinda?

Did they not understand how vulnerable the girl would be without Sybil?

Hopkins grinned and Sybil realized that she'd played into his trap. "You know I cannot say who spoke against you." There was a condescending note to his words. "But today, I *will* have your confession."

The words chilled Sybil. The memory of Edith's raw, bleeding feet rose in her mind.

Hopkins nodded to the guards in the room. Two stood by chairs on either side with two more men in the middle between them.

Dread swirled low in Sybil's gut. The room was silent, but the anticipation of what was to come vibrated in the air, like the frenetic moment before lightning strikes the earth.

"Go to that chair." Matthew Hopkins indicated the one across the room.

Sybil stiffened. "I would prefer not to."

Hopkins curled his fingertips in a beckoning motion and two guards in the middle ran like dogs to comply.

The tall one slapped a cudgel against his palm. "The chair. Now," he barked. He jumped toward her, as though meaning to strike.

Sybil lunged toward the chair.

The guard there spun her round and shoved her back, sending her sprawling in the direction of the other chair.

"Back the other way," the larger guard said, trotting beside her. "Quickly."

She ran back to where she'd started.

It was a foolish game, something children would play. For the first hour—maybe more—Sybil dashed about back and forth, running out her rage, stretching her legs after being too long locked inside a crowded cage.

Any time she slowed, one of the men shouted in her ear, face close enough to fleck her skin with spittle. Once, she stumbled and fell, and the men were there, bellowing for her to stand and slamming their cudgels so near her head, her ears rang.

All the while, Hopkins continued the barrage of questions, ridiculous and relentless.

Was the Devil her lover?

Did she attend the Sabbath with him?

Did he give her familiars?

Did she curse the cows to yield sour milk?

Did she blight the crops?

To each, she answered no. And for the moments she had to pause to first catch her breath, there was a red face in hers, demanding an expedient response.

After the first hour, her energy waned, and her pace slowed. The yelling only increased.

Eventually, time lost all meaning. There was not a single window in the long, narrow room by which to gauge the hours or note when day turned to night. Perhaps if there had been a window, she might have thrown herself from it.

An eternity dragged on as she trod between the chairs. Although now, all the shouting in England could not quicken her steps. Her feet throbbed in her shoes, the wooden heel of one latchet had broken and left her lurching unevenly back and forth, and back and forth, and back and forth.

Air rasped from her dry throat, making it stick together. "Water," she begged.

"Not until you confess," Hopkins replied in a bored drawl.

She hated groveling, but she could think of nothing but slaking her burning thirst. "Please."

"Run," a guard barked from behind her back. She jolted forward, hobbling as quickly as she could.

She did not know how much more time passed then. But she could not help recalling how Edith had been gone three days before she was finally returned.

Had it been a day yet?

Was it night now?

How much longer must she endure this torment?

Her head was light, her body heavy, and her exhaustion so great, she closed her eyes into blackness each time she reached one of the chairs.

A cudgel slapped against her arm in a pop of pain. "Move!"

Her eyes snapped open, and she limped to the other chair.

Hopkins's smooth voice followed her. "Did you take the Devil as your lover?"

No.

Her steps faltered and her lids drifted closed even as she continued to propel herself forward.

"...the Devil with dark hair and a pointed beard..."

An image swam in her mind of a handsome man with dark hair and a pointed beard.

"Did you attend the Sabbath with the Devil?"

No.

Her head nodded forward in a snatch of sleep despite the ongoing plod of her steps.

"Did you dance around the fire with Edith with ribbons streaming from your hair? Red and gold and black."

She could see the scene in her mind, a great fire as she and Edith danced with ease around the flames, the red, gold, and black ribbons twirling, tangling.

No.

"Do you have familiars?"

Brixton leaped into her mind, his wide, trusting brown eyes. Oh, what men would do to an animal they presumed guilty. She flitted back to awareness with horror.

No!

On and on the inquiries went.

No and no and no and *no*.

She replied only with no. No matter how many times she was asked. No matter how often her mind went dark with exhaustion as she continued to run while Hopkins planted pictures in her mind.

"Are you telling me the truth?"

The "no" froze on Sybil's tongue and her brain whirled around the question, one that had changed shape, one meant to make her falter.

The bones of her feet felt as if they were broken, her stomach snarled its outrage, and her throat was so dry, she could scarce speak her single word replies.

But this question was different.

"Answer, you slattern." Someone shoved her shoulder, sending her sprawling. "Answer now."

She fell to the floor, weighed down by the manacles at her wrists, too weak to even catch herself. Her skull cracked upon the floor sending stars dancing in her vision.

Darkness washed over her, and she welcomed it, desperate for the velvety embrace of nothing.

"Are you telling the truth?" a voice barked in her ear.

She startled awake, an automatic "no" sluggishly flipping to accommodate the question. "Yes. Yes, I am telling the truth."

Rough hands hauled her upright, her knees buckling under her weight several times before straightening to fully support her.

"And did you love your husband?" Hopkins's question transcended time, blurring with that of the magistrate as he asked the same question again and again.

Emotion knotted in Sybil's throat, bone dry, but stubborn just the same. A sob creaked in her chest.

"Did you kill him?"

Then she saw it in her mind—Henry's death.

Because it had been her fault.

A painful grip pinched her shoulders and shook her. "Did you kill your husband?"

The weight of her fatigue had her eyes slipping closed even as her teeth clacked with the force of her shaking.

Her thoughts faded to a memory, as visceral as the day when Henry's eyes had shone bright with fever and his skin blazed. Immediately Sybil knew he was infected with plague seeds, the same as those many dying souls she'd tended in St. Peter's Church.

But while she could avoid the pestilence after her mother survived with Sybil in her womb, Henry had no such resistance. In fact, he had been feeble, vulnerable.

He was no laborer with a body firm with muscle and vitality, but a scholar with elegantly tapered fingers and a brilliant mind.

If she had insisted Henry not come to the townhouse in Bury St. Edmunds with her, he would have lived.

If she had not put the deaths of many over the lives of her loved ones, he would have lived.

She had not cursed him with the Devil's powers, nor plunged a knife into his aged chest. But she had killed him all the same.

"Is this your confession?" Hopkins's triumphant voice made Sybil's eyes snap open.

"No," she said, now fully awake once more. "I did not kill my husband. I did not say that I did."

Had she?

Oh God—*had she?*

Hopkins simply smirked and went to his desk, lifting his quill.

"I did not say I killed my husband," Sybil protested.

"That will be all." Hopkins waved his hand dismissively, lowering his head to his work.

"I did not kill my husband." Sybil's eyes stung with tears her body was too depleted to produce. "I would never say that I did."

But had she?

Her pleas fell on deaf ears, first with Hopkins, then with the guards who pushed and prodded at her, forcing her to walk on feet that ground brokenly against the floor with every step.

Had she, in her state of delirium, given up the source of her greatest guilt?

If so, they would see her burn.

Soon.

She was running out of time.

CHAPTER THIRTY-FIVE

Sybil

Sybil remained on the floor of the cell, face pressed to the filthy rushes despite Edith's tender cajoling. At some point, Sybil's body managed to produce several tears which leaked into the damp straw beneath her cheek.

"I think I gave them what they sought," Sybil said miserably.

"Oh, lamb..." Edith stroked her back. "What did you say?" There was a hoarseness to her voice, exhaustion and defeat wearing her to nothing.

"I know not." Sybil shook her head, cheekbone rolling over the floor. "My exhaustion was so great, my dreams blurred into wakefulness."

Edith issued a pained exhale. "It was the same with me. As was likely their intent."

"But what did I say?" Sybil's chest blazed with a fire that could not be extinguished. One that grew greater as she whispered her utmost fear. "What will they do to Jacinda if I am accused?"

"Sybil Brantham," the guard called.

She shrank into herself, wishing to be small enough to disappear.

She couldn't go back. Not yet. She needed strength and had none left to give.

The gate squealed open. "Sybil Brantham."

"You saw to her mere hours ago," Edith protested in as strong a voice as Sybil had ever heard, pushing to standing though she wavered on her feet.

She knew what such defiance cost Edith.

"Quiet your mouth, hag." The guard drew his fist back.

Sybil pushed herself to sitting. "I am here." The room spun, but she remained upright.

"Don't hit her." Another guard nudged his elbow into the other. "That old witch is already ugly enough."

Edith ignored the jeer, the same as she always did. But despite her seeming indifference, Sybil knew the cut of those sharp words. She squeezed Edith's hand as her friend helped her to standing.

Pain radiated through Sybil's feet, as if the bones were shattered and the muscle shredded down to the nerves. She wobbled, her weight shifting around agony.

"Be strong," Edith mouthed.

Sybil closed her eyes in gratitude even as everything inside her shrank back in fear.

"Come on then," the guard growled.

Sybil opened her eyes and stepped forward on soles that protested her weight. An unbidden cry came to her lips.

The guards, impatient with her slow movements, gripped her by the arms, setting the iron manacles at her hands clanking and biting into her wrists.

Once more, she was dragged to that hated room. The one where so many had been broken with starvation, thirst, and sleep deprivation. And where only an hour before, she was made to walk.

"I'll need your confession." Hopkins held the quill in his hand in expectation as she was plunked into the chair across from his desk.

Having the weight off her feet made them pulse in time with her rapidly beating heart.

"I said I did not kill my husband, and I have not cavorted with the Devil." Sybil infused conviction into her voice.

Hopkins sighed. "We do have other ways to establish that you are indeed a witch if you do not confess."

"More torture, I presume?" Sybil asked harshly.

Hopkins straightened, affronted. "My dear Mrs. Brantham, have you been subjected to thumbscrews? Have you had knives and hot pokers implemented upon your person?"

"Is being starved and left to die of thirst not torture? And being walked without rest to the point that my feet feel broken?"

"A bit of hunger is a kindness compared to being bowed in the Scavenger's Daughter." Hopkins shook his head. "Truly, Mrs. Brantham, your claims are nothing short of theatrical."

Anger flashed like hot lightning. "You will get no confession from me," she hissed. "I have had no dealings with the Devil, nor did I kill my husband."

Heedless of retribution, she continued. "There is a child in the prison downstairs, starving and filthy. She is innocent, as is every soul beneath your feet, whom you torture with the intent to murder." She locked eyes with him, allowing all the rage coursing through her to radiate from her glare. "What you have wrought upon the innocents of this region should bring you shame!"

Hopkins leaned back in his chair, his gaze hardening to ice.

A chill crawled over her flesh.

He addressed the guards behind her. "Bring in the searchers.

Mrs. Brantham will be their first. Remove her stockings and shoes. Bind her feet."

Sybil jerked upright, trying to stand, to escape, but the guards held her down. One of them tugged off her shoes, his efforts hindered by her swollen feet. Days might pass before she could fit them on once more.

A guard's hand went up her skirt. She flinched away, but another held her in place.

"Nothing I want to see up there," the guard muttered indignantly.

Sybil turned her head, unable to watch as he pulled away the woolen stockings from her calves, leaving her skin bare in a moment of brutal intimacy. A heavy clanking sounded from the floor and the chill of iron clasped around her skin, resting sharp upon her jutting ankle bones.

But in securing her feet, they freed her hands, removing the manacles there and revealing torn, angry flesh at her wrists.

"The searchers will find the truth." Matthew Hopkins grinned at her with a cold, unfeeling malice.

Despite her resolve, whatever they meant to discover made Sybil tremble to her core.

CHAPTER THIRTY-SIX

Lilith

Sunlight pulsed through Lilith's slumber, rousing her.

She stretched, letting the dormant quiet of her muscles flex awake against the cool glide of her sheets. Dragon was nestled in the crook of her neck. A purr rumbled from his warm body as he snuggled closer.

Opening her eyes, she looked up at the ceiling and felt…rested.

She absently pet Dragon and tried to recall what she'd dreamed the night before. There hadn't been a single nightmare. No mirrors or fires or Jacinda begging for help.

Last night was blank, an empty canvas upon which her body could paint a restful night of restorative sleep. The bag of dried hops under her pillow was a miracle.

Or…magic?

Lilith sat up abruptly.

The manor and the pouch of herbs called to her with an urgency that sent her leaping out of bed.

Asher was already up with a cup of coffee when she and Dragon made their way to the kitchen. A smile hovered on his lips when he saw her and Lilith ducked her head shyly to hide her blush.

He'd almost kissed her.

She'd *wanted* him to kiss her.

"No need to make breakfast today," she said. "I was thinking I'd head to the manor this morning, if that's all right."

His silence made her look up to find his brow furrowed before he nodded slowly. "Yeah—right, that's fine."

It was an awkward acquiescence, but she'd take it.

"And don't forget your tea," Aunt Jacqueline called from the table. "I trust you slept well?"

"And I trust you already knew that." Lilith grinned at her.

Aunt Jacqueline laughed. "The cheek on this one!"

Before Lilith could return to her room, Dragon pawed at her ankles with the pouch of herbs dangling from his sharp teeth. The clever little guy.

She took it in her palm and the soft hum that had started after Mama's death intensified.

"What's that?" Asher nodded toward.

"Nothing you need to worry over," Aunt Jacqueline said before Lilith could stammer out a nonsensical reply.

But Lilith scarcely heard them. The manor. She had to get to the manor immediately.

The urgency returned with intensity, tightening the muscles along the back of her neck, tugging her onward with purpose.

Was it the herbs in the pouch? Was this actually working?

Dragon cooed and pawed at her shoes.

"I think he's impatient to go," Aunt Jacqueline said with a smile.

Lilith hastily poured hot water into a Kindred Creatures tumbler with a couple pouches of peppermint tea to steep and waved a hasty goodbye as she followed Dragon out the door.

Outside, Lilith had to squint against the sun's brilliance. Insects hummed around her, louder and louder, a crescendo that drowned out her footsteps. The lush fragrance of foliage mingled in an exquisite aroma of rich earth, making her almost heady with the perfume of nature.

Her senses were alive, her heart full with a sense of being exactly where she was supposed to be.

She had to walk very fast, because that skinny little cat navigated the terrain as if he'd been to the old building before. As if he, too, were pulled toward Brackenmere Manor.

The manor seemed larger somehow, the structure more imposing, the rot and decay less pernicious.

Lilith withdrew the iron key from her pocket, its weight suddenly more substantial than before, the touch of the metal sending the world into flat silence.

This visit was so much more important than previous ones. Before, she'd been curious, uncertain of what everything meant.

While she still didn't know exactly, she now understood the price of her failure.

And just how little time remained.

Hands trembling, she unlocked the door and gave a nervous laugh. "How did you know the way here, Dragon?"

He squinted up at her like a sage old man.

She opened the door and set the key aside as if it burned her. The hum rushed back to her like a siren song, alluring and impossible to ignore.

The past was more vivid than before, though still blurred against the stark clarity of the present. The muted veil of tapestries on the wall was now bolder with vibrant blues and reds and golds. She breathed in, drawing in the yeasty, homey scent of baking bread. Underfoot, the rushes were fresh and sweet, but also slippery against the soles of her shoes. A fire flickered in the hearth between the two Grecian figures, its warmth evident on Lilith's skin.

As if the house was awakening from a long hibernation.

Dragon stepped into the room and sniffed around. Lilith glanced at the pouch clutched in her palm.

Rosemary to draw the potency of the earth to your senses.

The world had been extraordinarily *alive* on the walk over. Was that from the rosemary?

Heads of a snakeroot plant to amplify your need.

Laurel leaves to increase success.

Was this why the room appeared so much crisper?

Were the partial ingredients for the charm already taking effect?

Had they actually worked?

A woman entered the room, more visible than ever before, her shape crisper. Her fingers twisted at the maid's apron over a plain brown dress. Lilith approached her. "Can you hear me?"

The woman continued on, oblivious, nearly walking through Lilith.

So far, only Jacinda had been able to hear and speak to her.

Which meant Lilith had to find her again.

A quick search indicated she was not anywhere Lilith had been before. She approached a set of stairs leading up to the third floor. Where she was not supposed to go.

Before she could back away, Dragon darted up the stairs in a streak of black.

Well, now, she truly had no choice but to follow.

"Sorry, Asher," she muttered as she made her way toward the forbidden area.

The rooms were smaller on the third floor, possibly servant's quarters given the echo of the past reflecting simple beds and nightstands. One room was painted pale blue with a wobbly painting of a giant blue dog on one wall.

Was that Blue's Clues?

Toys were neatly tucked into a shelf against the wall with Lego castles and Transformers arranged artfully. From the top of the shelf, the tongue of a Hot Wheels ramp drooped downward, ending at a mini garage full of metal cars.

This was a child's room from only a couple decades ago.

Was it…Asher's?

Had he lived in the house?

From somewhere downstairs, a pan clattered to the floor. Lilith strained to listen, ready for the shatter of glass that followed. The shatter came at the same time she glanced at her watch and confirmed it was 12:03.

Lilith finished her search of the third floor without finding Jacinda, though the remainder of the rooms were filled with moldering pieces of furniture, a rabbit-eared TV with a crack in the corner, and boxes laden with dust.

The attic stairs loomed before her.

"Go big or go home," she said softly to herself and put her foot on the first step.

Whispers of the past revealed a place where herbs had dried, the bunches swaying like specters overhead. But she scarcely noticed them for all the canvases. A series of them were braced against the right wall, as if to dry thoroughly.

Each one looked exactly the same, an image of Brackenmere Manor.

Lilith clicked on her flashlight and leaned closer to inspect the first canvas. A figure showed in the second-floor window in every canvas. The corner-most library window. Leaning forward, she studied the image, making out a woman with honey-colored hair, wearing a dark T-shirt and jeans. Was that…her?

The next painting showed the woman, this time as a shadow. On and on, the paintings were lined up to show the woman growing less visible in the window.

A final painting remained on the easel. Lilith approached, her throat gripping her heart.

In the last painting, the window was empty.

As if the woman had ceased to exist.

CHAPTER THIRTY-SEVEN

Lilith

Lilith fled the room in her panic to escape the paintings and nearly toppled down the stairs. Dragon raced after her, watching her with wide green eyes.

Those paintings…*her*…was that what Asher hadn't wanted her to find?

He was right—she shouldn't have been there. She shouldn't have seen the canvases, the confirmation that she was going to fade from this world.

Her heart clattered against her ribs, sharp and hollow.

She ran down the stairs to the second floor, around a servant bustling by with a pitcher in her hands, and into the room that called to her the loudest.

The library.

She shoved the books aside and wrenched the lever so the trap door flew open, issuing a complaining creak at her urgency.

This is where she ought to have been since discovering Jacinda's absence.

Lilith rushed into the hidden room with Dragon at her side. The candles flickered to life, revealing the grimoire still flipped to the same page as before.

Place into a satchel to wear upon your person:

- *Crystal to amplify intentions*
- *Amethyst to elicit power*
- *Rosemary to heighten your senses*
- *Heads of snakeroot to amplify your need*
- *Laurel for success*

Bring these together by the light of three candles with focus and intention.

She opened the drawstrings of the pouch, her fingers trembling as she added the clear quartz and amethyst to the herbs she'd gathered the day before. Her heart jackhammered, still in chaos mode.

In this moment, Essie would tell her to ground herself.

"I'm in a small room." Lilith filled her lungs with enough air to expand her diaphragm. "I am in a small magical room with an ancient book in front of me and I'm fixing to do a charm."

The frantic sputter of her pulse smoothed out, calming under her words.

"Thank you, Essie," Lilith whispered.

She put the small pouch over her chest, the lumps of crystals pressing into her breastbone. The candles flickered.

She hesitated. How did one "call the earth"?

Squeezing her eyes shut, she concentrated. "Earth, Mother Nature, please help enhance my gifts."

A gentle breeze stirred her hair.

Something in her chest loosened, as if her heart physically opened.

"Please help enhance my gifts," she said again.

A pleasant tingling started at her birthmark and spread through her body.

She opened her eyes in time to see her veins shimmer beneath her skin, the way the grimoire had when she first touched it.

Something innate within her bade her repeat the phrase a third time. "Please help me enhance my gifts." Her voice was louder, stronger, filled with the yearning to learn.

The candles flared, washing her in heat.

She stood still for a moment, suddenly aware of the room in a way she hadn't been before. Every mote of dust in the air shone like embers and the crystals on the table lit from the inside with a strange glow.

The grimoire pulsed with energy, drawing her. She placed her palms on the spread pages, vitality flowing beneath her touch. There was so much learning still to be had within those pages.

Before she could embrace the beauty of her gifts, a sense of dread fell over her like a weighted blanket, leaving her heavy, paralyzed.

Dragon hissed at the entrance to the secret room.

At something he wanted her to see.

But when she walked closer, he trotted off, tail up so a slight crook at the tip seemed to beckon her to follow. Like she had a choice.

As she kept up with him, she took in her surroundings with new eyes, eyes that showed the past strongly visible with the present now cast beneath a veil, obscured by what once had been.

They descended the stairs where the air grew thick and heavy, settling in her chest and made her heart strain to beat.

She'd felt this way last time. Right before…

Boom, boom, boom!

A heavy fist pounded at the door.

Fear punched through Lilith with a similar force.

A maid tentatively opened the door, her expression pinched with unease. A man entered, his stride purposeful, black robes snapping around him. His presence filled the capacious Great Room, blocking the light so everything suddenly went dark.

Ominous.

Dragon arched his back and loosed a savage hiss.

Lilith's veins prickled with ice.

Those robes, the way they billowed like a carrion bird, the hard set of his eyes and the mean determination gleaming there.

She knew this man. From her dreams.

The odor of smoke filled her nose, her mouth, and a scream went off inside her head, body alight with the reminder of the flames and their indescribable agony.

His hand had been the one to hold the torch. *He* had tossed it upon the pyre, setting the kindling ablaze. Setting her on fire, to burn alive.

He was the man who would kill Sybil.

CHAPTER THIRTY-EIGHT

Sybil

The "searchers" were two women, both of whom Sybil had tended in the past with her mother's remedies.

Mrs. Jones, with wide, bright blue eyes, who had anxiously approached Sybil three years before seeking a posset to help the child in her womb who had ceased to move. And then later, after Sybil confessed there was naught to be done, she'd stemmed the blood from the loss of the woman's babe.

The second, Mrs. Williams, wore the somber dress of a Puritan, her hair pulled back in a braid as severe as the look in her steely gray eyes.

Sybil recalled how exuberantly she had protested *The Book of Sports*, a government-issued book of games allowed on Sundays some ten years prior, going so far as to snap the sticks children used in Morris dancing.

Mrs. Williams had also been the one to plead for Sybil's help when her youngest son fell ill with the plague, and how she'd wept with gratitude when his fever broke after Sybil's teas took effect.

There was no gratitude in her level gaze now.

A shiver skittered down Sybil's spine.

Hopkins pushed up from his desk. "I leave you with these women." He bowed low as a courtier, a mockery of respect.

The guards followed him from the room, leaving her alone with Mrs. Jones and Mrs. Williams. The latter thinned her lips as she regarded Sybil. "Remove your gown."

Shock drew Sybil instinctively back. "I will not."

Mrs. Jones appeared less certain. "Perhaps we can check without—"

"No." Mrs. Williams tossed down a heavy leather bag which clinked inside upon landing. "We will find a witch's mark on her no matter where it has been hidden." She nodded to Sybil. "Remove your clothes or we will seek help to do so."

Sybil took another step back.

Surely they were not serious.

"The magistrate is near." The hardness in Mrs. Williams's eyes told Sybil she knew exactly the type of man he was.

Tendrils of fear closed around Sybil's throat.

How could a woman be so cruel to another?

Sybil pulled at the ties of her bodice, hands shaking. A stubborn knot refused to pull free and Mrs. Williams hissed in impatience. She stalked toward Sybil, steps biting loud and hard into the wood floor. A pair of shears screeched open and sliced through the once-fine bodice before Sybil could protest.

The gown sagged open and dragged down her body, stopping only when the sleeves caught at her arms.

An astonished cry escaped Sybil, and she tried to back away, shackles clanking and catching, preventing her steps. Mrs. Williams caught her with a merciless grip, the shears working in rusty squeals.

Sybil twisted and wrenched, but was no match for Mrs. Williams's vice-like grip. Starvation had weakened Sybil's body, and the last of her resistance bled away.

Too weak with hunger to fight back.

The grinding snick of the shears filled the room as her stays were cut away, then her petticoat, so she stood in only her shift. Her nipples pebbled beneath the thin fabric and she crossed her arms over her chest, cheeks burning with mortification.

"Take it off." Mrs. Williams puffed from exertion. "Or I'll cut it away and leave you in prison without a stitch on you."

Sybil looked to Mrs. Jones, but the other woman averted her wide blue eyes, turning away her shame.

"How can you do this to a fellow woman?" Sybil's voice cracked.

"You're no woman." Mrs. Williams spat on the ground, a globule of white foam landing near Sybil's feet. "You're a witch." She held up her shears like the weapon they were. "The shift."

Choking back a sob, Sybil drew the hem of her shift over her head and released it quickly to cross her arms over herself.

The white fabric floated to the ground like a flag of surrender.

Mrs. Jones now stared intently at the floor. Not Mrs. Williams. Her gaze descended over Sybil's nakedness, consuming her skeletal legs and arms, the flatness of her breasts, which had deflated as she starved, the concave scallop of jutting hipbones, where even her womb seemed to have been carved away.

Perhaps Mrs. Williams was correct.

Sybil was not a woman.

Not any longer.

With her oily, tangled hair and emaciated body, she was barely even human.

She had not only been stripped of her clothing, but also her dignity. Her identity. She was bared, vulnerable down to her very soul.

Mrs. Williams stepped closer and Sybil drew back again. The wall hit the back of her heel.

What more could they want?

Mrs. Williams charged at her with cold, grasping hands, ruthless as her icy fingers crawled over every inch of Sybil's naked body. Lifting, parting, probing…

There would be nothing found. Sybil knew this. She had been born with no marks upon her body.

When Mrs. Williams finally backed away, violent shudders wracked Sybil's body, from the damp chill in the room, from the intensity of such violation.

"There's a witch's mark to be sure." Mrs. Williams crossed her arms over her chest. "We just need to find it."

Sybil remained where she stood, knees bent together to brace herself upright, arms folded over her withered breasts, shoulders curled forward over her torso, so her hair draped like an onyx curtain over her nakedness.

"We can look harder," Mrs. Jones said in a quiet voice from where she stood. She hadn't joined Mrs. Williams in the search but had slowly edged toward the door as if she meant to flee.

"We knew this might happen." Mrs. Williams cast a disparaging look at the other woman. "You said you could do this."

Mrs. Jones nodded. "I'll get the pricker."

Sybil shrank against the wall. "What do you mean to do to me?"

Her poor exhausted body trembled, muscles quivering with the threat of failure. Even as her spirit rallied to keep fighting, everything else begged to give up.

Mrs. Williams rummaged in that awful bag once more and produced a pair of sheep shearers, the two wicked blades catching in the candlelight. "We must rid her of all that hair."

Sybil shook her head. "No. Please."

This time, when Mrs. Williams approached, Sybil did not

possess the energy to fight. She sagged back in utter defeat as the blades nipped over her skin, as hair sifted around her in a detached black cloud.

Her scalp chilled against the air, save the parts that burned where the blades cut too close. Next, Mrs. Williams set to Sybil's under arms. And after that, Sybil's most private area until all of her was shorn and pink and vulnerably exposed as a baby bird.

Sybil stared at the floor, imagining the worn wooden slats were gone, replaced by packed earth. Like the cottage she'd lived in with her mother.

In her mind, Mother brushed Sybil's hair, sweetly humming that lullaby she used when the sounds of the forest made Sybil afraid at night. Later, that cadence was a tune echoed by nature when Sybil came into her gifts as a daughter of the earth.

She wrapped herself in that tune as it played out in her head, oblivious to the voices that floated nearby.

"Prick her."

A cold point pressed into Sybil's skin, sharp enough to pull her attention. Her gaze shifted, slow and lethargic, but not so delayed as to miss how the needle disappeared into the shaft. Poking, but not wounding; a trick meant to give the appearance of sinking deeply into her flesh.

Mrs. Williams pulled the needle back so the shaft pushed out from the hollow handle, appearing whole once more, absent blood. A sure sign of witchcraft to be pricked with a bodkin and not bleed.

Privy to the trick or no, Mrs. Williams gave a victorious cry. "There. You see? She is a witch. Something truly evil."

Sybil closed her eyes, knowing herself condemned.

Of one thing, the old Puritan had indeed been correct. There was evil in the room that day.

And it was Mrs. Williams.

CHAPTER THIRTY-NINE

Lilith

Lilith stepped instinctively back from the man in the entryway of Brackenmere Manor, the man who would kill Sybil. Nausea churned in Lilith's belly, that awful sense of being sucked into one of her dreams.

Her thoughts swam as the room darkened around the edges.

She clenched her hands into fists. She would not faint, not now.

A nudge at her shin made her look down to where Dragon swept figure eights around her legs. The action broke her gaze from the man, giving her a chance to breathe.

Restored, Lilith looked up as the scene played out in front of her, the birthmark at her arm practically burning as if shouting.

This. She needed to see *this*.

And Lilith saw it all: Sybil alone with the man in black, the magistrate, how intimately he pressed her until the dagger in her pocket finally made him back away. How the guards were abruptly called into the room and pulled Sybil's hands forward to clasp in iron manacles.

The weight of those rasping manacles tugged at Lilith's own wrists.

All at once, a subtle glow around Sybil that Lilith hadn't noticed before winked out.

Jacinda was there, crying out in protest. The maids went to her, struggling to hold her back at Sybil's insistence.

Her gaze found Lilith's, those hazel depths filled with horror, with pleading. And though the other woman did not speak, Lilith heard the words clearly in her mind.

Save her.

The door slammed closed, and silence descended, stark with shock and fear.

A brown-haired maid named Anne led Jacinda upstairs.

The room flickered, like Lilith's brain was short-circuiting between the past and the present.

The past came back clear once more, and Lilith followed, stopping before a door where muffled sobs were rife with a heartbreak that echoed in Lilith's soul.

She knew the chasm loss opened inside a person, a yawning gap that couldn't be filled. She'd experienced that pain when Daddy died.

Unable to stay away, she entered the bedroom, plush with blue velvet curtains framing the bed and a richly polished wardrobe and vanity. A bird sat on a stand near the window, its black eyes drilling into Lilith.

The past dimmed away and the present rose to the forefront, revealing a different four-poster bed, one that sank into itself, posts crookedly leaning to the center while the remnants of a mattress drooped to the floor.

Jacinda was a filmy apparition as she wept into a pillow at its center, back shuddering with the force of her sobs.

A metal bracelet sat heavy and dull on the small table beside her bed.

Another flicker of Lilith's vision and a dull pain bloomed behind her eyes.

The past came into focus once more and Jacinda sat up, swollen tear-stained eyes fixed on Lilith. "You knew this was going to happen."

Lilith nodded, knowing she had been lured to the manor for help before even anyone knew help was needed.

"How do I recognize you?" Jacinda bit her lip. "I've seen you..." She shook her head as though trying to clear it. "Like in a dream remembered out of order."

"I'm Lilith and I have spoken with you before." Lilith hesitated, knowing how strange her words were. "I keep seeing the same day over and over, as if I'm meant to notice something."

"From your past," Jacinda whispered. "In my present."

Lilith nodded and was relieved when Jacinda seemed to be considering this idea rather than rejecting it.

"Did you find what was in the library?" Jacinda asked abruptly, clearly beginning to remember.

"The secret room?"

"A secret room...?" Jacinda said softly to herself. "That's what she's been hiding."

Dragon batted at the base of the bird's stand and those glittering dark eyes slid down to the small black cat. Lilith scooped him up.

Ghost or not, she wasn't taking any chances.

"You think Sybil will be burned alive at the stake?" Jacinda's voice wobbled and Lilith kicked herself for her frankness on their last meeting.

Helplessness built up with uncomfortable pressure in the back of Lilith's throat. "I don't know. I think I'm supposed to stop it, but I don't know how."

Jacinda tilted her head at Lilith. "You were there when she was arrested. What was said?"

Lilith explained what she'd seen, how the magistrate lorded over Sybil, how she'd remained strong. The poppet that condemned her.

"That's it." Jacinda sat up straighter. "The poppet. The only one who could have turned it in would be someone within the household. Someone here at the manor denounced her. If we can find out who…"

A flare of heat blazed at Lilith's birthmark. She hissed and put her hand over it. "I think you're on the right track."

Jacinda's gaze followed Lilith's actions and her brows pursed.

"Maybe something in the book will help," Lilith said, more to herself than Jacinda.

"What book?"

"The grimoire."

Jacinda shook her head in confusion.

"I'll show you." Lilith waved for Jacinda to follow.

The ache in Lilith's head was impossible to ignore, like her brain was trying to squeeze out from her skull.

Together, they went into the library with Dragon trotting after them. "There's a lever here." Lilith moved the books aside and pulled the bar set in the bookshelf. The trap door drew back, and Jacinda gasped.

"The room is in here." Lilith ducked into the secret room, but when the candles lit upon her entry, Jacinda was not there.

"Jacinda?" Lilith went out into the library, but the teen was gone.

Likewise, the past had faded once more, revealing only the dusty, dilapidated room and Dragon, who sat by himself, his tail coiled perfectly around his four paws.

"Where did they go?" Lilith asked.

He gave a little chirp and ran into the secret room.

Alone and more determined than ever, Lilith followed. The

candles flickered to life and the sweet scent of those eternal flowers greeted her with an ineffable fragrance that hovered between floral and herb—that fused real life with something otherworldly and coiled into her soul.

A golden glow framed the grimoire, the words shimmering as she approached. Had it been that way last time?

She unfurled her hand from the necklace pouch, the pink velvet crushed into the shape of her curled fist, and read the page before her, a different location than before.

The more you know yourself, the more guidance you will receive from the earth.

A groan escaped Lilith. Because she had never known herself. She'd always been a chameleon, trying to fit in, but always somehow altering to the wrong environment, so she stuck out.

She put a fingertip to the page in an effort to turn it. The page stuck fast.

Embedding her fingernail between two pages midway through the book, she tried again. The pages clung together as if glued.

Apparently, this was the entry she needed to read.

CHAPTER FORTY

Sybil

Sybil did not recall when she had finally been thrown back into the cell, nor when the gift of dreamless slumber offered a reprieve from the horror she'd endured.

When she woke, light spilled from the crude window, revealing a new day. She sat up and a dirty shawl peeled away from her torso where someone had covered her. A shard of light revealed the familiar Lavenham blue beneath the grime, bringing the realization that it was the pretty young woman's shawl.

Sybil looked across the crowded room, finding the woman with her arms folded across her chest, and nodded her thanks. The young woman inclined her head in return, a silent acceptance of a truly selfless gesture.

Something shifted in the rushes beside Sybil, and she turned to find Edith sitting quietly beside her with the little girl curled in her lap.

Sybil's feet were cold as ice. Her woolen stockings and shoes had not been returned. Not that she could have squeezed her battered feet into the latchets regardless. Even now, the tendons of her toes weren't visible beneath the swelling and mottled bruising of her feet.

"I have your bread ration for you," Edith whispered, pulling two pieces of bread from her waistband.

Sybil lifted her gaze to the bread. Edith extended a cup of ale, fuller than usual. Likely partly her portion as well as Sybil's.

Edith pushed both toward Sybil, her actions gentle to keep from waking the girl. "They were generous this time."

There had been no food or water after Sybil had been walked, nor before she had been so stripped and prodded.

"Liar," Sybil croaked. "That is yours."

Edith's brow pursed. "Your need is greater than mine."

"You give all your food away," Sybil accused, hating how desperately she truly did want the bread. And the ale.

Oh God, the ale…

Edith truly looked at her then, studying Sybil from the crown of her roughly shorn head to her battered feet. A sheen of tears shone in Edith's eyes. "Please, my friend. Eat."

Sybil did not protest again but fell upon the gift with zeal. Her desperate, breathless gulps echoed back at her from the hollow of the mug and never had anything been more delicious than the cool liquid slaking her parched throat. Next, she tore into the bread, her teeth barely able to chew before her stomach demanded the food be forced down in greedy swallows.

The meal was scarcely satisfying after having gone so long without, and she could have sobbed for want of more. Instead, she thanked her friend for the great sacrifice and lay back in the rushes, her abused scalp stinging where the bits of hay dug into fresh cuts.

How she longed to sleep. To forget.

"Sybil Brantham."

She jerked at the sound of her name, alarm bells clanging through her skull.

Edith placed a comforting hand on Sybil's shoulder.

"Sybil Brantham," the young guard called, louder this time. "You have a visitor."

She lifted her head, suspecting a cruel trick. After all, this was a place without hope. She would do well to remember as much.

Rising unsteadily to her damaged feet, Sybil made to smooth her hair, fingers skimming her bald pate.

Her heart lurched in horror.

At the memory.

What she had endured assaulted her memory, playing again with details she wished she could forget.

Her fingertips trembled as they ran over the plane of her skull once more, some areas prickled with patches of hair, unevenly shorn, others scabbed where the blade had cropped too deeply.

And who would come here to see her thus?

Robbed of the only feature she'd been proud of, gaunt, filthy. Defeated.

A hand curled around Sybil's. She looked down to find Edith gazing up at her.

"Have hope," she whispered.

Walking slowly on feet that could scarcely hold her weight, Sybil was led to a square room where manacles hung from rusty nails, and several buckets lined the side of one wall. All were visible by the narrow cut in the stone that allowed in a scant amount of light.

A cry wrenched from her throat.

For there truly was someone there to see her.

Jacinda.

Her eyes went wide, the shock of Sybil's appearance written as plainly on her face, as if in stark black ink upon a page.

"Sybil?" Jacinda approached slowly, cautiously.

Sybil nodded. Tears blazed in her eyes.

She wanted to apologize for her appearance, to tell how they had stripped her bare. How she had been thusly violated as they picked and preened over every bit of her scraped skin. How she had been so weak, she'd given up.

Instead, she simply nodded. Such horrors were too great to give voice to. Some were best locked inside, where a key could twist them shut forever.

"You have only a few moments," a guard called from the corner.

Jacinda blinked, brought round by the reminder.

Sybil shifted her weight from one agonized foot to the other, the manacles around her ankle bones clanking. "Jacinda." She choked out the single word, barely a whisper.

The guard stared with bored disinterest, his heart numb or missing.

Jacinda gazed at her shoes. At the wall. Anywhere but at Sybil.

But Sybil was not offended. She understood she was a hard visage to take in, her shorn head nicked and scabbed, her body skeletal beneath her shift.

"It has only been a fortnight," Jacinda said brokenly. "How could they have done this to you in so short a time?"

"They are persuasive in their efforts to encourage a confession of witchcraft." Sybil tried to give a wry smile, but her lips had split from lack of moisture.

Jacinda shook her head, incredulous. "Why?"

"They sought a witch mark," Sybil replied. "When one could not be found, they insisted there must be one beneath my hair. There was not."

Jacinda covered her mouth with her hand, suppressing the emotion welling in her eyes. "They arrested you for Henry's murder."

Jacinda had loved Henry. For a girl who had never known

her father, he had easily stepped into the role, guiding her, educating her, marveling at her cleverness and making her feel worthy of praise and affection.

Sybil nodded. "I know."

"But he died of the plague," Jacinda cried.

"He did. But a woman tried as a witch is merely hanged, and a woman who has killed her husband is burned alive."

Jacinda shrank back. "No."

"It is what they want. To make an example of me."

It is what *he* wanted for her repeated rejection.

Robert Walsingham. The magistrate.

He had not been by to see his handiwork. Not yet. Sybil knew it was only a matter of time.

"One of the servants denounced you," Jacinda said, her words inflamed with a wrath that could make the entire town burn. "I will find who did it."

Sybil shook her head. "It matters naught now."

"It matters," Jacinda said between clenched teeth. "There has to be a reason why. A way to stop this."

Sybil continued to shake her head. "Please…keep to yourself, stay to the manor, wear your bracelet. See Kat."

"She has been by," Jacinda said softly.

The tension drawing Sybil's shoulders to her ears relaxed some. Kat had made good on her promise. Of course she had. "Kat has been given instruction to see to your care."

Jacinda put her hand to the iron bracelet on her wrist and nodded again.

Sybil glanced to the guard, wishing she could say more. How she longed to tell Jacinda she would remain strong in prison to keep suspicion from turning to her, how Jacinda must refrain from using her gifts.

A knot swelled in the back of Sybil's throat.

There was so, so much to say that she had put off for too long.

"Mind Kat," was all she could manage.

If anyone could corral the enormity of Jacinda's power, it was Kat—a woman used to navigating life around the tantrums and chaos of seven children, all while trying desperately to establish herself as a seamstress in the village. Kat hadn't the time for impatience or hesitation.

Jacinda nodded and surreptitiously looked to her right, where the guard watched them with bored disinterest. With shaking fingers, she pulled the iron bracelet from her wrist.

The scent of the earth's power teased at Sybil's nostrils despite the heavy iron manacles at her feet—a wet, pungent fragrance, like the moments before a rainstorm in a garden thick with fragrant blossoms.

Though she wanted to tilt her head back and revel in the aroma, to strain her ears for its hum, doing so was far too dangerous.

She reached for Jacinda's wrist when the image of the guard wavered, like heat rising from flame. A blocking charm.

Alarm prickled through Sybil's entire body, stinging every nerve ending. "Don't. Not here."

"Quick." Jacinda passed a bladder of ale to Sybil from her basket. There was authority to her tone, an understanding of caution. A note of maturity.

In Sybil's absence, the girl was finally starting to become a woman.

And though Sybil wanted to decline the offer, the slosh of liquid was more than she could resist. She put the mouthpiece to her lips and drank and drank.

Sweet and bright and gloriously wet, she gulped until her thirst was slaked. Jacinda then brought a sack of food from the basket.

The guard wore a strange dreamlike expression on his face, as if he could not keep his eyes open.

Sybil looked at the food and hesitated. "You can't do this. If you're caught with what you're doing to him..."

"It is already done." Jacinda pushed the basket forward. "Now hurry."

There was cold chicken, tender and still juicy and crusty bread with a soft center. She had almost forgotten how fine manchet bread could be and regretted every moment she'd taken it for granted in the past.

The remainder of the food, Jacinda hurriedly helped tie to the inside of Sybil's knee, hidden from view beneath her chemise.

The wall separating their movements trembled and Jacinda hastily slipped her bracelet back on. The guard blinked as though his vision had blurred.

"Jacinda, know that..." Sybil hesitated, uncertain of what Kat might have said, uncertain of what she could safely share. "Know that I love you. But that you cannot come back."

Doing so was far too risky.

"I will be back," Jacinda vowed, stubbornly defiant as ever. "And I will find out who denounced you."

"Do not," Sybil cautioned. "Please. What's done is done. Just stay in the manor and obey Kat."

Jacinda shook her head, eyes bright with unshed tears. "I will do anything to save you." She touched her bracelet. *"Anything."*

A chill raked over Sybil's skin. For there were enchantments that might be begged of the earth, powers great enough to save those who were condemned.

But they scraped against the grain of nature, an abomination.

And there were grave consequences indeed for engaging in the forbidden.

CHAPTER FORTY-ONE

Lilith

Lilith leaned over the grimoire, committing each word to memory.

> *The more you know yourself, the more guidance you will receive from the earth.*
>
> *After all, it is not uncertainty which shows a path, but confidence.*
>
> *The earth's memory is long, able to recall the abuses suffered by women, and ensures we will once more be strong.*
>
> *You must welcome that which flows in our veins without restraint, without protest, without question of worth. This is the legacy in our souls.*
>
> *In order to accomplish great tasks, we must fully accept that legacy. That we will honor the earth by cherishing our gifts and pass our knowledge to our daughters that they might be as strong as we have become.*

The flower does not seek permission to grow. The sun does not issue an apology as it rises. The moon does not feel shame when it glows. These are beautiful in their own right.

You, too, are beautiful, my dearest Sybil. You are a daughter of the earth, and someday, I hope you claim your birthright.

There are charms that have been passed down from mother to daughter for generations. Those have been scribed into this book, for your knowledge and for you to pass on to future generations.

But I pray you experience your surroundings for strength. Let the sweetness of honeysuckle melt on your tongue, bask in the light of the moon, bathe in the cool water of a spring rain. See where your own gifts guide you. Only you will know what is in your soul.

This simple spell will help you claim your legacy, and honor yourself:

Pink quartz to accept your soul

Blossoms of a fragrant flower to sweeten your life

Moonlight to ease your weary mind and quiet your uncertainty

Be confident in who you are, my daughter, and know you are worthy.

CHAPTER FORTY-TWO

Lilith

Lilith ran her fingers over that poignant line in the grimoire.

After all, it is not uncertainty which shows a path, but confidence.

She had become lost in the grimoire after that, learning about the phases of the moon, how great power could be achieved when it was full and bright, and how a dark new moon was ideal for setting intention.

There had been in-depth detail on how colors aided charms, with white for purification and cleansing; red for courage, passion, and power; and information about every color of the rainbow in between.

There were runes, and crystals, and herbs—each with its own purpose. At the end of each entry, Lilith found the ingredients for charms that encompassed anything she might need from good health to prosperity, as well as love and protection.

On and on, she read, pausing only to feed Dragon.

She read until the knowledge cramped in her brain, yearning to unfurl and stretch into the world.

A nudge at her calf pulled her from the text.

She startled and looked down, seeing Dragon gazing up at her, his green eyes almost luminescent. He gave a quiet coo and trotted to the door where he pawed impatiently.

Lilith opened the door, and he tore off. When she did not follow, he stopped and looked back impatiently at her.

"I guess you want me to come too?" she asked.

He blinked at her.

Compelled by instinct, she quickly scooped up the remaining stones from the table and a few herbs, tucking them into her pockets.

Dragon waited for her by the doorway, then resumed his steady gait from the library.

The house was dark, the moonlight muted where it valiantly attempted to stream through the dusty windows, revealing a dizzying mix of past and present that made her headache throb back to life.

She thought back to the grimoire's words as she followed Dragon.

Confidence was needed.

Lord, she was lacking that…

A glance at her phone indicated it was well past midnight. The ideal time for charms for banishing, healing, and self enhancement.

She shoved aside her doubt and hoped the fake-it-till-you-make-it confidence would work for now.

The force of the moon welcomed her outside, waning

gibbous, with vitality radiating from its half-shielded face, leaving Lilith with a sense of quiet power.

Dragon turned in the opposite direction from the bed and breakfast, where they ought to be heading, and continued onward.

Lilith hesitated. "You're going the wrong way, you silly thing."

Dragon stopped and sat, eyes narrowing to slits.

Well, he certainly knew how to get what he wanted.

And color her a sucker, because she didn't hesitate to join him as he so clearly intended.

He didn't move when she approached but batted at her shoelaces instead.

Ah, yes, she was supposed to press her bare feet to the earth.

Lilith toed off her shoes and tugged off her socks. As soon as her naked soles connected with the ground, something loosened inside her that she hadn't realized had been curled up and withdrawn.

She closed her eyes and tilted her face to the moonlight, empowering her with the harmony of nature. A gentle breeze stirred her hair, tickling her cheeks, but she kept her eyes shut, focusing on the world around her.

Something cold and wet touched the top of Lilith's foot.

She blinked her eyes open to find Dragon nudging her.

He turned and slinked over the grass, his coat gleaming like a raven's wing in the muted light. They continued into the forest, navigating over tree roots and thick clusters of ferns.

Bracken.

A common foliage in England often used to ward off witches. The thick flora created living barriers to skirt around.

Lilith almost laughed as a frond tickled over her ankles and left her skin humming from the contact.

After a lifetime of Mama telling Lilith to wear shoes when she didn't want to, she'd have thought her feet would be tender. But the rough ground seemed gentle. The forest was alive around them, and the partial moon glowed like magic in the vast, inky sky.

A canopy of foliage came into view, the path seemingly blocked by a wall of hanging branches of what appeared to be weeping beech trees. A honeyed vanilla fragrance filled the air.

Lilith slowed down, but Dragon plunged ahead through a gap in the branches.

Ducking, she followed him into a clearing framed in a tangle of honeysuckle bushes, their vines lush with yellow-white petals, the air heady with their unique floral perfume. All this was housed within the protective circle of weeping beech trees. A supernatural strength pulsed within the grassy clearing as the moon's glow flared, flooding the clearing with sacred light.

In a world filled with bustle and noise and chaos, this place was peace. It was beauty.

It was home.

The thought came to her, unexpected and with a finality that settled inside her.

Moonlight to ease your weary mind and quiet your uncertainty.

"You knew what you were doing," Lilith teased Dragon.

He tucked his paws under himself and squint-blinked at her in that wise old man way he did.

She had been exhausted before, but now energy radiated through her.

Energy and desperation.

If she did this, she would be accepting her legacy.

Life would never be the same again.

That at some point, she must have a daughter to pass her legacy on to.

She hesitated, flinching from the idea of motherhood, hating that it still scraped against everything natural within her.

No, there must be no reservations.

And she wasn't like Mama.

Again, she thought of the journal, how Mama went through so much of her life feeling like something was missing. How empty that must have been. And how sad to constantly seek ways to fill that unrelenting void.

The weight of Lilith's lifelong anger eased somewhat.

This was what she needed. To yield to her gifts, to let her hurt go.

Lilith closed her eyes, lips lifting in a soft smile, giving her whole self, sacrificing whatever was needed for this beautiful gift.

A slight hum at her back pocket made her start. Without thought, she withdrew the rose quartz.

As soon as her fingers grasped the crystal, a pleasant warmth infused her heart. She curled the stone into the cradle of her palm and recalled the enchantment from the grimoire.

Pink quartz to accept your soul.

The fragrance of the honeysuckle intensified, so rich, its honeyed perfume was sweet on her tongue.

Blossoms of a fragrant flower to sweeten your life.

She hesitated. Creating a charm to love herself felt so small.

But, as the grimoire had said, uncertainty would not find the path, and she needed to know where she was going. If she couldn't love herself, how could she save Sybil?

"Here goes nothing," she said under her breath.

She approached a honeysuckle bush, gently extracting several blooms. They came away easily, surrendering to her the way she had to the earth.

If this was the first gift meant to be bestowed upon her, she would accept.

Cradling the blossoms and the rose quartz in her hands, she closed her eyes and opened her senses. She relished the distant buzz of insects, the caress of a gentle breeze against her skin, the rich soil beneath the floral notes of honeysuckle.

Let me love myself.

Memories came at her in a whirling assault.

The way other children had thrown away her binders in school, how they refused to sit by her in class, calling her a freak. But also the way Essie had always stood up for her.

How Mama's face contorted in disgust when she told Lilith she would never amount to anything.

A college dropout.

A worthless daughter.

Tears stung behind Lilith's closed lids.

"Let me love myself," she pleaded, her voice thickening.

Because there was also Daddy who had been there to pick her up when she fell, how he'd blow on a scrape after a swipe of rubbing alcohol. How he'd beamed with pride at her, eyes filled with love.

Then there was the now. Lilith's reeling life without purpose, aimless, useless.

A job that easily moved on without her.

The nudge of a warm, furry body against Lilith's shin and a delicate purr that sent vibrations limned in gold through her mind.

In every situation in her life, she hadn't cared for herself. She had let others hurt her. And yet, there had always been someone there to love her.

She had to see herself the way they did.

Drawing in a shuddering breath, she poured the whole of her wounded heart into her words. "Let me love myself."

Her chest lifted in a deep inhale, free of the constraint of her own self-doubt, liberated from castigation. And the lie of her insignificance cracked open.

She was kind. And strong. And worthy.

Exactly as Daddy saw her, and Essie, and even little Dragon.

She blinked her eyes open. A milky glow shimmered over

her skin, a sheen of power enveloping her. A gift she was worthy of.

She was beautiful.

She was powerful.

And she could do this.

She hadn't realized she'd started to cry until the wind brushed her damp cheeks.

In this world, where she had never felt like she belonged, she understood now that she was exactly who she was supposed to be.

And perhaps if she hadn't been comfortable in her own skin, if she hadn't been picked at for being strange, if Mama hadn't ridden her like she did, maybe then the rightness of this place—of Lilith understanding her own power—wouldn't stretch so soul deep.

"I *can* do this," Lilith declared aloud.

But first, there was something calling to her—a thread pulling at her that she needed to follow, and she headed back to the manor.

CHAPTER FORTY-THREE

Sybil

Sybil hobbled back to the prison, trying to push the sounds of Jacinda's weeping from her ears. The bag of food strapped to her knee made Sybil's gait off-kilter, but the stiffness of her abused body masked the awkwardness.

By the time she returned to the cell, Edith was gone.

"They took her not long after you were called away," the pretty young woman said.

Sybil thanked her and the woman's nostrils flared. "Did you confess?" she hissed. "I smell ale upon your breath."

Sybil shook her head. "My sister came to me." She beckoned the young woman to follow her to the corner, where the little girl sat in the shadows. "She brought me food." Sybil spoke in an almost silent whisper. "Sit before me."

The young woman complied, blocking Sybil from the view of others. Sybil opened the bag and handed a bit of chicken and bread first to the girl, then to the young woman, sharing before she could yield to the temptation to keep the food and drink for herself. Hopkins and his mercenaries could do what they wanted to her body, but she refused to allow prison to change the woman she was inside.

"Keep your food for yourself." The young woman shook her head, her eyes filling with tears. "You know nothing of me."

Sybil pulled from her memory, recalling the guards as they spoke. "Your name is Margery, is it not?" Sybil nudged a hunk of meat toward her. "Eat."

Margery pursed her lips. "I confessed. My soul is damned."

The little girl's eyes widened as she shoved chicken into her mouth.

"I know you confessed," Sybil replied. "I smelled the ale on you the same as you did me just now."

"I didn't do it for food." The young woman sagged back. "They threatened my husband's commission if I did not confess. All he has ever wanted in this world is to be a soldier. I couldn't take that from him. I love him too greatly."

Her voice choked off, and she cleared her throat before continuing. "It was my steadfast love for him which condemned me to be here from the first."

Chill bumps crawled over Sybil's skin. If they exploited love for confessions, how soon might Jacinda's name be brought up again. Especially after she had been inside the prison, using her gifts.

"Jacob Neech denounced me." Bitterness hardened Margery's lovely features. "He waited until my Bran had left with the other Parliamentarians and he set upon me, bade me take him as my lover. I told him I would take no lover. Day after day, he came to me, until he refused to hear my reply."

Sybil's fists tightened at her side at the familiarity of the woman's pain, of the helplessness from the brutish nature of some men.

"I would never lie with another man," the young woman said vehemently. "I am no cavalier."

Everyone knew the cavaliers, the women whose husbands were at war and so they assumed a masculine role. Not only at home, but in pubs, consuming strong ale, speaking like sailors, and taking men to bed.

No one would ever mistake Margery for one of those women.

"I knew he would be by again," she continued. "I…I had hidden a knife in my basket, you see."

"You killed him?" Sybil asked.

"I wish I had." Her eyes flashed with hatred. "But I injured him well enough for his thigh to be stitched closed. Then he accused me of witchcraft, saying I was a lewd woman. I finally agreed to have conspired with the Devil to keep my Bran safe." She pressed her hand over her heart. "I have given my soul so that Bran might keep his commission. May God forgive me."

She wept then, in breaking gasps that caught at Sybil's heart. She embraced the young woman, cradling the bony body in her own thin arms.

Such was the cost of love in their world.

When Margery's tears had finally dried, Sybil encouraged the young woman to take some meat and bread. "We must all keep up our strength."

No sooner had she uttered the words than the door to the cage was opened and a figure was thrown within. Edith lay upon the rushes as Sybil had, her head bald and bleeding, patched with tufts of gray hair. The warts that plagued Edith's face dotted her scalp as well.

The little girl's eyes locked on Edith, and she crept closer, holding out a hunk of chicken.

Edith's eyes filled with tears as she shook her head. "Keep it for yourself, dear."

Sybil helped Edith up to sitting and carefully blotted away the blood.

"They say I have no witch's mark, and I refuse their entreaties to confess." There was a wooden quality to Edith's voice.

As if she were outside of herself.

Sybil understood. Letting one's thoughts drift away was the only escape from such pain and humiliation.

"I have some meat and bread," Sybil whispered to her dear friend. "Come fortify yourself."

But Edith did not move from where she sat, her poor feet still blistered and bleeding from when they had walked her. "Save it for yourself and for others. I have no future."

Sybil shook her head, not understanding. "Please, Edith, you cannot give up—"

"I am to be put to the swimming test."

Whatever low conversations hummed in the prison went silent, as if every ear heard Edith.

"No." Sybil continued to shake her head, refusing to believe the words. "They cannot."

"They can," Edith said. "And they will. I will be swum in two days' time."

"God save your soul," a frail voice called from the other cage. The old vicar stood by the bars and folded his long, skeletal fingers around them. He alone understood how terrible the water test could truly be.

Sybil embraced Edith, knowing her fate was a death sentence. Either she would float and be denounced a witch and hanged. Or she would die by drowning and be declared innocent.

Sybil tightened her hold on Edith, as if doing so might protect her friend from the inevitable. For either way, Edith would die.

And soon.

The unfairness of what they endured wound tight in Sybil.

The way women were overwhelmed by men, their words of protest ignored.

Twist.

The confessions forced through torture and extreme deprivation.

Twist.

The innocent lives condemned by unjust means.

Twist.

Tighter and tighter, until Sybil knew, at some point, she would snap.

CHAPTER FORTY-FOUR

Lilith

Power shot through Lilith, a potent draw toward something she had to see despite the late hour. She led Dragon to Brackenmere Manor, her path marked with purpose.

The manor lay in quiet slumber, lit by a gleaming slice of moonlight. The invisible thread tugged at her gut.

This was the ideal time to explore, to orient herself with the rooms. Her heart constricted in her chest, a recurring sense of dread.

The reminder of how swiftly she was running out of time.

Silent as the black cat shadow at her side, she examined the first floor where the scullery maid slept on a pallet in the kitchen. The remaining rooms on the ground floor were entirely devoid of people.

Creaking floorboards sounded overhead. Someone else was moving through the house.

Lilith rushed into the Great Hall in time to catch the sweep of a white nightdress and red-gold hair on the second floor, along the railing.

Jacinda.

Lilith rushed up the stairs. A glance at Jacinda's bedchamber revealed she was not there. The groan of a door being opened sounded down the hall.

The library.

Dragon was already darting in that direction and Lilith hastened to follow. The door stood ajar, allowing her to glimpse inside as a white nightdress disappeared into the secret room. The door fell into place, shielding its existence from view.

Was this the moment that would echo through generations, impacting lives of all of Jacinda's descendants, including Lilith's?

A chill raked down Lilith's skin, a premonition of an enchantment that scraped against their gifts.

She wasn't just watching history, she was witnessing her own legacy, the thing that had shaped every second of her life.

The thought spurred Lilith forward, into the library, into the secret room.

She stopped, blinded by darkness.

"Jacinda?" Her voice was loud in the small, quiet space.

She crept forward, heart thudding. If she could just speak to Jacinda…to understand.

The candles flickered to life and Lilith's stomach dropped.

The room was empty.

Jacinda was not there.

Lilith stepped toward the table, noting the handwriting on the open page of the grimoire was different than previous entries. The fat loops bespoke of a girlish hand.

Jacinda's?

Lilith began to read.

What I have done is forbidden.

CHAPTER FORTY-FIVE

Sybil

Sybil woke with a leaden heart on the morning of Edith's swimming test. They slept beside one another in the rushes with the little girl safely tucked between them, their warmth shared as their lifelong friendship neared its end.

Commotion roused within the prison.

"Ye'll let me through, or I'll tell them how ye roughly handled a woman with child."

Kat.

Edith and Sybil looked at one another and clambered stiffly to their feet along with the girl.

"Don't ye touch me. I'm well enough to walk on my own."

And then Kat was there, outside the bars of their prison, resplendent in a yellow gown, with her flame-red hair and bright green eyes. A length of blue silk lay over her forearm, and she hefted it higher so they could see. "I brought something for ye."

They were herded into the small square room where Sybil had met with Jacinda.

"Kat, you shouldn't have come," Edith whispered. "It's too dangerous, and those men don't do well when spoken against."

"Edith." Kat swallowed and shook out the garment, revealing the finest gown she had ever sewn. "I had to. I've been working on this for ye since I heard…"

Blue silk embroidered with honeysuckle flowers and woodlarks, each stitched with the finest detail.

"It's too fine." Edith gaped. "Kat, it's far too fine for me."

Kat's eyes watered. "It isn't fine enough for the likes of you."

Sybil touched a hand to the silk. "Put the gown on, Edith."

Kat stepped closer to their friend. "Please."

Edith blinked away a sheen of tears. "I can't. I'm filthy."

"It's meant for ye." Kat reverently placed the garment in Edith's bewildered hands. "I want ye to wear it today." Her voice caught. "It's for ye, as I said."

Still Edith hesitated. "But I won't be able to give it back. Kat, I—"

"I know." Kat nodded and swallowed thickly. "Go on now."

The guard turned to allow Edith the opportunity to strip off her overdress, which hadn't been cut away as Sybil's had.

Edith's strength had waned in those last two days, and both Sybil and Kat aided their friend into the gown.

When she was properly laced, Kat smoothed the bodice and adjusted the skirt, then stood back to admire her handiwork. "What do ye think?"

Edith looked down for a long time. The silk was the exact summer sky blue as her eyes, making them stand out with startling clarity. Kat had sewn a white linen cap for her, which hid Edith's shaved head.

When she finally lifted her gaze, her eyes were brilliant with tears she could no longer hide. "I've always wanted to be beautiful." She pressed her lips together then whispered, "I feel beautiful."

Sybil took Edith's hand. "You *are* beautiful."

"I feel it in this gown." Edith swallowed and gave them both a watery smile. "Thank you, Kat. Thank you for this gift."

Kat caught her in an embrace.

"Enough," the guard called out. "It's time."

Time.

Time for Edith to be marched away, to be dunked in the River Lark, to be murdered today or another day, depending on the result.

Sybil shook her head, unable to even form the words.

"My life never had love in it until I met you both." Edith clasped their hands.

They embraced, the three of them, the final circle of their sisterhood made whole. "May the earth guide you," Sybil whispered, quiet enough that the guard would not hear.

"Now," the guard said testily, earning him a sharp look from Kat.

Before she was sent away, her hand slipped into Sybil's, placing a small glass vial against her palm.

Edith straightened her back, head lifted like a queen. A woman who felt beautiful.

That confidence led her from the room as Sybil was forced back to her cell and Kat was sent back home.

Outside, the crowd clamored in a frenzy as Edith was led to the cart that would take her near the abbey ruins where River Lark flowed.

Hag.

Witch.

Ugly.

Their insults were knife points in Sybil's heart. She only

hoped that Edith kept her head lifted, that she continued to feel beautiful.

For Edith truly was the loveliest soul to ever walk the earth.

When the shouting abated and the footfalls outside went quiet, the waiting began.

The entire prison fell silent, save for the occasional shifting of vermin in the rushes. But even their activity was subdued, as if they sensed the grave mood.

From the men's cage, the old vicar prayed for Edith's soul, for her strength as she endured the test that broke him. In between his prayers, he wept.

Margery remained by Sybil's side, as did the little girl.

An hour passed.

Two.

Eventually, light faded to dark, and still, Edith did not return. Sybil took that moment to uncap the vial and sniff, the earthy odor reminiscent of bad cheese.

Valerian root.

A draught upended in mugs of ale would send the guards into a deep, incoherent slumber. Such a gift might prove helpful indeed.

Sleep eluded Sybil that night, interrupted by a heaviness in her chest. The assumption to Edith's prolonged absence.

News of the swimming test did not reach her ears until the following afternoon, told by a guard who appreciated the attention of so many as he recanted the tale he'd heard through another.

It was said that Edith remained upright and proud in the cart, her face lifted to the sky.

Sybil could imagine her friend, elevated by the lovely silk gown, soaring over the insults and the hate. Knowing she was truly loved.

It was said they bound Edith's right big toe to her left thumb and her left big toe to her right thumb. In this position, she was shoved into the river.

It was said she bobbed about, coughing and sputtering, enough that an impatient few deemed her a witch. But before she could be fetched from the icy River Lark, she sank like a stone.

It was said they waited for her to rise once more, spitting and cursing them all. But she did not. The trail of bubbles where she descended melted into the current and the gleam of her white cap showed beneath the water.

It was said there was a lark song in that moment, the most mournful one to have ever been heard.

It was said the mood turned somber as Edith's innocence spoke for itself with her death, when all recalled the goodness she'd bestowed upon others. How she tended to the infirm and the aged, how she gave to those who had none. Solemn beneath the weight of such knowledge, the crowd dissolved as a woodlark swept from the trees, carrying with it that sorrowful tune.

Sybil had asked then if the shackles remained clasped around her friend's ankles. The guard confirmed those heavy iron cuffs had been removed.

At this, Sybil's spirits lifted somewhat.

Edith had died with the hum of the earth in her heart, radiating in her soul, drawing her into an eternal embrace. In these last moments before Edith's death, she had been allowed to revel in life.

Even with such knowledge, Edith's loss was a blow. To the entire prison, but especially to Sybil. She had lost one of her dearest friends, a light in a world of darkness. Whatever future Sybil faced was mean and bleak and empty.

In the quiet hours of early morning, when the ember of loss burned in Sybil's chest, something warm slipped into her hand. She looked down and found the little girl had clasped hands with her and gazed up with large, sorrowful eyes.

That comfort, given by a child who had so little consolation of her own, was nearly Sybil's undoing.

Sometime in the night, Sybil finally drifted off to sleep, but was awoken by a tingling at her right arm.

Her awareness pricked with recognition, with understanding that, despite the barrier of the iron shackles, her body had been imbued with the power of the earth.

She pulled up the sleeve of her shift where a beam of moonlight revealed a strange mark on her forearm, just below the crook of her elbow. A strawberry-colored crescent moon.

In the back of her mind came the clang of a warning bell.

This was no ordinary enchantment. Not when its power transcended the iron dulling the earth from reaching Sybil.

This was something that went against the earth's gifts.

Something forbidden.

Something only a daughter of the earth could accomplish if she had extraordinary power.

Jacinda.

What had she done?

CHAPTER FORTY-SIX

Lilith

The hairs on Lilith's arms rose as she read the next passage in the grimoire.

What I have done is forbidden.

I embarked on my endeavor knowing its wrongness, both through what I have read here in the grimoire and the stark emptiness inside me when I created the enchantment. My request was too great.

And yet, my power is also great.

Was great.

I defied the bounds of our gifts. The power in me wanes already, an atrophy that began the moment the incantation left my lips. It is the cost of my actions.

And yet, seeing Edith die… I could not allow such a fate to befall Sybil.

Lilith, if you read this, you were correct: You must save Sybil.

This is your destiny. A path laid out before you by me—a path you marked as surely for me to find when you led me to this hidden room. An endless spiral through time, the two of us tangled in the same fate.

One where I lose the earth's power, a worthy sacrifice to save Sybil. One where you must save a life or risk your very existence.

One where our legacy is at risk if I have set you up to fail.

Lilith, I am aggrieved that you must be ensnared in this destiny with me. It is my hope that you will someday read this passage.

In this world where women's power is not revered, but denigrated, women of strength and intellect are persecuted. Murdered.

Like Sybil will be as well if she is not saved. Like we all eventually will be.

I found this room, this book, because of you, Lilith. Reading what has been so carefully written in these pages revealed so much about who I am, where I come from. All things Sybil withheld from me. I suspect there are still more secrets for me to learn.

Lilith, I now put down the rest of these words for you to read:

As you have learned in this grimoire, ours is a gift that spans generations. Centuries. The power of the earth has protected the women of our family.

This forbidden enchantment has cut a swath through that force. If Sybil can be saved, our line will be protected, allowed to continue after a dormancy stretching between the loss of my gifts and the awakening of yours.

You must find who denounced Sybil. I believe it is the only way to save her.

And if you cannot, the failed enchantment will not only wither my powers, but also my body. I will not survive the year. I will not bear children.

You will not exist.

This linking spell is rare, one that can only be done by a woman of incredible power. Mine started as far back as I can remember, the way the earth spoke to me, how the wind blew secrets into my ear and shared the beauty of the world.

The magnitude of my gifts made Sybil afraid. I understand that now. Even now, she implores me to wear a bracelet of iron to cut my connection to the earth.

I wear it when she will see me, but I dread the muted silence that descends once it touches my flesh. As if I am living, but soul dead.

Despite my reduced power, I am still stronger than Sybil or any of the others. I believe several weeks will be required to fully sever my tie to the earth.

I mourn the loss of my gifts already. But I would mourn Sybil more. I am prepared for the punishment my actions demand.

The linking enchantment is meant to tie Sybil to someone who may help her, a daughter of our line who has been born under the brilliant, open face of a full moon. Sometimes that daughter is born within months. Other times, centuries will pass. Given your strange attire, I presume the latter has occurred.

You have been tied to Sybil since you were born. I suspect you have seen her in your dreams, felt her in your heart. Tasted the fear of her final moments. I am sorry for this—it is the nature of the spell.

I also suspect your mother is no longer of this world. A mother's sacred charge is to protect, and her spirit will have safeguarded you from the full force of your power with the earth to ensure you are ready. When the earth claimed her soul, that shield fell, allowing you to step into your power. And thus begins the full extent of your need to save Sybil. Before you reach the date of her intended death.

27 August 1645

I can scarcely breathe even as I write such harrowing words.

Perhaps it is well that my powers are fading.

Now is not a time for women of the earth. Not when men seek to rob us of our strength, to pin us under their thumbs with lies and murder.

Someone has betrayed Sybil, someone residing within Brackenmere Manor.

If you find who has spoken against her, we can understand why. My own inquiries have left me uncertain who I can trust. The energy from the earth can only aid us so much. Having this knowledge will fortify our ability to spare Sybil from the pyre.

I assume you have received little to no education about your gifts. You will find all you need in this grimoire, the very book you guided me toward.

When in doubt, listen to the world around you.

And my final message to you is one of sincere apology. I knew your face when I cast the spell, for I realized your destiny in helping Sybil as well as my own in speaking the enchantment that would forever find you through time.

I apologize for the burden I settled upon your shoulders and for the peril I lay at your feet.

It is my hope that I may reunite with Sybil, and that you will step into the legacy that has been laid before you. That our line will not fade from the imprint of time. That you will become a woman of the earth and carry our power into a new generation.

For the task you are charged with, in equal parts, I beg your forgiveness, and I thank you.

Eternally,
Jacinda

CHAPTER FORTY-SEVEN

Lilith

Lilith closed the grimoire and returned to the bed and breakfast, her mind a live wire of questions.

Every part of her life had been influenced by the linking spell, set in motion the moment she was born under a full moon. The tease of her powers, straddling between two worlds, never fitting into either, leaving her on the outskirts.

And Mama...

She'd blocked the full force of Lilith's gifts to protect her, whether she knew it or not. In doing so, she had been robbed of her own legacy.

Both Mama and Mama's mama had felt like something was missing in their life. Was that why?

A twist of pain radiated from Lilith's chest.

Mama never felt the beauty of power threading through her veins, shimmering on her skin, connecting her to the earth.

No wonder she always felt incomplete.

Rage and sorrow, hurt and confusion all muddied up into one great mess, like a kid making a new color by using every crayon in the box.

Lilith sank onto the bed and pulled out her phone.

Three missed calls from Asher.

She grimaced. Checking in with him at some point would have been the polite thing to do. Not that he needed to get a call from her now in the middle of the night.

Instead, she opened the photo app, intending to study the pictures she'd taken of the grimoire.

Her photo count changed from 10,501 to 10,495. She blinked as the numbers continued ticking down, like the seconds descending toward something momentous.

Frowning, she skimmed up to pictures of Essie with Amara cuddled in her lap from a few weeks prior, at one of the various story hours. There were also a few pictures of blooming camellias in Johnson Square.

No pictures were of Lilith.

Pulse fluttering, she swept her thumb down, scrolling through dozens of images at once before finally seeing a selfie with her and Essie and a few snaps of Lilith suggestively holding a cocktail that Essie had insisted she take for a possible dating profile.

The pictures dissolved before her eyes, while those of coffee cups and trees scooted upward to take their place.

Erasing her.

Like a mirror with no reflection.

A quiet erasure.

As if she had never existed at all.

Hands shaking, she opened her texts, tapping out a message to Essie.

I'm scared.

Her finger hovered over the send button, trembling.

Never had she needed someone more, to remember her. To let Lilith know she was still seen.

For Lilith to reaffirm the knowledge that she *did* exist.

Finally, she hit send and her body tensed.

With hope.

With fear.

Three dots appeared and disappeared as Essie began to type then stopped, then started again. This repeated several more times.

Then came the reply:

Who is this?

CHAPTER FORTY-EIGHT

Sybil

Sybil still could not sleep the following night despite her exhaustion. Edith's loss that sat heavy in her chest, the emblazoned new mark of a crescent moon on Sybil's skin, how such a mark placed Jacinda in grave danger. It was all too much.

"Sybil Brantham," the guard called.

Her heartbeat staggered to a stop.

What now?

The key clanked in the cage. "Another visitor." The barrel-chested guard churlishly waved her out, clearly vexed at the interruption to his day.

Jacinda?

The thought was met with a dizzying rush of hope and fear. Mayhap she had arrived to confess to the spell that marked Sybil's arm, to ask how it might be undone.

If the enchantment could be broken, mayhap Jacinda could

be spared the loss of her gifts for committing such an egregious enchantment.

But when Sybil was led to the small square room, her visitor was not Jacinda, but a man in dark robes.

The magistrate.

Her breath caught and she stepped back so quickly, she nearly tripped on her shackles.

The door closed and locked, the guard on the other side.

Leaving her alone with him.

Again.

Fear rattled loose in her chest.

She was not strong enough for this.

But then, the man turned, and surprise snatched the air from her lungs.

John Griffin. The man who had ensnared her heart with tender words and pretty promises he could not make good on.

And oh, how she had loved him. That young, unfettered girl she'd been, dreaming of traveling the world at his side, of having a bevy of children and lying awake every night to talk about everything and nothing.

She had made her love weep when last they'd met. When he vowed to defy his father's demands to abandon her, choosing love over legacy.

But Sybil would not have allowed him to exact such a cost on her behalf any more than she could stomach his father seeing her as filth.

And now…

Her hands fluttered over her face, across the stretch of skin over gaunt cheeks, the patches of dark hair and clumps of scabs upon her scalp. Though Margery's shawl embraced her shoulders, her thin shift cast her form in shadow, revealing her skeletal body.

If she had thought herself vulnerable and exposed at Mrs.

Williams's hands, that degradation was nothing compared to this unexpected moment of standing before John.

She hadn't a care for Mrs. Williams or her opinions.

But John…

He knew the feel of her supple body in his arms. He knew the silky texture of her hair gliding through his fingers. His lips had moved over her skin as he whispered poetry that made her feel beautiful.

Standing before him now, his father's words ravaged her mind.

She was filth. Scarcely a woman. Barely even human.

Worthless.

In that moment, she was drowning in a deluge of shame.

"Sybil." John whispered her name, soft, tender.

The way he had done so many times in their youth, and she hated the tears welling in her eyes, the painful yearning for that carefree life, for the simplicity of those girlhood days.

She shook her head, unable to bear his presence.

She had never thought to see John again, had never anticipated he might look at her with such soul-reaching depth. And she had never expected to be as she was, so broken and withered.

Why had Kat not simply passed on Sybil's message?

Instinctively Sybil shrank back, curling her shoulders forward, wishing she could bury herself in the indignity and humiliation. "You should not have come."

CHAPTER FORTY-NINE

Lilith

Lilith stared at her phone in horror, reading Essie's message again.

Who is this?

Had she already been erased from Essie's memory? A lifetime of friendship dissolving the way Lilith's pictures had on her phone?

It's Lilith.

Three dots appeared.

Lilith held her breath, tethered to the gray bubble of a forming message. Almost too afraid to see Essie's reply.

Finally, it came.

OMG, where have you been? My phone deleted your number, and I haven't been able to contact you.

Another message immediately followed.

What is happening? Why are you scared?

A series of texts immediately followed, rapid-fire.

Is it Mr. Darcy?

You send me his picture. I'll have it to Interpol before you can say cretin.

Talk to me. Tell me what is going on this instant.

Answer me right now because you're totally freaking me out.

Lilith choked on a shuddering breath at the normalcy of Essie's reply. Still the same Essie.

The same Essie who had not forgotten Lilith.

It's not Mr. Darcy—it's not a person, but a... Lilith hesitated then continued typing. How much time do you have?

She imagined Essie's busy life. Play dates, meetings and dinner parties with the partners of her firm, keeping the household running while Eugene worked late hours at the police central precinct on Bull Street.

What time was it in Georgia anyway?

Before Lilith could google it, Essie had already replied.

I always have time for you.

And she did.

Lilith's fingers tapped over the screen. This is going to sound absolutely insane.

With my life, insane is my specialty.
Hit me with what you've got.

Lilith's smile was a flash on her lips before fading as she did exactly as Essie asked and hit her with *everything*—the manor, the ghostly figures repeating that one day in history over and over, the grimoire, the spells, the way she was fading from reality.

Check your photos. Lilith texted at the end. The ones with me are disappearing.

There was a long pause and Essie replied back.

WTF? Lil...

Lilith choked back a sob. I know.

Three dots appeared and disappeared, then appeared and disappeared. The phone buzzed in Lilith's hand and the screen lit up with a picture of Essie and Amara, faces pressed cheek to cheek as they grinned at the camera. A picture from a normal day getting Byrd's cookies at City Market.

Lilith slid her thumb over the screen to answer the call.

"Essie?"

"You still sound the same, thank God. How the hell did you get wrapped up in this?"

Lilith gave a shaky sigh. "It's the birthmark, this whole linking spell."

"This is otherworldly insane, Lil."

"Literally." Lilith laughed as tears burned in her eyes.

"Look, you are still alive. You are still existing. And that means you can do whatever necessary to save Sybil."

"But what if I can't?" Lilith whispered, putting a voice to the fear tearing at her insides.

"You've always been a fighter," Essie replied in a firm tone. "Like the time when we were kids and that boy with his stupid bowl haircut…"

"The one that shoved you," Lilith finished for her, knowing this story like the back of her hand.

"Yes! That punk shoved me on the ground. You shoved him right back, and then you said…you…you said…" Her voice faltered.

An icy wash of dread poured over Lilith.

"Oh God," Essie said breathlessly. "I can't remember now…"

Lilith pressed the phone to her face, her throat too tight to speak.

"Lilith." This was Essie's mom voice. The one she used when Amara tried to run out in the street. The one she used when she turned around once and didn't see Amara at her side at City Market. The one she used when love scared her so deeply, it brought out a rage of fear.

"Lilith, don't you dare let me forget you, do you hear?" There was a catch to Essie's voice. "You have been the constant in my life, the one who was there for the new kid on the block living with her nana because her parents had just been killed. You've been there ever since. When I was in sixth grade and swore I'd marry Gill, and he broke up with me the next day. When I got my period before you and thought I was dying. When I graduated from college and was so happy I drank a handle of vodka to celebrate and puked my guts out. You held one of my legs when Amara was born because that epidural made me forget the lower half of my body, and Eugene was chasing down some drunk guy through Chippewa Square."

She pulled in a hard breath. "I can't tell a story in my life without you being in it. You are stitched into the very fabric of my existence. I *can't* lose you." Her voice broke. "I love you, Lil."

Lilith's face stretched with the force of her pain, hot tears running silently down her face. "I love you too, Ess."

Lilith didn't know when she fell asleep, but the chime of her alarm went off way too early at 4:00 a.m. Early enough to return to the manor before the household from the seventeenth century could wake.

She looked at the world clock on her phone, confirming it was 11:00 p.m. in Savannah. Essie would still be awake, likely waiting for Eugene to get off work, so she could keep him company while he ate his warmed-up dinner.

Lilith's phone was practically a new device, all the text messages gone, hardly any photos remaining. But she'd had Essie's number memorized for well over a decade and tapped out a quick message.

Thanks for talking to me last night.

Dots danced to the left of the screen as Essie replied right away.

But when the message came through, a frisson of fear tightened through Lilith.

Who is this?

Lilith tightened her grip on her phone and replied: Lilith. Did my number delete itself again?

Her phone buzzed with a reply, and Lilith's heart slithered down to her toes.

Sorry, hon. Wrong number.

A chasm ripped open in her chest. But there was no time for tears. No time for grief. She had a job to do.

Grabbing a pair of jeans and a fresh shirt, Lilith dressed hastily and stopped in the kitchen to grab a bottle of cinnamon for amplification, some more bay leaves, and a few cans of cat food.

She would fight for Sybil's life, for her own existence, and for all the women who came before her.

And she would fight for Essie.

There would be no leaving the manor until she had answers.

CHAPTER FIFTY

Lilith

The scullery maid was the first to wake, yawning as she slowly plaited her wheat-blond hair.

Lilith bristled with impatience.

One day.

She had one day to discover who had betrayed Sybil.

The scullery maid's tasks were mundane, stacking wood in the hearth to light. Filling a cauldron with water and hooking it to the crane to hang over the flames, all while still rubbing the sleep from her eyes.

Lilith listened in the Great Hall for the telltale groan of the floorboards above to announce someone else had roused.

Silence.

Dragon nudged Lilith's calf, and she bent to stroke him. "I need your help today, bud."

He squinted up at her, and she rubbed the underside of his chin, earning her a grateful purr.

A creak came from above.

Someone else was awake.

A final glance back in the kitchen confirmed the scullery maid was still setting about her mundane chores. Lilith took off, booking it up the stairs.

On the top floor, three maids moved around rooms, and two male servants did likewise down the hall.

The buxom maid named Bess was clearly in charge, ordering the women about as they made their beds and dressed, lacing one another's gowns and pinning their caps into place. Bess didn't flinch as she entered the men's room despite their state of partial undress, ordering that the corners on beds be tucked tighter.

Within minutes, the five descended the stairs and dispersed in opposite directions.

This was what Lilith feared the most. She was one person, tasked to monitor a household with almost a dozen servants in the manor and another in the barn.

She looked to Dragon, deferring to his sage wisdom, but his head moved back and forth at each departing person, just as confused.

Lilith withdrew a stone from her pocket, one she'd initially mistaken for quartz. Upon closer inspection, she had noticed splotches of yellow, like tea stains embedded in the stone. Citrine.

Or yellow quartz as it had been known in the seventeenth century. Notable for its ability to bring good fortune and prosperity, increasing the likelihood of success.

The pink necklace pouch was still in contact with her body, stuffed in her bra to keep the contents against her skin.

Lacking any other receptacle for the new enchantment, she cupped the stone in her palm and added a sprinkling of bay leaves for success. She reached into her pocket and took out a pinch of cinnamon.

She sprinkled the cinnamon powder into her palm and the

concoction pulsed to life with warmth. The whisper of the earth was too quiet. She stepped out of her shoes, letting her bare feet touch the floorboards. It wasn't the same as having the naked earth against her soles, but the telltale vibration still echoed through her regardless.

Show me what I need to see.

She folded her hand around the mix of herbs, crushing them to the stone. Her brows pursed with concentration.

Show me what I need to see.

The world around her sharpened.

Show me what I need to see.

Footsteps were discernible, not only where she stood, but on all the floors of the manor. The damp air stirred with movement. The savory scent of the roasting meat that would be dinner mingled with the yeasty aroma of bread being kneaded, along with the herbal notes of the rushes on the first floor.

The house came alive in a concert of activity, and she was in tune with every note. Every pitch.

The padding of four delicate paws drew her eyes open.

A birdlike chittering sent Dragon racing off to Jacinda's room. Lilith followed, finding the girl standing by the window in a long white nightgown.

"I received the letter you wrote for me in the grimoire," Lilith confessed.

Jacinda turned, mouth parting in surprise. "The letter?"

Lilith touched the birthmark on her arm. Jacinda had not written the letter yet—at least not in any way that obeyed time. Something in Lilith told her to be vague in her reply. "It was a warning…an apology."

Jacinda watched her with unease, as if something Lilith said pressed against a truth that had not yet formed.

"We need to find who denounced Sybil, like you said." Lilith took a slow steadying breath. "I'm running out of time and so is Sybil."

Jacinda pulled a cloak on over her nightdress. "I'll help."

Lilith and Jacinda separated with Lilith starting on the first floor.

Three maids were in the kitchen, the scullery maid cutting a piece of knobby root—ginger by its sharp scent. Bess stood by the young maid named Anne, whose face was almost as pale as the white cap covering her dark hair.

"Mayhap something I ate..." Anne moaned.

Bess's mouth tucked back at the corners. "Go on and have a lie down if you must."

"I'll be fine." Anne's slender hand rested on her stomach. "I'm feeling better already."

The scullery maid shoved the bit of ginger at Anne, who eagerly put it in her mouth to suck.

Bess narrowed her eyes, hands fisting on her hips. "Is there something I ought to know, Anne?"

The maid widened her brown eyes and shook her head vigorously, setting her mob cap flopping almost comically against her narrow face. "Just something I ate."

Bess nodded, her action slow and measured with skepticism. "Off with you now."

Anne nodded, color showing in her pale cheeks as she rushed off so fast, she nearly ran through Lilith.

Lilith darted back in time to avoid the unwanted collision.

A place inside Lilith's gut twinged, drawing her attention to how Anne gently held her lower stomach, as if cradling something precious. Exactly the way Essie had done when she was pregnant with Amara.

Likely Anne would be someone to follow. No sooner had

the thought nagged at Lilith than the scullery maid gave a sly look toward Bess, who was busy watching Anne depart.

That sly look caught at Lilith's conscience, pulling her back. Surely such an expression was not unwarranted.

Bess bustled from the room in that officious way of hers, leaving Lilith alone with the scullery maid.

A shadow passed by the window as a figure strode swiftly by.

The scullery maid snuck over to a door with a key jutting from its lock. She clicked the handle, shoulders flinching at the sound before the larder creaked open. With one last glance over her shoulder, she slipped inside, taking a lit candle with her.

Lilith followed her into the small space, hating how voyeuristic it felt to be watching someone who didn't know of her existence. Especially when the hunch to the scullery maid's shoulders seemed like a reflexive instinct from that primitive part of the brain that lets someone know they're being observed.

The maid shifted a jar and drew something toward her. Lilith leaned around the woman to see what it was.

Another jar, one that revealed glossy orange spheres in a syrupy liquid when the lid was removed. The fragrant perfume of peaches filled the air.

The scullery filched one out, pinching the slippery fruit between her thumb and forefinger before letting it drop in her open maw. Her eyes closed in pleasure as she chewed, savoring that simple extravagance in a way that made Lilith wonder if she'd ever eaten something she'd enjoyed with as much pleasure.

The door opened and Sybil entered, her form clearer than Lilith had ever seen her. No longer a ghost from the past, but a real person—living, breathing. Someone in need of saving.

Sybil's dark hair was lustrous where it hung down her back

in a thick braid. Golden light from the rising sun spilled into the room and caught at the gleaming strands.

"Good morrow, Elspeth." Sybil's voice was lightly husky, adding to her commanding presence in a way that felt both authoritative yet welcoming.

Elspeth gulped down the fruit, a line of juice trailing from the corner of her mouth.

"I came down for some ginger and saw the door was open." Sybil smiled, her eyes compassionate, avoiding the open jar of preserved peaches. "I didn't mean to intrude."

Elspeth shook her head. "Not at all, ma'am. There's some ginger on the block I can get ye. Are ye feeling poorly?"

"No, it's for a basket I'm making for someone."

Elspeth looked at her feet. "I was stealing a peach, mum."

"I know," Sybil said kindly. "I won't tell Bess." Then she closed the door softly, and the sound of her footsteps clicked away.

The young woman was honest.

Too honest.

Lilith knew with utmost certainty that Elspeth was not who she sought. And from Sybil's reaction to seeing the scullery maid stealing what was likely valuable food back then, it was likely Sybil didn't make many enemies in their home.

Who would denounce her as a witch?

Lilith slipped back into the kitchen, heavy with regret. She had followed the wrong thread.

Dragon raced around the corner and dashed a quick loop around Lilith's bare feet, then darted off once more. Clearly wanting her to follow him outside.

Lilith exited the house through a smaller, plainer door meant for the servants and drew back with an audible gasp.

Anne, the sick maid, stood outside, in the shadows of a stack of firewood. She spoke animatedly to a figure in dark clothing.

Lilith went still, frozen where she stood.

She knew that man.

The one from her dreams. The one who would arrest Sybil within hours.

The magistrate.

CHAPTER FIFTY-ONE

Lilith

Lilith forced herself to step closer to the shadows, where Anne spoke to the magistrate. Apprehension hummed like electricity in the air.

"Bess knows," Anne said to him, her hand once more caressing her lower stomach. "I've tried to be so careful."

"Mrs. Brantham will not employ you much longer." There was a coldness to the magistrate's tone.

Anne's cheeks went red. "My position here would not be in peril were it not for you."

The magistrate lifted a brow. "I don't recall your complaints at the time when you tried to trap me into marriage with this by-blow."

Anne looked down at the ground, clearly shamed by his words.

Revulsion tightened Lilith's jaw.

Oblivious of her presence, the magistrate lifted Anne's chin, forcing her to look back up at him. "I'll help you, of course. But, Anne, you know what you must do."

She shook her head, large brown eyes welling with tears. "Please don't ask this of me. There has to be another way."

The magistrate's eyes hardened. "There is no other way. Not for you."

Lilith scoffed in disgust.

"But my family depends on me," Anne whimpered. "And Sybil has been so kind."

"Enough of your sniveling." The magistrate's lip curled. "Will you do it or not?"

Anne's face crumpled as she reached into her pocket and withdrew a small cloth poppet, tied with red twine. The very one that would soon be used to condemn Sybil. She shoved the offending object toward him, her eyes averted, as if to lessen her culpability.

The magistrate snatched the poppet from her. "You've done this with quite a bit of skill. Are you certain you aren't a witch?"

Anne's gaze flew to the magistrate's in horror.

He smirked. "Don't worry, Anne. I won't turn you in, you little fool." He opened his coat and withdrew a folded page from a pocket. "You will agree you had this confession scribed for you?"

"You'll give me money to support the babe and my family when I am released from Brackenmere Manor?" she shot back with a spine Lilith wished she would show more of. Especially with the likes of the magistrate.

"Yes, yes," he muttered irritably.

Anne's fingers linked over her belly, her brows thrust together as she gave a reluctant nod. "I will."

"You ought to read it." He thrust the papers toward her. "In case you're pressed to go into further detail."

Her cheeks scorched with color. "I can't."

"Of course you can't." He rolled his eyes and returned the pages to his pocket. "It doesn't matter. Agree to anything on the stand. If you flounder, they will assume it is due to your ignorance."

Anne's fierce blush darkened.

Lilith wanted to scream at Anne to refuse, to burn the poppet and run. But she knew she was only an observer to what transpired hundreds of years before. She was here to witness history, not alter it.

At least, not in this moment.

"And don't get it into your head that the child will bear my name. My surname is one of pride and elevated social bearing. A bastard will never be graced with the Walsingham name."

The air seized in Lilith's lungs. That name hit like a blow.

Walsingham.

Wasn't that...?

She pulled up her phone and went back to her contacts. Yes, there it was: Asher Walsingham.

The magistrate was related to Asher.

Her stomach dropped.

Was this why Asher had been so cagey? Why he'd been loathe to let her come to the manor?

Had he known and intentionally kept the truth from her?

The magistrate strode away, leaving Anne alone. She put her hands over her face and sobbed, this poor woman who had been forced to become a traitor.

Lilith had her answer, the culprit who had spoken against Sybil. And she had the reason why. Now she just needed to find Jacinda.

Lilith dashed inside, leaving Anne weeping piteously in the shadows. The scullery maid was the only occupant on the first floor, now hard at work making what appeared to be a pie.

Upstairs, Bess moved through the bedchambers with an

efficient energy, bustling about with dirty linens trailing behind her. Jacinda was not in her room. Nor was she in the library.

In fact, a sweep over the entire household proved Jacinda was nowhere to be found.

There was one last place to look.

Lilith went to the library and opened the secret room. Heart racing, she slipped inside.

The candles flickered to life, revealing the small space.

But no Jacinda.

The grimoire waited in the silence, like a held breath.

Lilith approached the ancient book. "What else do you have for me?" she muttered.

After all, she had the solution she'd been tasked with finding.

Now, how to relay the message to the past?

Lilith flipped through the grimoire, but the pages were all the same as they had been previously, not revealing anything new.

Not until…

A page slipped off the back of another as if what had been stuck together released to reveal a new entry in yet a different style of handwriting.

Another woman's story. Another secret revealed.

CHAPTER FIFTY-TWO

Sybil

Sybil stared at John Griffin, wishing he had not come. Regretting most miserably that he should see her in such a broken state.

Those familiar gray-green eyes she had never forgotten now searched hers in a way that made the tight fist of her heart unfurl. "I have been waiting seventeen years for a word from you," he said softly.

She blinked.

He had been waiting for her?

All those difficult moments in her life when she had longed for him to be at her side. That painful year after he left. Her mother's death, having to scrape together skill enough to sell tinctures and simples to keep herself and Jacinda fed.

Even her marriage to Henry and their vow to one another, to respect and care for the other, knowing love to be impossible. And after Henry's death, the pain of his absence, the guilt of her role in his demise.

"Sybil, I love you." John stepped closer.

But she pulled away, overly aware of the sharp odor of her person. "I'm…I'm not the same woman anymore."

"But you are," he protested. "Strong. Caring. Opinionated. Beautiful."

A sob choked out of her, unbidden.

He approached again, slowly, cautiously, and lifted his hands to her face. "The same full lips I dream of at night and those golden hazel eyes that see me in a light no other has since."

"My hair—" Her voice caught.

"Will grow back, as lovely as it ever was." There were new lines next to his eyes, a sunburst of crinkles she had not known. Carved from laughter she had not heard and smiles she had not witnessed. Those lines transformed him from the boy of her memories to the man he was now.

So much had changed since that boy and girl who fell in love.

And yet, as he stroked his fingertips over her jaw, as her body responded with a hitch of her breath and a quickening of her pulse, she realized some things had stayed exactly the same.

She thought of Edith then, so convinced that she was ugly. How to those who loved her, she was beautiful.

Her loss struck Sybil anew in a blaze of agony.

Hot tears trailed down her cheeks before she could stop them.

John opened his arms, and she fell into them. The rasp of his wool robe scratched at her cheek, and she breathed him in. He still smelled the same, fresh like a rainstorm with the underlying spice that was so unique to him. And when he put his arms around her, she still fit perfectly against him.

He whispered her name as he held her, his voice warm with quiet affection. Slowly, his words melted into her heart, bolstered her spirit. Until a semblance of her humanity finally returned.

When at last her sobbing ran its course, she straightened and apologized for having wept so unabashedly on his robe. The dark stain of her tears showed against the wool.

"I worried I would take too long to arrive," John said. "I was in Ipswich when I received word from Kat. Then I was waylaid by storms, and my horse threw a shoe. I thank God I am not too late. Surely there is something I might do."

He had not let go of her hand, and she did not pull away. "You cannot beg for my release. It is far too dangerous. But you can speak out against the atrocities that are being committed. They are starving us, walking us between chairs for days at a time, having women bared and shorn—"

The words clogged in her throat. She could not give voice to such memories. Doing so made them too real when she would rather they fade into the fog of her mind.

"They pricked me with a trick bodkin with a hollow handle and claimed I did not bleed, stating it was proof enough." Sybil took his hand, reveling in the warmth and strength of his long fingers. "John, I am condemned."

He shook his head fiercely. "No, there has to be a way—"

"There is not."

"I'll preach against what is happening with my parish and to anyone else who will listen," he vowed. "But you, Sybil, there must be a way to set you free?"

She was about to shake her head when a thought came to her. The valerian extract.

Sybil sniffed away the vestiges of her tears. "Mayhap, but it would be through escape." She lowered her voice and glanced toward the door, as if expecting the guard to walk through at any moment.

"I told him you wished counsel from a vicar," John admitted sheepishly. "I think they hope it means you will confess."

"I will never confess," Sybil said vehemently.

"See there?" John grinned. "You are still my same Sybil. Resilient and with an iron will."

My same Sybil.

How she cherished those words, and the way he saw strength in her that she had not felt in far too long.

Mayhap his seeing strength in her might bring it into existence once more.

"Come again tomorrow," Sybil said. "See if you can find some clothing like the guards wear. Meet with a young woman named Margery and give her the clothing to secret into the prison. And bring ale for the guards." If the guards drank enough, they would not taste the bitterness of the valerian root. "A lot of ale."

"I shall return on the morrow." John studied her, his gaze like a caress. "I will speak to people of what they have done here," he said quietly. "Of how they persecute the innocent. Of the unfairness and the brutality of Edith's death."

Sybil looked quickly away, unable to yield to her sorrow once more lest the loss consume her. Now was not for mourning.

Now was for fighting back.

For doing what she could to keep anyone else from dying.

John turned to go, but she caught his arm. "There is something I must tell you." Her heart fluttered erratically and suddenly she was breathless, lightheaded. "In case…"

In case the attempt to escape went awry and she never had the opportunity to speak to him again.

"What do you know of my life?" she asked. "Of me and my household?"

He tilted his head in that inquisitive way of his that conveyed she held the entirety of his attention.

"Jacinda," she said.

It was so difficult to breathe. Her heartbeat thundered in her ears. Her thoughts racing.

He nodded. "Your sister."

"Not my sister." Sybil pulled in a deep inhale and clung to John's hand. "My daughter." She stared deep into his eyes, knowing her next words would forever change how they saw the world. "Our daughter."

CHAPTER FIFTY-THREE

Lilith

Lilith stared down at the new pages the grimoire had revealed to her, a confession not meant for her, but one she could not stop reading regardless.

I, Sybil Brantham, have a confession to make in these final pages of the grimoire. A confession to Jacinda.

I am to be arrested. The earth has whispered signs to me that this will come to pass and this may be my only chance to offer my admission.

I must tell you about a man named John Griffin, a landowner's son whose future had already been laid out for him until he fell in love with me.

What we write for our hearts is not always read kindly by the world. His father wanted more for his son than the daughter of a local healer. He wanted a good name, reputation. A dowry.

I had none.

When our relationship was no more, I vowed none would ever think less of me. I rode high on my convictions, until reality struck.

Until the day the child quickened in my womb, and I realized I had not bled for several moon cycles. My heartache had been great, too distracting to notice the changes in my body.

I created a tincture that would bring my courses once more, but the idea sat bitter upon my soul.

Because it was not just a babe growing within my womb, but love. This child was a piece of the man who I loved, a child created through an act of selfless affection and admiration.

Such beauty could not be allowed to end. Instead, I let our love grow within me, knowing the result would be a soul I could cradle in my arms and cherish for all eternity.

However, when the babe was born, my mother feared persecution for myself. I begged her to allow me to keep the babe, but she said her reputation was already sealed and mine was still open. There was so much more of my life to live.

And there was.

I met Henry when he took a fascination in my mother's herbal remedies, citing her cures as fascinating and ingenious rather than provincial. He did not know of her death until sometime later. When he found out, he immediately offered marriage to care for me, to educate me. Not only me, but also the child who had been raised as my sister.

The Book of the City of Ladies *by Christine de Pizan was one of his favorite books. In it, women were educated as men, resulting in brilliant minds and creations that might never have been otherwise. The text is now one of my favorites as well.*

But the girl he knew as my sister was actually my daughter. Jacinda, you are of my blood and my heart.

I ought to have told you before this moment, but the time was never correct, and as you grew older, so too did your resentment toward me, simmering under the surface. I was afraid that rage would make me lose you.

Someday you will read this, and I hope you will understand.

But what I want you to know without question is the depth of my love for you, the way our hearts cleaved together when you were in my womb and how we are still connected.

I love you, my beautiful daughter. I wish I could teach you all you need to know. Mayhap I am wrong and this letter is for naught.

You will find the learning you need in these pages. I was hesitant to come into my gifts, just as I have been hesitant to impart such wisdom upon you with yours. Fortunately for both of us, my mother was prepared.

She always knew what to do.

What I will close with is the reminder she always whispered to me:

No matter what happens, seek solace in the honeysuckle grove.

CHAPTER FIFTY-FOUR

Sybil

Sybil's trust in John was not unfounded. He arrived the following day, as he said he would, with several jugs of ale for the two guards on duty, the awful one with the scarred eyebrow and the youngest one. As planned, John met with Margery under the auspices of hearing her confession. In this meeting, he secreted a guard's uniform to her, apologizing that there was only one. This she hid under her skirts.

Sybil buried the clothes in a dry patch of rushes. "One of us can dress as a guard and lead the way for those being smuggled out."

Margery nodded, but the wariness in her expression indicated skepticism. She had been unconvinced from the start. Uncertain that the little girl could be fast enough to slip the valerian root into the ale. Uncertain that, upon their departure, their small group would not be chased down like dogs.

Then there was the question of who might join them.

If every prisoner escaped, the attempt would be that much harder. They would be too easily seen. But how could they leave everyone else behind?

And yet how could they risk being caught?

These questions twisted back and forth, tangling around one another.

In truth, Sybil had her own doubts. But there was too much at stake not to try. Once she was free, she would take Jacinda and flee from this town. They would be safe.

For the first time since she had been arrested, there was a semblance of hope.

"He said to tell you he is grateful for what you said to him," Margery whispered to Sybil after her meeting with John Griffin.

It was obvious Margery did not understand the message she conveyed, but to Sybil, those words were a balm to the ragged parts of her soul.

Were their places reversed, and he had kept the knowledge of their child from her, she did not know that she could be so forgiving.

But then, she had been the one to know what he missed, witnessing Jacinda grow from a babe to a beautiful little girl with curling red-gold ringlets. How her inquisitive nature evolved into defiance and a strength Sybil found equal parts inspiring and infuriating.

Hours later, the guards wasted no time imbibing the gift bestowed upon them. Mugs frothed with foaming ale, and the sweet scent hovered in the air, making every prisoner's mouth water with longing.

By evening, the guards were staggering around the room, jabbing their cudgels into the cages and jeering at the prisoners. The one with the scarred eyebrow approached Sybil and wavered outside the bars, glaring at her.

"You do not have to be so cruel," Sybil said boldly, knowing she would stoke his ire.

From behind her back, she waved a hand, the sign for the little girl to slip between the bars with her vial of valerian root.

"Oh, but I do." He sneered, his face ruddy with drink. "You *witch*."

"I am no witch." Sybil lifted her head. "I am a woman. One who has never done harm to anyone." From the corner of her eye, she caught the little girl's slight figure slip between the bars.

A quick glance confirmed the other guard was busy harassing the male prisoners, his back to the table where the two mugs of ale sat beside the jug.

Sybil could not have planned their distraction more perfectly. The guard's vicious natures would be their own downfall.

A scoff drew Sybil's full attention back to the guard. "We'll see tomorrow."

Her body quivered in response despite her resolve. "What do you mean?"

What more could they possibly to do her?

"You are going to trial tomorrow."

Sybil shook her head, scarcely feeling her own body. "Without the assizes?"

Bury St. Edmunds was too small to have their own court system—like many towns—and relied on the traveling court to oversee trials. With war ravaging the country, the men of the assizes were not traveling.

How could there be court with no men to act as judge and jury?

The guard simply lifted his shoulders in an uncaring shrug. "They'll deal with the likes of you tomorrow. You and the pretty one." He nodded to Margery, who stiffened at her side.

Behind him, the little girl hid under the cover of the table and poured half the vial into each mug with trembling hands. Just as she was returning, the guard began to turn back around.

"All of us?" Sybil asked quickly.

His brow furrowed. "Of course not all of you. No one has the time to see to the lot of you in one day." He rolled his eyes, thoroughly convinced she was a fool.

When he turned round once more, the little girl was back in the cage.

He lifted the mug of ale, and drank so deeply, his entire body leaned back. When he lowered the mug, there was a scowl of disgust on his face.

Valerian root *did* have a strong taste, even when rivaling good ale.

Fortunately, the guard didn't seem to mind overmuch and went to drink again when the younger guard knocked into him, sending his ale to the ground. Sybil's stomach fell along with the mug as it shattered to a hundred pieces amid the frothy splash.

"Oy, you wasted my ale," the guard growled.

The other guard was practically a boy and already staggered with drink. He lifted his own off the table and handed it to the scarred jailer. "Take mine."

Without a word of thanks, the scarred man swept the ale to his lips and drank thoroughly.

Within minutes, he slumped into the chair, his head resting heavily upon his fist.

Eventually, the younger sank into the other chair, his own head nodding.

While he had not had any of the valerian root, apparently, he'd had more than enough ale to see himself to a drunken slumber.

Sybil held up her hand for the little girl to wait, to ensure they were both truly asleep. The elder of the two would not wake until dawn, not with the dose he'd received.

Finally, she nodded, and the little girl was through the bars, attired in the guard's clothes as she crept toward the two jailers.

Every person in the cages tensed.

"Get the keys," someone whispered.

Before she could even try to reach for the guard's belt, another prisoner cried out, "Free us."

The younger guard sat upright and glared over his shoulder at the old woman who was still keening. "Enough out of you," he slurred. "Or I'll give you cause to cry."

The little girl ducked under the table, and by the time the younger guard turned and lowered his head to the cradle of his arms, she was out of sight.

Sybil waved her back. After a second's hesitation, the child crawled out from under the table and slipped back through the bars into the cell.

"You can't do this," Sybil said in a voice loud enough for all to hear. "The risk is too great. I cannot put you in danger."

The prisoners were too desperate. Too eager for escape themselves.

The girl shook her head, her small brow pursed with a resolve no child should ever be burdened with.

"My trial is tomorrow," Sybil said. "Margery's too, along with several others. Our absence will be noticed."

The girl looked between them and her eyes widened with horror.

"You have the guard's clothing," Sybil lowered her voice, whispering so none could hear but the child. "Wait until everyone falls asleep and slip through the bars like you do. The vicar John Griffin will be at one of the local parishes. Do you think you can find him?"

Despite the girl's wary expression, she nodded.

"Go to him," Sybil said quietly. "He will protect you."

The girl's face crumpled, her large, dark eyes filling with tears.

"Come now, be a brave girl." Sybil opened her arms, and the girl fell into them, her small body trembling with the force of her embrace. "Let us pretend to sleep and wait for the others to quiet."

They lay in the rushes, the little girl curled into Sybil's side as she'd once done with Edith.

Around them, the murmur of excitement gave way to exhaustion. For empty bellies and raging thoughts made for terrible fatigue and they all found themselves sleeping more and more as the days dragged on.

Finally, all was silent.

Sybil lightly squeezed the girl's shoulder. Her eyes were already open, staring at Sybil. She sniffed, the sound wet with tears.

But she nodded and rose quietly.

Silent as a mouse, she slipped through the bars. She shrank down as she passed the guards, as if she could make herself small as a mouse as well.

The younger guard stirred, and she froze.

Sybil's heart lurched from where she watched.

After a long pause, the girl stealthily stepped forward to the barred entry leading to the open bay. One set of doors from there and she would be free.

As if sensing the girl's nearness, the younger guard snapped awake, just as the girl was about to leave the room of cages.

He stared at her, incredulous.

Sybil's heart throbbed a frantic beat, and she slid her leg through the bars, to see if she could glide through as well, only to be stopped by her hip bones.

All she could do was continue to watch, helpless.

The little girl shook her head, eyes wide and fearful. And then, a single word escaped her lips. "Please." She put her hands over her chest, and she gazed up at him with a hope so visceral, even Sybil felt its charge. "Please."

The young guard's shoulders softened. Then he turned away from the girl and lowered his head to the cradle of his arms.

Sybil almost gasped with relief.

The girl looked back at Sybil one last time. Then the child who had been such an incandescent spark of hope was gone, fading into freedom.

Sybil hoped that little girl spread her wings and soared into the world she was meant to have. That she could cherish life for them all.

For Sybil knew the outcome of her trial before it began.

Death would come for her soon.

CHAPTER FIFTY-FIVE

Sybil

The prison was silent the following morning, heavy with threat of the impending trial.

In the place of the traveling assizes, oyer and terminer had been granted—a court approved to hear special criminal cases with a group of men gathered with the intention of condemning the witches to death.

With so many imprisoned, only two dozen could be seen in the one day. Sybil was among them, as the guard had claimed. As was Margery.

The courthouse had been stuffy, overcrowded, filled with the men and women she'd cared for in past years. Women whose children she had assisted in delivering when a midwife was not available, men whose farming injuries she helped heal, parents to children she saw through the pestilence and the starvation that followed.

These townsfolk who had once been grateful for Sybil's aid

now watched her trial, eyes gleaming with bloodlust as the accusations were hurtled at her feet: curdling the neighbor's milk, spreading sickness and war, and killing Henry. This abomination had been signed by a member of her staff. As yet still unnamed.

Sybil stood in the box of the accused, damned by their judgment, as she was charged first with witchcraft—a crime punishable by hanging—and was found guilty.

The blow had left her staggering under the weight of the conviction.

Then came the charge of having used witchcraft to kill Henry, drawing the plague seeds to him, resulting in suffering and death, leaving her a wealthy widow. The punishment for this crime of petty treason was being burned alive.

She was found guilty.

Her world swam around her, fading in and out in the moist heat of the courtroom, the air rank with judgment and stained bloodred with malice. With hate.

She would die in the most horrible fashion, lashed to a stake amid a pyre and set alight like a bit of kindling. And like kindling, she would peel and split in the flames.

The horror of her future curled around her shoulders. Her death would be slow. Awful. Witnessed by those she had so freely given her time, her coin, and her love.

A metallic taste rose in the back of her throat, polluting each word, each swallow, with the tinny taste of fear.

Her lashes fluttered and the world dimmed. There was not enough strength in her to think of such horrors.

Thoughts of Dido from *Heroides* filled her mind. How the independent widow had given herself to a lover who had cruelly betrayed her. Sybil's love had been the townspeople, and they too betrayed her.

Through the course of that mockery of a trial, judgment was

meted out with an unfair hand. The punishment would be exacted with haste. The lot of them would die the following day.

The remaining six score prisoners would be tried within a sennight.

Sybil and the others condemned to die were broken off from the rest, stuffed into a smaller cell, mixing the seventeen women with the two men. This was a kindness to the Everard couple who had been separated into cages opposite one another these last several difficult weeks. They fell into one another's arms and held tight. The rest of the prisoners turned their gazes away, as much for privacy as for the inability to bear the envy of such comfort in those final hours.

For the rest were a miserable lot indeed.

Destined for death, devoid of all hope. Alone.

Some wailed their misery, some begged the guards to let them out, bargaining with all their world possessions. Some, like Margery, wept for what they would lose in death, for her inability to ever see her beloved husband again.

Mary Bacon's husband had continued to fight for her release and had been arrested that day, now contained in the men's cell. So close and still so far. She wept with pity for him and hope that their son might make his way to the New World, to be free of such unfair persecution.

The old vicar bore the weight of everyone's pain on his frail shoulders. He prayed until he was hoarse, and then he kept on until his voice was thready and breaking.

And some, like Sybil, sat in quiet regret.

Regret that she had not told Jacinda the truth when she was younger, that she missed so many moments of her life, observed as a sister rather than relished as a mother.

Regret that she would not walk upon the cool moonlit grass once more, that the powerful energy of the earth would remain forever silent, muted by heavy iron shackles.

Regret that she would never again feel the sun's glory warm upon her face, its radiance reflected in her soul.

Sybil had read once that the last moments of life were brilliant and vivid and meant to be savored.

Except in the prison, they were surrounded by starvation and the promise of death.

Sybil remained awake through the night. Nearly all of them did, save for the few who were so exhausted, they could not stop their eyes from closing. Silver moonlight crested and she wished she could stretch high enough to reach the window, to breathe in the freshness of the night air.

Eventually, sunlight peered into the cell, spilling golden light on the righteous. The wrongfully accused.

The other prisoners had received their rations that morning, but the barrel-chested guard approached them empty-handed. "No use in feeding the dead. But if you have kin and they've come, you'll be called to see them."

Though they would die with hunger rasping in their bellies, the small mercy to see their loved ones was an expected and precious gift.

And it meant that Sybil would be allowed to speak with Jacinda one final time. To finally confess the words that had been building in her heart for the entirety of Jacinda's life:

I am your mother.

CHAPTER FIFTY-SIX

Lilith

Lilith reread the last line of the grimoire.

No matter what happens, seek solace in the honeysuckle grove.

She knew that clearing, recalling how the night before, it had been awash in moonlight, brimming with an unmistakable hum of power—otherworldly.

Was that where she needed to go?

The candles flickered and went out abruptly, before she'd even left the room.

While strange, she couldn't focus on that now. Not when she needed to get to the clearing.

She rushed from the secret room and came to an abrupt halt at the figure standing in the middle of the library.

Asher.

Asher, who had not told her early on that the magistrate had been his ancestor. No wonder he had been so cagey about the manor, so evasive with her questions.

The rush of anger was instantaneous and blistering.

His eyes widened when he saw her. "Lilith, what—?"

"You lied to me," Lilith snapped.

Asher frowned, blinking.

"Don't you dare ignore me." She stomped over to him, her feet somehow muted on the wood floors.

She stopped in front of him, and he put his hands out. "Lilith? What is the matter with you?"

"What's the matter with *me*?" she repeated. "I'm angry that *you* failed to tell me that the magistrate's last name was Walsingham, the same as yours. Your ancestor murdered Sybil Brantham."

He shook his head. "You didn't know that? But can we talk about—"

"Is this why you've been so cagey about coming here?"

He pulled his head back in surprise. "No, I didn't think it was of any consequence. Lilith, it happened nearly four hundred years ago… But why are you—"

"Then why do you act all weird about the manor?" She softened. "Asher, did you live here?"

He rubbed the back of his neck and exhaled a defeated sigh. "I did. For most of my childhood. I was the creepy kid who lived in the old haunted manor." He looked away, shamefaced.

"I went on the third floor," she confessed. "And the attic."

His gaze snapped back to her.

She held his stare. "I saw the paintings."

"I'm sorry you saw those." He rubbed a hand over his face.

"Wait—you painted those?" Lilith asked in shock.

He sighed. "I wasn't honest before about the house. I…I didn't want you to leave." He offered a helpless shrug. "I didn't want to lose you."

Lilith pulled in a quiet breath and the heat of her anger cooled into something that twisted in her chest. "Why would you lose me?"

"My father obsessed over the legacy of Brackenmere Manor. When he died, the manor became everything to me."

"You obsessed over it too?" Lilith asked in a whisper.

Asher nodded. "Aunt Jacqueline had the other house built and moved me out. But there was this draw, this need to be there. Until you."

Lilith swallowed. "Me?"

"Since you arrived, the house has let me go. I don't feel its pull and I don't have that dream anymore."

Her heartbeat quickened. "What dream?"

"The one where a woman fades into the house." He gave her an odd look. "It's why I painted the canvases. But now…looking at you…"

Lilith arched a brow. "What do you mean?"

"Why are you…?" He lifted his palms toward her in presentation. "Why are you…almost invisible?" There was a crack to his voice, a pitch of fear.

"Huh?" Lilith glanced down at herself and saw the floor through her feet, the wall through her ribs.

Terror gaped within her, a black hole she fell into.

"I'm…disappearing." The explanation came out of her mouth in a soft whimper, one of helplessness and raw understanding. "I'm ceasing to exist." Those familiar words caught in her throat.

Asher's eyes bulged. "What?" He shook his head. "How? Why? Aunt Jacqueline didn't…disappear? Did she?"

"What happened to Aunt Jacqueline?"

"She's missing." Asher shook his head. "What is even happening right now?"

Lilith's birthmark stung, the sensation sharp with urgency. "We have to find her."

A breeze swept through the room, fluttering her hair.

"I'm not missing, you silly fools." Aunt Jacqueline appeared in the doorway, nightdress belling out around her skinny frame, her hair unbound and floating around her shoulders like finely spun cotton. At her feet were three familiar animals: Lord Wimbleton the third, who sat in front of her like a squat pile of white and black fur, with Toby and Dragon on either side of her.

Aunt Jacqueline tsked at Lilith. "Look at you—you're already fading. We're running out of time."

"What is this all about?" Asher demanded. "Aunt Jacqueline, where have you been? What are you doing?"

Aunt Jacqueline stepped closer, sure-footed and confident as she lifted a metal lantern. A thick plume of gray smoke billowed from punctured holes. With a slender, aged hand, she swept the smoke toward Lilith, the scent of burning bay leaves both acrid and fragrant as the smoke washed over her.

"Be seen," the older woman intoned in a melodious voice. "Be seen. Be seen."

A sense of reassurance coiled through Lilith. Closing her eyes, she breathed in the aromatic smoke, inviting its infusion of strength.

"That's better," Aunt Jacqueline said with evident satisfaction.

Lilith opened her eyes to find Asher gaping at her. She looked down, relieved to see her body entirely visible once more. The swirling pit of despair in her stomach downgraded to a bubbling simmer.

"The effect is temporary," Aunt Jacqueline cautioned before Lilith could allow herself to embrace a sense of relief.

"I need to find Jacinda," Lilith said. "I discovered what she wanted."

Aunt Jacqueline shook her head. "You won't find her here. Not now, not after Sybil's arrest."

Lilith blinked. "How do you know that?"

"Stop," Asher said vehemently. "Will someone explain to me what is happening right now?"

Aunt Jacqueline gave Lilith a soul-suffering look before addressing her nephew. "I'll tell you on the way to the honeysuckle clearing."

CHAPTER FIFTY-SEVEN

Sybil

Sybil shifted her weight from one foot to the other, the shackles around her ankle bones clanking. Jacinda stood before her one last time, containing a lifetime of secrets. A lifetime of love.

Sybil knew what her loss would do to Jacinda. The pain of that understanding was overwhelming, ineffable. "Jacinda." She choked out the single word, barely a whisper.

The guard cast a look of caution before departing, leaving them alone.

"They told me…" Jacinda's words clotted with emotion. "They told me you are…"

Sybil pulled in a deep breath, letting the agonizing pain in her chest curl inside itself, wrapping into a fragile shell of indifference.

"That I am to die," Sybil finished, her voice wooden—dull—knowing that if she infused life into her words, they would swallow her whole. In these last few moments, she was a coward.

Too afraid to yield to the intricacies of a life where she was condemned to die.

Jacinda's expression broke in anguish as she gasped around a harsh sob.

There was much Sybil must convey. And too little time remained.

So little time.

"The house will be taken by the king," Sybil continued flatly. "The land, the wealth, all of it will be gone."

Jacinda jerked her head up, eyes flashing with the quick, incandescent rage of youth in the face of injustice. "I care not for the house, or the coin."

Sybil calcified her expression, necessary to silence Jacinda's tantrum. "You will. Henry had a solicitor in London. You will find his information in my desk. Seek him out. He will aid."

Jacinda stubbornly thinned her lips.

"There is another matter I must speak of." The admission caught in Sybil's dry throat. "I should have told you long ago." Her voice wavered, the shield crumbling.

Jacinda's thumb nail dug into the ragged cuticle of her middle finger where there was nothing but torn flesh to pick at.

The armor of Sybil's apathy splintered apart, and misery consumed her, so great, so vast, she could scarce draw breath. "You've been raised all this time as my sister—"

"I know."

Sybil went mute, stunned into silence as Jacinda regarded her, eyes wide and full of expectation. Full of understanding. Full of love.

"I know." Jacinda repeated. Softer this time, reverent. "I read it in the book Mother left you." She shook her head and corrected: "*Your* mother left you."

"Then you know everything." The words were almost too fragile to say aloud.

Jacinda nodded and Sybil's exhaled sob resounded off the cold stone walls.

"My daughter." Her voice trembled. She could no longer hold back her tears. She opened her arms, catching Jacinda in an embrace, relishing the way her red-gold hair smelled like sunshine, how the warmth of her daughter nestled so perfectly against her heart.

They clung to one another, mother and daughter, newly united despite a lifetime spent together.

"You could have told me," Jacinda said in a thick voice. "All this time, I mourned having never known my mother as I was so young when she died. Now I realize I have known my mother all this time, perhaps better in some ways than I know even myself." Something quivered in her tone. Hurt? Anger? Betrayal?

She had a right to any one of those emotions.

"Your father," Sybil said. "I told him only recently that I had kept you a secret."

"The man on the street some years ago." Jacinda hesitated. "The vicar. With hair the same color as mine."

Sybil nodded. "You saw him?"

"I saw you see him. The way you looked at him, like your heart had leaped into your eyes." She gave a sad smile. "That and I've never seen someone else with the same color hair as I have."

In that moment, Sybil realized exactly how much she'd deprived Jacinda of by keeping her secrets. Not only a mother, but also a father.

How many nights had Jacinda succumbed to the pain of being an orphan?

All these years, Sybil thought she was protecting everyone she loved, but truly, her own wounds were what she sheltered.

For everyone else, she had deprived them of a chance to love with the whole of their hearts.

"His name is John Griffin," Sybil said. "Seek him out after…" She balled her hands into fists and let her ragged nails bite into her palms. "He will help you."

"I know his name," Jacinda said.

"The book." Now Sybil understood. "The priest hole—how did you…?"

"There was a woman who helped me." Jacinda bit her lip, the way she did when she knew she'd done something she ought not. "A woman not from our time."

The birthmark.

"I presume this woman has a similar mark on her?" Sybil pulled up the sleeve of her shift. "Jacinda, what did you do?"

"I was trying to save you." Tears filled her large hazel eyes. "I told you I'd find a way to help."

"But at what price?" Sybil demanded in a whisper. "You will lose your connection to the earth. And the woman… She could not have known she would be implicated. Every descendant until her will suffer. My child, there are repercussions."

"I knew that before I performed the enchantment." Jacinda nodded solemnly. "The cost is one I do not take lightly. I would do anything to save you."

The conviction of her words plunged into Sybil's heart. Jacinda was young, impetuous, she hadn't had enough experience in the world to realize how heavy such wrongs could be. And she'd done it out of love.

The door opened. "Enough."

Pain splintered open in Sybil's chest, deep and raw. Their time was over far too quickly. Not only these scant precious moments, but their life together. Once seeming to stretch on for eternity and now ephemeral.

As if afflicted by the same visceral thought, Jacinda threw her arms around Sybil.

"I love you," Sybil said around the knot in her throat. "I have only ever wanted the best for you, my daughter."

The sound of Jacinda's weeping muffled against Sybil's shoulder, her skin beneath the shift wet with the girl's tears.

They held each other thus, a moment to love before being forever separated by death.

"I'll save you," Jacinda whispered under her breath.

"Don't." Sybil said in a tone that brooked no argument.

She would do anything to keep her daughter safe, and that included dying.

The door opened. Jacinda pulled from Sybil's embrace and turned away, looking over her shoulder as she did so. Likewise, Sybil watched her, memorizing her daughter's face, the way a dimple appeared in her right cheek, the stubborn set to her jaw.

Even without the earth's gifts, that girl would be a force to contend with someday.

These thoughts of maternal pride squeezed at a wounded place in Sybil's heart. Mayhap that was why she did not see the figure who entered until Jacinda was gone and the door closed.

But there he stood.

Black robes, a fierce expression.

Her heart stuttered to a stop.

The lock clicked in the door.

And Sybil was alone once more with the magistrate.

CHAPTER FIFTY-EIGHT

Sybil

Sybil could not mute her horror as the magistrate strode toward her in the small room.

There was no penknife in her pocket for protection. No servants to give him pause. No elevated status to lend her power.

Her strength had been whittled away for far too long, leaving her a shell of who she'd once been.

She was alone with him, vulnerable.

Afraid.

And he knew it.

He sucked air between his teeth as his eyes devoured her. "Prison has not been kind to you."

"It is disagreeable." She kept her gaze locked on his, refusing to break contact, playing the only card she had. "As are the circumstances that have placed me here. All falsehoods as you are aware."

He lifted a brow. "Am I?"

She didn't deign to reply.

"You could have avoided this." His head tilted to the side in a condescending show of disappointment.

"I prefer this prison to the one with you."

The back of his hand replied for him, connecting with her jaw like a brick. Her head snapped hard to the right and the world spun for moment, knocked off its axis.

Before she could recover, his hand curled around her throat, cutting off her air.

"I could do anything I want right now." His teeth were yellow this close, his breath fetid, noxious against the dizzying scent of ambergris and musk and nightmares.

He was not wrong. Even if she cried out, no one would come to her aid.

She was entirely at his mercy.

Panic fluttered in the back of her mind, at her inability to draw breath, and her vision began to darken. Eyes gleaming with malice, he lifted her by the neck, so her toes swirled and kicked in the air for purchase.

All at once, the pressure at her throat loosened and she dropped to the ground. Her bony limbs landed hard, but the gift of air was greater than the pain in her body and she sucked at the air in great, heaving gasps.

He withdrew a rope from his belt as he stood over her. "Give me your hands."

Before she could lift them, he yanked her right wrist, which he bound with the coarse rope. This was followed by the left.

From his pocket, he withdrew a metal key.

Her breath froze as she realized what he planned to do.

Not just her breath, but her heart, even the very blood in her veins—all went still, afraid to disrupt this impending miracle.

He knelt and inserted the key into the lock at her ankle where the shackles left the skin chaffed and mottled with bruises. The iron clattered to the ground, the air kissing her tortured flesh. As he unlocked the second, his lip curled in disgust. "You aren't worth the loss of these shackles when you burn."

The iron fell away from her skin.

The power of the earth that had been suffocated into silence at the first touch of the shackles now rushed into her like the crescendo of an orchestra. Humming and singing and throbbing and pulsing and vibrating through every part of her being. A reminder of all the strength she once had and never thought again to possess.

For all the times she'd been deprived of food and water, never had she been more ravenous with need as she had been for *this*.

For the beauty of the earth pouring into her, fortifying her with the strength of centuries of women.

Her skin glowed to her own eyes, shimmering with the force of the energy charging through her.

She did not know how long she would have this power. Mayhap a minute. Mayhap until the flames consumed her.

Her death would be easier to bear with the earth to guide her from agony to a place of eternal rest. But she could not waste this one opportunity. She had to try to save as many as she could.

For that reason, she did not cast a spell for herself. Nor did she compose one for the other souls condemned to die within an hour alongside her.

There were so many left to save. Women who would be persecuted for being different, and the men who stood up for those women. The many who would suffer the fate of false accusation, persecution, and death.

Sybil stood, rising up like a phoenix from the ashes, like Elizabeth from Shakespeare's *The Famous History of the Life of King Henry the Eighth*. In a strong, clear voice, she began her enchantment, infusing it with the entirety of the earth's power.

"May the earth afford you, Robert Walsingham and Matthew Hopkins, the treatment you have granted others."

He scoffed. "Quiet yourself."

"May the earth afford you, Robert Walsingham and Matthew Hopkins, the treatment you have granted others."

Not a curse. Not a blessing. But a promise. That the earth would cycle back to Walsingham and Hopkins with the heavy debts they'd accumulated.

Uncertainty flickered in the magistrate's eyes.

Fear?

She said the words a final time. "May the earth afford you, Robert Walsingham and Matthew Hopkins, the treatment you have granted others."

A rush of cool air whipped through the room, ripe with the fragrance of honeysuckle blossoms.

If the earth was good, these men would be rendered impotent through accusation. Unable to convict any more innocent souls to death.

The door to the room slammed open and the magistrate startled, a clear sign she had indeed unnerved him.

Matthew Hopkins swept in like a winter storm, brittle with cold indifference. "Why did you take off those shackles?"

"They'll melt and become unusable."

"Better than the rope burning and letting her free." Matthew Hopkins examined Sybil. "The time has come."

Then he quit the room, leaving the magistrate to comply with his order. The shackles clapped onto her ankle bones once more. The immediate silence so stark and empty compared to the euphoria she'd felt only moments ago that she could not help but weep.

She had run out of time.

CHAPTER FIFTY-NINE

Lilith

Honeysuckle flavored the air with a honeyed sweetness long before they reached the clearing.

Lilith followed behind Aunt Jacqueline, careful not to trip over Dragon as he darted between her feet. "How do you know Jacinda wasn't in the house?"

"She never is within an hour after Sybil has been arrested," Aunt Jacqueline answered matter-of-factly.

"You can see it all too?"

"See what?" Asher asked.

"Of course I can. Every daughter of the earth can see spells at work," Aunt Jacqueline said. "We have to connect to Jacinda through the clearing. It is the only way."

"And who is Jacinda?" Asher's voice strained with exasperation.

Lilith disregarded his question, too fixed on the importance of the task ahead. "You know how to reach her?"

"It's not an easy enchantment, and there are…sacrifices." Aunt Jacqueline strode toward the weeping birch trees, her little skunk trundling alongside her.

"Sacrifices?" Lilith stiffened.

"Spells that tear the seams of time are forbidden."

"No." Lilith gasped. "That means if you do this…"

Aunt Jacqueline paused and regarded Lilith. "I will lose my gifts, yes. Lilith, we are both bound to this linking charm. I have spent my entire life preparing for this moment."

Lilith shook her head. "You can't… I can't let you…"

"I am the descendant of the man who did this to your family." Aunt Jacqueline lifted her head like a queen. "I absolutely can and will."

Asher looked between them. "So, you're what…witches?"

"Daughters of the earth, as we were once called." Aunt Jacqueline resumed walking. "But, yes, witches. Men stole that word from us when they persecuted and killed women who held even a modicum of power. Only in recent years have we begun to take back the word, to make it powerful. But women aren't the only ones with the earth's gifts…"

Asher slowed and Toby gazed up at him, snaggy underbite on full display.

Lilith gaped. "Do you mean…Asher too?"

"Oh, yes." Aunt Jacqueline beamed proudly. "My nephew is of the earth as well. Males are not commonly chosen, and their powers are a fraction of ours. But when they are born into the line and their souls are sensitive and open, the earth shares its gifts." She tossed a coy look over her shoulder. "Why do you think animals love you as much as they do?"

The sweep of birch trees rose before them and the mirth melted from Lilith's mood, replaced at once by the weight of reality.

A delicate hand settled on Lilith's shoulder, and she turned to find Aunt Jacqueline at her side. "You can do this."

Lilith nodded.

Aunt Jacqueline gave Lilith a squeeze. "It's dangerous."

Lilith frowned. "Excuse me?"

"Nothing is without sacrifice, as I said." Aunt Jacqueline dropped her hand and trudged through the bracken toward the curtain of foliage. The scent of honeysuckle drew them like ambrosia. "Not only mine, but yours as well. Your power is strong enough to survive it." She hesitated. "I think."

Then she ducked beneath the heavy branches and slipped into the darkness beyond.

Lilith shared a shocked look with Asher, her heart racing with a shot of adrenaline.

He took her hands, and something sparked between them, something warm, pleasant, and altogether too enticing.

The kind of enticing that could make her want to stand there forever on a moonlit night in the forest, gazing into his deep blue eyes, forgetting the danger.

She wanted warmth, comfort.

He held her gaze. "You can do this."

The way he looked at her reminded her of that night when they shared too much wine, when she thought he might kiss her. Her heart skipped. He leaned toward her, his eyes closing.

"I can't do this if you aren't both here," Aunt Jacqueline called out in a singsong voice from the other side of the tree line. "Yes, Wimbleton, I *know* I'm too old to do this enchantment myself."

Lilith opened her eyes and found Asher grinning at her like a kid caught doing something he shouldn't.

"Aunt Jacqueline is killing your game," Lilith murmured.

He gave a sheepish smile. "To be fair, I'm not sure I've ever had 'game.'"

Regardless, Lilith appreciated the moment of levity in a situation with too much weight. She eased through the branches and emerged in the clearing. The moon was darker than the night before, as if someone had scooped a section away.

Aunt Jacqueline sat before a small campfire with Lord Wimbleton the third happily curled in her lap while she fiddled with a bowl containing several items. Some Lilith recognized, like rosemary and thyme and…

"Is that elder wood?" Lilith asked, referring to the sticks.

Aunt Jacqueline nodded and patted the ground beside her. "Yes, an elder tree whose permission I requested."

"Three times," Asher mumbled almost to himself.

"Ah, you remembered." Aunt Jacqueline's smile was one of pride. "There's more of the earth in you than you realize, my boy."

Lilith sat beside the older woman, who indicated each item in the bowl. "We also have yarrow to lift the veil between our worlds and selenite to prevent anything from blocking our entry. Elder wood and labradorite to help connect us to where we need you to go. Rosemary for memory and recall, so you don't forget where you came from. And thyme to ground you and call you back."

Dragon nestled against Lilith's side as the firelight reflected something inside the bag hanging from Aunt Jacqueline's shoulder. Lilith frowned. "Is that a knife?"

Aunt Jacqueline indicated Asher sit between Lilith and herself, completing the circle around the fire, before answering. "Of course it is. You can't ask the earth for so much power and not be willing to offer something in return."

"You are already sacrificing your gifts for this," Lilith said softly. "Is that not enough?"

Aunt Jacqueline offered a gentle smile, one of acceptance at her own fate. "That is my sacrifice. You, my dear, require just a bit of blood."

"Do I need to offer blood too?" Asher asked.

Toby dropped his whole weight into Asher's lap, and Asher's breath came out in a grunt.

"I am leading the spell and Lilith is sliding back in time, which is why we must sacrifice," Aunt Jacqueline replied. "You are here only for your power. No sacrifice needed."

"Sure, that makes sense," Asher replied with a tone that suggested it made no sense at all.

Aunt Jacqueline ignored him and handed Lilith the knife. "Just enough to dribble onto the plants."

"Dribble seems like a fair amount of blood," Asher muttered.

Lilith accepted the knife, startled by its weight. By how solid the handle appeared against the transparency of her hands. "Whatever it takes." Flexing the fingers of her left hand outward, she positioned the blade over the heel of her palm.

"With intention," Aunt Jacqueline said vehemently. "And make sure the blood catches the moonlight."

Lilith took a deep breath and adjusted her position, so the moon bathed her left palm in silvery light.

Closing her eyes, she focused her thoughts.

Let me see Jacinda so I can tell her what I know, so Sybil may live. So, I may continue to exist.

The force of her longing sent a pang through her chest even as a prickling sensation warmed over her birthmark, echoing her intent.

She pressed the blade to her skin, shocked how easily the razored edge slid into her flesh. Blood trickled out, landing *pat, pat, pat* against the herbs. The metallic scent mingled with honeysuckle into a macabre perfume. Lilith moved her injured hand, ensuring every item in the bowl was sufficiently spattered with blood.

Aunt Jacqueline nodded and took the knife before handing

Lilith antiseptic and gauze, a kind consideration given Lilith was still dripping everywhere.

While the old woman assembled the items in front of her, Lilith hastily wrapped her hand. The wound burned, the discomfort pulsing in time with her heartbeat, like her birthmark, all throbbing to the same rhythm.

With a graceful swirl of her wrist, Aunt Jacqueline spoke in a low voice, the tone melodic as before. "Let the thread of time unwind, to reveal what we must find. Return her once all is said and please ensure she is not dead."

Lilith gaped at Aunt Jacqueline.

"Was that really necessary?" Asher asked dryly.

Aunt Jacqueline shrugged. "You don't get what you don't ask for."

A white glow glinted in the bowl and blue flames licked over the herbs and stones, bathing the offering in a brilliance that made Lilith squint. The pungent fragrance of herbs filled the air and motes of light danced up from the bowl.

Aunt Jacqueline held out her hands, which Lilith and Asher each took before clasping their own, completing the circle.

A flash of memories flickered through Lilith's mind, ones that did not belong to her. Asher as a small boy, making his own breakfast amid a deteriorating kitchen littered with empty bottles, a couple shouting in the background. Children laughing, mocking. The frenzy of paint on canvas. A young woman who disappears…

Then there was a girl, Aunt Jacqueline, being told she was not good enough for the legacy of Brackenmere Manor.

These experiences tangled with Lilith's own past, sending a spear of agony at her most painful memory. Daddy's death. When she'd used a bowl of water to scry in high school and saw his death in the mirrored surface. The next day, he'd ignored her plea to go the hospital, instead meeting with a wealthy client as Mama pressed him to do.

According to Mama, if Lilith had never said he'd have a heart attack from all that foolish magic, he wouldn't have been worried all day. He wouldn't have taxed his heart. He would have lived.

Memories of her heavy shame followed. She never opened herself to magic again. Not until that fateful day at *Enchanted*.

The memories continued to pour in, including when Asher had walked Lilith to her room, that lingering pause when he almost kissed her. Lilith's heartbeat fluttered. Another recollection, this time of only moments ago, her hands in the protection of his, the yearning in his gaze.

"Oooh," Aunt Jacqueline chirped.

Lilith grimaced.

"Focus," Aunt Jacqueline said in seriousness. She closed her eyes and intoned, "Let the thread of time unwind, to reveal what we must find. Return her once all is said, and please ensure she is not dead."

"Seriously, please stop saying that," Asher said irritably.

Aunt Jacqueline peeked an eye open, glaring at him, before closing the eye again and repeating the line a final third time.

Lilith likewise closed her eyes and opened her mind to the words, losing herself in the chant.

Nothing happened.

She clenched her teeth. *Please let the charm work. Please let the charm work.*

She could not afford for it not to.

Please let the—

All at once, the world spun around her, and her stomach plunged like a roller coaster drop.

She clenched her hands into fists and suddenly realized she

was no longer holding on to Asher and Aunt Jacqueline. The air was cooler, the grass damp under her feet.

How was she standing?

A moment of fear ensnared her, and she blinked her eyes open. The moon overhead was larger now, a waxing gibbous moon rather than the waning crescent she'd left behind.

"It's you."

Lilith turned to the sound of the voice and the birthmark on her arm thundered in time with her heartbeat.

Two women stood by the fire, and one of them was Jacinda.

CHAPTER SIXTY

Sybil

Sybil was forced outside and pushed onto a wooden cart. Her eyes ran with tears against the brilliant sunlight, trying to adjust after being so long in the darkened prison.

Still squinting, she took in the condemned women and men alongside her, their faces drawn, haggard with exhaustion.

Crowds of people pressed against the cart as it rolled forward, making slow progress. They'd come armed with rotten food and insults to hurl with vicious abandon.

After only several minutes, the cart stopped before a small, narrow building, just outside the market.

Sybil had spent much of her life in this area, procuring food and sundries. Then there was the Maypole in the spring, and at Christmastide in winter the mulled wine and hot roasted chestnuts that Jacinda always burned her fingers on in her haste to get to the sweet nut within.

These memories clogged in Sybil's throat, blazing with the realization that there would be no more.

Rough hands grasped Sybil by the shoulders, hauling her from the cart with such force she stumbled.

Several women descended upon the prisoners with scissors. Sybil looked up at the woman before her, recognizing her wide blue eyes.

"Mrs. Jones?" Sybil asked as the woman took her hands.

The woman looked up, her brows lifting in startled recognition. "Mrs. Brantham."

Mrs. Williams was there, as cold and steely as she'd been when shaving Sybil's hair from her body and prodding at her with a hollow bodkin. She shot a hard glare at Mrs. Jones.

"Forgive me," Mrs. Jones whispered.

Before her arrest, Sybil had softened her cuticles with lavender and calendula-infused rose oil, her nails kept clean and perfectly rounded. Now they were black with grime, the cuticles ragged, the brittle nails uneven and chipped.

With surprising care, Mrs. Jones snicked the broken nails into a brown jar and twisted the cap into place.

Likewise, the other prisoners were having their nails hastily clipped. The ones who still had hair lost locks that were crudely shorn and stuffed into jars.

Those brown jars would be tucked into the basement of the building, separating the nails and hair from the witches being killed. For those not buried whole would be denied entry into heaven. Or so they believed.

Once the jars had been sealed, the men and women were crammed back onto the cart. Margery's hair had been hacked with intentional cruelty, an obvious attack against her beauty.

She clasped Sybil's hand and squeezed her grip. Sybil squeezed back. For strength, for comfort.

Beneath the jeers of the mob pressing around the cart, the unmistakable murmur of the vicar droned on in prayer, begging mercy for their souls.

When they finally came to a stop on Thingoe Hill, a crude wooden beam awaited them, affixed with eighteen ropes. To the right was a pyre of split logs with a stake jutting from the center. For Sybil.

Beside her, a woman whimpered, and a puddle formed beneath her feet.

Though many townspeople followed the procession of the cart, many more were already waiting by the gallows. Hundreds.

Mayhap even thousands.

Lightheadedness overwhelmed Sybil and she swayed on her feet.

A breeze stirred from the east, and she closed her eyes, letting its sweetness wash over her cheeks, savoring the moment of nature, breathing in the verdant fragrance of sun-warmed grass and late summer blossoms.

Oh, how she longed to have her shackles removed, to let the earth embrace her into death.

The wind picked up, whipping her shift against her body.

She blinked her eyes open. Clouds crowded the horizon, ferociously dark in contrast to the clear sunny day only moments before.

Unnatural.

Frantic suddenly, she searched the faces of the gathered crowd when Margery's hand was abruptly ripped from hers. Too late to stop, Margery was pulled away along with the other condemned until only Sybil remained.

The women and men were marched to the gallows in a single line and nooses were looped around their necks. A charged silence descended on the crowd and lightning flickered in the clouds.

Matthew Hopkins stepped forward. "You die today for your admission and evidence of witchcraft. As of this day, the world will be rid of your wicked ways."

The crowd cheered, a cry of savage bloodlust.

The executioner slid behind the row of prisoners, a black hood masking his face.

He stood behind the first woman—Mary Bacon, whose husband had recently been arrested for trying to help her. Just that morning, she had learned her son had, indeed, embarked on the journey to the Connecticut Colony in the New World.

With a single shove from the executioner, she flew from the platform. Her scream was cut short by the brutal snap of the rope. Her feet thrashed as her body swung, jerking in helpless spasms.

The masses roared with approval.

Sybil gripped the splintered railing of the cart.

The horror had begun.

The executioner did not wait for Mary Bacon to die before he moved on to the next soul, the old vicar whose mouth still moved in prayer, no doubt offering support to those around him until his last, dying breath.

Next…

A sob choked in Sybil's chest.

The executioner stopped behind Margery, her beautiful hair jaggedly hacked, her face crumpled. Her voice rose above the crowd in a desperate pitch. "Tell my husband I love him. Please. Tell—"

She flew forward and was yanked back by the rope about her neck. Her legs kicked in desperation, body swinging like a fish on a line.

Cheers erupted at the death of a woman with too much life left to live.

Nausea churned in Sybil's stomach, and she turned away.

She could see no more.

But though her eyes stopped the horror, her ears caught every groan of the taxed wooden beam. Every gurgled choke as the rope caught. Every effusive cry of excitement for another innocent murdered.

Thunder rolled overhead and rain spit down at her.

When the final victim had been sent to their death, the creak of the cart opening once more drew Sybil's attention.

Two guards hauled her to the grass, her feet heavy and awkward in her shackles. At the gallows, eighteen bodies swayed as the wind whipped about Thingoe Hill with a frenzy.

She knew that kind of storm. And the young woman who could cause it.

Please not today.

Even as she thought it, she caught sight of reddish-gold hair in the mob.

Jacinda.

Sybil's blood ran cold.

Jacinda should not have come. And certainly, she should not be brewing this storm before an excited crowd who would eagerly see her swing from a rope.

Regardless of what Jacinda intended, it would not be enough. The risk she placed upon herself was in vain.

Sybil would be dead within the hour and no longer able to protect her daughter.

CHAPTER SIXTY-ONE

Lilith

Lilith stepped closer to the two women dressed in old-fashioned clothing. "Jacinda?"

The young woman nodded. "And this is Kat, a fellow daughter of the earth. I could not perform the spell alone."

A squirrel sat on the woman's shoulder, almost lost in the riot of red curls. "It worked." She cast an incredulous look at Jacinda. "The linking spell actually worked."

"And is as yet incomplete." Jacinda looked pointedly at Lilith, old eyes in a young face. A familiar bird perched on a tree behind her, those glittering black eyes fixed like a predator. "Did you find who spoke against Sybil?"

Lilith nodded. The world around her spun, time tugging at her like poorly fitted clothing. "Anne."

Jacinda rocked back on her heels. "Anne?" She shook her head. "Were it not for Sybil's generosity, Anne's family would have perished during the plague." Her gaze searched the air, her head still shaking in a rhythm of disbelief. "How?"

"The magistrate," Lilith replied. "Anne is pregnant."

"That bastard," Kat growled. "I've a mind to curse him so his—"

"He threatened Anne?" Jacinda asked, expression hard.

Lilith nodded. "The child is his. He refused to help her unless she betrayed Sybil. He implied she would lose her job once they found out she was pregnant. I…I don't think she had a choice."

"Apparently people in the future are soft," Kat said without sympathy. "There is always a choice."

"Mayhap she did not consider Sybil's mercy well enough." Jacinda tapped her fingers to her lips. "Desperation can alter a person's reasoning."

Unease twisted in Lilith's gut. "Do you think knowing Anne denounced Sybil is enough? Will this mean you can save her?"

"The truth will lie in Anne's response," Jacinda replied solemnly.

"And how we manage the situation." There was fight in Kat's words, enough that Lilith hoped she could find a way to use the information to save Sybil.

Jacinda looked at Lilith, her face softening with a look of apology. "Sybil's fate, your fate, and every woman born between me and your birth hangs in the balance."

Lilith bit at the inside of her cheek. "That's not very reassuring."

Jacinda drew in a pained breath. "No. But I vow to do all that is possible. For Sybil. For you. For the legacy that will follow you."

Jacinda's words cut deep. "What if…" Lilith swallowed. "What if I'm not worthy of this line?"

Jacinda tilted her head in quiet contemplation before replying,

"That isn't for you to decide. You were born into this line because the earth deemed it so. There is no question of your worth."

"But I don't want children." The words were raw as they left Lilith's throat, rendering her hollow with a fear she had not dared voice.

That she was a failure as a woman for not wanting to have children, yet another way she did not fit into the world.

"I've been trying to be okay with accepting our legacy, but… I've never wanted children," she offered meekly. "Not after how my mother treated me." Under the bandage, her palm throbbed in time with her pulse.

"Women are more than the children they bear." Jacinda smiled softly, revealing how very young she truly was. "I am indebted to you for what you have done for me." She stepped closer to Lilith. "I give you the gift of choice. That you may decide to pass on the legacy." She swept her hands over Lilith's face, down her neck and over her collarbones.

Warmth followed the motion and the tension eased from Lilith's muscles, draining away beneath the graceful sweep of Jacinda's fingertips.

A patter of something wet sounded by Lilith's feet. She glanced down to find the bandage stained bright red, blood dripping from her hand.

"Should we see to that?" Kat asked.

Jacinda shook her head. "We've tarried for too long. Lilith must hasten back."

A jolt of terror struck Lilith. "I don't know how to go back." The trickle of blood at her hand ran hot and steady now, pouring from her as time slipped away.

Was this the cost of the spell?

"I might be able to offer aid," Jacinda said. "You must trust me."

Lilith gave a sardonic laugh. "As if I actually have a choice."

Kat tsked. "There's always a choice."

Jacinda frowned at Lilith. "I'm sorry."

"Just save Sybil."

Jacinda nodded. "Close your eyes and let yourself fall back."

Lilith closed her eyes imagining the library at Brackenmere Manor with Dragon at her side, cooing as he nuzzled her shins for affection.

Hands closed over her shoulders, pressure followed by a shove, and she toppled backward.

"This might hurt," Jacinda cautioned.

Before Lilith could ask what she meant, there was an explosion of pain. As if every atom in Lilith's body was being sent in the wrong direction.

As if she was being ripped apart.

A scream tore from her throat, her teeth loosening.

"Focus," a voice hissed at her.

Lilith squeezed her eyes and mouth shut, fisting her hands, flexing her muscles. In her mind, she imagined her body like magnetized balls, clinking together, forming a tight mass.

Keep it together.

Her body shuddered.

Keep it together.

She imagined herself ripping into pieces. Pink mist and bone fragments.

No.

Keep. It. Together.

Her limbs curled toward her torso. A fetal position. Desperate to stay intact.

There was a final wrench that threatened to shatter her. She clenched her teeth, a whimper sharp in the back of her throat.

This would be how she would die, shredded between two centuries, scattered across a landscape of time.

Ceasing to exist.

CHAPTER SIXTY-TWO

Sybil

Even as Sybil was dragged toward the pyre, she could not pull her gaze from Jacinda. She stood at the front of the mob, absent her iron bracelet, wide hazel eyes brimming with tears.

Of all people to watch Sybil burn, Jacinda was the last person who should be there.

While Sybil had never been to a burning herself, she heard the horrific stories of how quickly clothing singed away, how long the flames licked at flesh before death finally prevailed. The strongest spirits were broken in such ways, resulting in terrified cries of anguish.

These could not be Jacinda's last memories of her.

"You have been charged as a witch," a booming voice announced.

Sybil turned to find the magistrate alight with the force of his wrath.

He held a torch in his hand, the flame flickering in the wind.

"You have used your evil to kill your husband. May Henry Brantham rest in peace." The magistrate looked out at the crowd, playing for his audience as he announced, "And now you will burn for your sins."

The crowd roared their approval and icy fear coiled in Sybil's stomach.

The clouds blackened and swirled overhead, thick and ominous.

Sybil wanted to shake her head at Jacinda in a silent plea. This risk was not worth the danger.

The guards grabbed Sybil by the arms and hauled her toward the pyre, her progress hampered by the shackles at her feet, the chain dragging behind, catching first grass and then logs. Their boots did not feel the jagged, uneven surface of splintered wood, but Sybil's did. Every scrape of rough bark and sharp edge, every miserable splinter across her battered feet.

She clenched her teeth to keep from wincing. How ridiculous to worry about the pain in her feet when she would soon be burned alive?

Her hands were unbound just long enough to lash together once more around a stake driven into the ground.

Sybil's heart crashed in her chest like a clap of thunder, her entire body quaking with anticipation.

These were moments she ought to cherish, and yet, the wind was too hard to snatch into her overactive lungs, her thoughts too frantic to settle on any one thing.

She would never feel the power of the earth again.

She would never see her daughter again.

She would die knowing she had lost so much time. So much wasted time.

A sob choked up her throat.

The rain came then, droplets cast from the swollen, angry clouds.

The efforts of a daughter of the earth whose gifts were waning. The cost of enlisting the forbidden.

But Jacinda's efforts would not be enough to put out the flames.

Sybil would burn that day.

All she could do was beg the earth that her daughter would not be next.

CHAPTER SIXTY-THREE

Jacinda

Jacinda ground her teeth so hard against one another, they felt as though they might splinter.

To summon a storm a fortnight ago would have been as easy as breathing.

Now the effort gouged her very soul. She glanced at the hill in hope.

The empty forest beyond pulled at her rapidly depleting energy.

Sybil's fear radiated from the pyre, leaving a metallic taste in the back of Jacinda's throat.

She had always been aware of Sybil's moods.

Indeed, she had long suspected Sybil was her mother before she had confessed. The way her gaze lingered on Jacinda's face with quiet pride, the persistent love that endured no matter how stubbornly Jacinda fought back against Sybil's rules.

The hurt that echoed between them the day after they saw Jacinda's father in the street that one time.

Exhaustion tugged at Jacinda. Her entire body was suddenly impossibly heavy.

The clouds overhead continued to churn, a storm simmering but not boiling.

Tears burned in Jacinda's eyes, a knot of frustration clenching at the back of her throat.

She needed only hold on a few more moments.

For Sybil. For Lilith. For herself. For the descendants she wronged so completely with the linking spell.

For every daughter of the earth who ever felt the weight of judgment and persecution.

A flare of energy roared through her, feeble by comparison to what she'd possessed in the days before. But a spark still amid her draining energy.

Rain came down harder, spattering against the tinder of the pyre, slapping at Jacinda's face.

As soon as the energy arrived, it ebbed, bleeding out.

It was too little. She could not help Sybil as she thought she might.

She was too weak.

The hot salt of her tears mingled with the rain.

Her eyes closed, yielding to the exhaustion.

"Wait."

Her eyes flew open at the familiar voice. At the direction the cry had come from.

She looked to the forest and her heart leaped.

Finally.

Kat had arrived.

CHAPTER SIXTY-FOUR

Sybil

"Wait."

A woman's voice lifted on the wind, carrying over the crowd, high and clear.

Sybil followed the magistrate's gaze as Kat strode over Thingoe Hill, a dark-haired woman behind her.

Anne?

Sybil's heart seized as she regarded her maid. Why was she here?

Kat braced herself against the savage gusts, her red hair blowing back from her fierce expression, black skirts snapping behind her. She looked like wrath itself come to exact vengeance. "Ye have committed a great sin, Robert Walsingham."

"The magistrate is not on trial," Matthew Hopkins said in a bored drawl.

The guards moved forward, but he lifted a single hand to

stop them. The crowd loved a spectacle. No doubt Kat would use that to her advantage as readily as Hopkins and Walsingham.

Sybil shifted her feet on the uneven logs, tamping down the hope that dared flicker to life.

"Walsingham ought to be on trial," Kat snapped. "It is his fault Sybil Brantham is on this pyre."

"This woman is a witch, and her death comes at no one's fault, save her own." Hopkins swept his hand at Kat in a dismissive gesture. "Enough of this. Let us proceed."

"You cannot." This time Anne spoke, screaming into the wind, her dark locks wildly blowing about her.

Kat nudged her forward.

The guards moved tentatively as well.

Anne staggered closer and looked first to Sybil, then out at the crowd. "She is innocent. If anyone is to be killed this day… it is me."

"No," Sybil whispered. Already there had been too much death.

The guards stopped as much from Kat's warning glare as Anne's startling admission.

The crowd, equally baffled at this unusual development, looked between Anne and the magistrate.

"Mine own hands made the poppet I claimed was created by Sybil Brantham," Anne cried. "I signed my name to a confession I did not speak. I didn't even know what the confession claimed." She shook her head, her doe-brown eyes catching Sybil's from across the expanse of the field. "I didn't know."

The desperation in the young woman's gaze pulled at a deep place within Sybil.

"Why would you sign a confession you did not speak?" Hopkins asked, frowning.

Anne hesitated, scrunching her eyes shut.

Kat's lips moved, but Sybil could not make out what was said.

"I'm with child." Anne cradled her belly with the palm of her hand. "The magistrate is the father, though he refused to help me unless I denounced Mrs. Brantham."

"This is a lie," the magistrate snarled. "A distraction to save her mistress."

"We all know how ye are, Walsingham," Kat said, her tone a singsong taunt. "Women lock their doors when ye're nearby. Husbands make a show of being home, shouting and carrying on so ye'll hear their voices and leave their womenfolk be." She spun around to the crowd. "Are ye not afraid of Walsingham?"

Silence met her demand. But a few faces tucked downward, hiding from speculation.

The magistrate scoffed. "I had this chit as a lover, it is true. She was desperate to climb into my bed in the hopes of grasping a rung higher in life."

"You said you loved me, and now..." Anne balled her apron in her hands, cheeks a brilliant stain of red. "Now I know you used me to punish Mrs. Brantham for refusing to marry you."

Sybil's heart squeezed in empathy for the young woman. Poor Anne, who had spent her entire life caring for others, who was so desperate to finally be cared for herself.

"Enough," Hopkins hollered. "Mrs. Brantham has been declared guilty of witchcraft and will die this day."

Sybil closed her eyes against the pain of his words, the inevitability of her death.

"No." Anne shook her head. "I stood idly by as she was taken for crimes she did not commit. I stood idly by when I heard she was starved and tormented in prison. I will *not* stand by now as she is condemned to die. She is no witch, and she did not kill her husband. He died of the plague, same as many of yours."

"Henry Brantham died so that many of yer kin could still be alive today." Kat added as she faced the crowd, her expression solemn. "How many of ye had family return from the pest-house because of Mrs. Brantham's care? How many of the family ye lost had words of comfort from her after ye abandoned them in yer fear, leaving them to die alone?"

One woman in the front cast a glance at Sybil, her eyes gleaming with sympathy. With shame.

"Probably a similar number to the men and women who Edith fed and tended to." Kat's voice broke. "The innocent woman ye tried to float in the river. The one ye declared after her death what a shame it was to lose so good a soul. *What a shame.*"

A man in the crowd covered his face with his hands while another woman looked away.

Kat pointed at Sybil. "And ye stand here now, before a woman who gave coin to the poor when the rich held their purse strings, a woman whose husband caught the very plague she tried to save yer loved ones from, a woman who has offered the services of her mother's healing when the lot of ye can't afford a physician's care. She never intended to take on her mam's work, but ye had need, and she was there, not charging even a tuppence for her efforts."

There was an uneasy shift among the mob.

Sybil would never have used her efforts with the townsfolk against their conscience, but Kat had no qualms with wielding Sybil's past deeds.

Kat put her hands on her hips. "And what will ye say when ye've a babe with a fever and ye cannot afford care? Or when there is naught enough coin for extra food stores when this war leaves us starving? Or when ye've got chilblains in the winter, or a backache at harvest? Ye'll think back to this moment and do ye know what ye'll say?" She looked pointedly at the mob. "Ye'll say, 'What a shame.'"

A young woman cradled her round belly, her face stricken.

"And when the magistrate finds a woman whose man is not there..." Kat prodded a tooth with her tongue. "Ach, what a shame."

A beautiful woman cast an anxious glance at the magistrate and crossed her arms over her chest, shrinking into herself.

No doubt she too knew the stink of ambergris and musk.

"This is ridiculous." Hopkins banged his hand on the railing. "Guards."

The guards remained where they were. The one with the scarred eyebrow, who had only days before taunted Sybil in her cell now looked directly at her, as if truly seeing her for the first time. "We sent my mam to the pesthouse, thinking she was not long for this world. She returned a sennight later. I hadn't realized...all this time, it was on account of Mrs. Brantham."

"My boy had a fever," a woman at the front of the mob said. "She made a tonic, and he recovered."

A murmur began among the throngs of people, snatches of their words caught from where Sybil remained with her hands painfully bound behind her.

Plague victims spared and consoled, babies born, comforts delivered to the elderly and the injured. Through it all, several women continued to glare at the magistrate, equal parts fear and hatred.

"But she's a witch," someone cried. "Burn her!"

"It is not her who must be stopped, but the magistrate." A woman's voice came from the crowd, harsh with desperation.

Hopkins lifted a brow.

"Save Mrs. Brantham," another woman cried.

Sybil's breath caught. Hope flickered anew. Hope and gratitude for the people who had not forgotten her in her time of need.

"Kill the magistrate," a woman cried. "*Kill* him for what he's done to us."

The violence of the cry summoned the bloodlust of the crowd. Gone was the uncertainty that had left them shifting their weight from foot to foot. Their faces were florid with outrage, their voices sharp with judgment.

With the need for vengeance.

"Guards," Hopkins shouted above the din.

The younger guard who had allowed the little girl to flee that fateful night put his hands out, blocking the other guards from coming forward. "My sister said ye touched her." He stared at the magistrate, his eyes blazing with hate. "I didn't believe her at the time…" He tucked his right fist into his left, popping the bones there, then he turned to the mob. "Kill the magistrate!"

The answering cry was deafening. "Kill him!"

Robert Walsingham looked out at the wrath calling for his blood and roared at them like a beast, spittle stretching between his teeth like cobwebs. Then he turned toward the pyre and flung the torch upon it with all the force of his rage—one final act of control before he lost it to the mob.

The tinder caught at once, despite the spit of rain earlier. Sybil jerked from the heat, held by the stake at her back.

The magistrate did not stay to witness his handiwork but dashed round the pyre to the open field leading to town. A coward with his back to those whom he had wronged. Those who now wanted revenge and gave chase.

Sybil stared at the pulse of light beneath the logs. Fire glowed in its depths, fanned to life by the sweep of wind. Flames erupted all around her and smoke clogged the air, filling her lungs, her nose, her mouth. She coughed, bringing a lungful of the polluted air even deeper.

A tongue of fire licked at the hem of her shift, flicking over her skin with intense pain.

For all Kat's efforts and the grief of Anne's admission, Sybil would still die.

CHAPTER SIXTY-FIVE

Lilith

"Enough," Asher growled. "I said enough."

A humming ceased abruptly.

"You don't have to be so dramatic." Despite Aunt Jacqueline's nagging tone, there was a note of terror.

Lilith's face rested on something cool. The ground?

The scent of rich soil and grass overwhelmed the delicate fragrance of honeysuckle.

"Lilith." Asher's voice again. Softer this time. "Lilith, talk to me. Open your eyes."

Were her eyes still closed?

Gentle hands took her shoulders and rolled her to her back.

The world rolled with her and Lilith groaned. A flutter of air tickled over her brow.

She blinked her eyes open to find Dragon sniffing her face and Asher only an inch behind him, concern in his eyes.

"Thank God," he whispered.

She tried to speak, to say his name, to assure him she was fine, but she couldn't get her teeth to stop chattering. A violent spasm wracked her body.

Strong arms came around her, pulling her toward a wall of warmth and the scent of clean laundry. Dragon lay the length of his body against Lilith's leg, rumbling with the force of his purr.

She absently recalled having once read that cats purred when they healed. Was he trying to heal her now with the force of his love?

"I have you, Lilith." Asher's voice was velvet in her ear. "I have you."

She closed her eyes and rested back against him, borrowing from his strength until the trembling in her body finally stopped.

"Why is she still so hard to see?" Asher asked in a tentative voice, as if worried about frightening her.

Lilith's eyes flew open, barely able to make out her jeans atop the dark grass. A sob bubbled up in her chest and emerged as a pathetic whimper.

She *was* still disappearing.

"We don't know if what she found has helped," Aunt Jacqueline replied sadly. "Only time will tell. If Sybil still dies..."

Asher's embrace tightened on Lilith, so protective, it made her want to cry. "Let's get back to the house. Can you walk?"

"I think so?" Lilith's voice was thready, even to her own ears. She tried to sit forward, but exhaustion overwhelmed her.

Asher got to his feet and bent over, scooping her into his arms.

Lilith gave a little shriek. "You can't carry me like...like a damsel."

"I have to make up for not catching you when you fainted in the manor that first day." He managed a small smile, too tense to make his words as flirtatious as he likely meant for them to sound.

"Wait till Essie hears about this—" Lilith broke off at the sudden splinter of pain in her chest. Because Essie wouldn't remember anything about Asher.

Because she wouldn't remember Lilith.

Lilith's head lolled groggily against Asher's hard chest by the time they arrived at the house. "I hope I'm lighter because I'm invisible," she muttered, half asleep.

"You weigh almost nothing." Worry tinged Asher's reply as he settled her onto the couch. She lay back on the soft surface and closed her eyes to keep from crying.

"Is there nothing you can do?" Asher asked urgently of his aunt.

"I've done all I can," Aunt Jacqueline replied in a whisper. "The rest must happen in the past. I have no control over that."

A shiver of fear trembled to life in her core.

"Lilith..."

She opened her eyes to the timbre of the familiar masculine voice and found Asher crouched by the couch.

"I'm here." He reached for her hand, which had miraculously healed. He hesitated only a second before cradling it in his warm fingers. "I'm not leaving you."

She nodded, her throat too tight to speak. Dragon hopped on the couch with her, curling up on her chest, his entire body vibrating with the force of his purring.

"When you arrived, I never expected this," Asher confessed.

Lilith's lips lifted in a sad smile. "That makes two of us."

"I'm glad you came," Asher said softly.

"Me too," Lilith replied, her voice thick.

"When you're visible again, I'd like to take you out...if you'd like—"

"I'd love that." Lilith smiled to herself. "Not just being visible. I mean going out with you."

"I'd love that, too."

"Come on the couch with me." She used the couch to sit up slightly to make room for him, careful not to disturb Dragon.

Asher sat on the couch and Lilith leaned back against him, secure in his embrace. From the floor, Toby grumbled at being left out.

The quiet reassurance of Asher's body against her, the rhythmic purr from Dragon, and surviving being slingshot between the past and present was more than she could bear. Her eyelids were too heavy to keep from closing.

"I'm tired, but I don't want to sleep," she murmured.

A hand gently brushed over Lilith's brow, sweeping away a lock of hair. "I'm not leaving you."

Despite his words, his fingers trembled as he touched her face. "I'll see you in the morning." Asher spoke so quietly, Lilith almost didn't hear him.

With the last of her energy, Lilith replied, "I really hope so."

CHAPTER SIXTY-SIX

Lilith

"Asher?"

Aunt Jacqueline's voice startled Lilith awake from where she lay against him. Sunlight streamed in through the window, nearly blinding her.

"Asher, why on earth were you sleeping on the couch?" Aunt Jacqueline asked.

Lilith sat up and looked back at him, her strength restored.

Asher frowned, his brow furrowed as he examined the room around him.

"That's my fault," Lilith said quickly. "I was too—"

"I don't remember." Asher blinked and sat up, accidentally upsetting Lilith's balance, so she had to catch herself to keep from rolling off the couch.

She stared up at him in horror.

Had she disappeared already?

Had Jacinda failed?

"Asher," Lilith whispered.

He continued to look around the room in utter confusion.

"Asher," she said again, louder this time, her voice pricked with panic. "Asher, you were with *me*. With Lilith."

He didn't respond. He frowned once more and turned away like she wasn't there.

As if she'd ceased to exist.

Her heart clattered in her chest, a rapid-fire beat she couldn't control. "Asher! Can you hear me? Can you see me?" Her voice cracked.

He continued toward his aunt, rubbing a hand over the top of his bald head in a way that would be impossibly sexy if this wasn't so terrifying.

"Asher," Lilith called. "Asher!"

He walked away, not turning back once. Aunt Jacqueline hovered in the room, her brow pursed like she was trying to find something before she, too, turned away.

"Aunt Jacqueline," Lilith cried. "Please, Asher! Anyone!"

The birthmark on her arm prickled. Not with the usual warmth, but with a chill.

An insistent pressure slid against her shin, and she looked down to see Dragon curling his body around her legs. Tears pricked her eyes.

At least she still had him.

She went to her bedroom, where the door stood open. Her suitcase was gone, the open closet empty, devoid of the clothes that had been hanging there the day before.

She paused outside the bathroom before entering, knowing what she would see.

And hating that she still clung to hope that her suspicions wouldn't be true.

She passed the threshold and—without turning the lights on—gazed at the mirror.

A sob tore from her throat.

The mirror offered nothing back. Not an outline of her body, not a glint of her eyes.

Nothing.

The nightmare had become her reality.

Bay leaves.

The idea hit Lilith's mind like lightning. She rushed to the kitchen to gather more bay leaves to burn, but her fingers could not grip the cupboard door to open it. Her fingers couldn't grip anything for that matter.

She could not leave the house until Asher left for work later that morning, then deftly slid past him when he opened the door.

Her rental car was gone, as were the tracks in the gravel from when she'd driven in.

Erased.

Like her.

She rushed to the manor, hoping she might be able to somehow enter the hidden room with the grimoire. Perhaps because the book was of the earth as she was, she might be able to hold it.

Except the door to the manor was closed, locked tight with no way for Lilith to enter. Defeated, she sank to the ground with a sob.

A cold wet nose nudged her hand, drawing her back from her pity party. She looked up, and Dragon gave a little chirp, the way he did when he wanted her to follow him.

"There's nothing more to do," Lilith said miserably.

He trotted down the steps and onto the path leading to the forest. Resigned, Lilith pushed to her feet and trudged after him.

This time, the familiar scent of honeysuckle did not bolster her spirits. Now it was merely a reminder that she was of the earth, and subject to its rules. That she was losing despite having worked so hard to win.

She ducked into the honeysuckle clearing. Unable to help herself, she drew in a lungful of perfumed air. A thread of strength tightened through her. Sunlight spilled on her skin with golden strength, bolstering her spirits with a fledgling hope that maybe Jacinda might have found a way to save Sybil.

Dragon sniffed around the clearing, pawing here and there, as if seeking some kind of cure-all for Lilith. He returned to her periodically, purring as he pressed his body to hers, green eyes wider than she'd ever seen.

As if he worried about losing her.

Around midday, Dragon sat up and looked about abruptly. All at once, his body sagged, no longer alert, and he turned to the edge of the clearing, walking away.

"Dragon?"

His right ear pricked and he partially turned back.

Hope whispered around her. "You can hear me? Dragon!"

He turned and loped slowly away.

"Dragon…" Her voice broke as she watched the little animal stride toward the edge of the clearing.

Her final connection to the earth—to life—had snapped.

The chill of Lilith's birthmark was like ice on her skin.

Jacinda had been too late. The world had gone on without her.

Lilith Legare had ceased to exist.

CHAPTER SIXTY-SEVEN

Sybil

Rain drizzled, alternating between strong and weak, as though struggling to do so. And yet the flames persisted, dancing closer to Sybil, tongues of fire determined to burn. To destroy.

"Let me through," a male voice called. "Sybil."

But Sybil could not look up, not when the fire leaped between the split logs and licked at her feet in blistering bites.

Her mind, unbidden, flashed to Margery, to what she must have suffered through in her final minutes on this earth. What terror.

And what might Jacinda face if anyone suspected she caused the storm?

Sybil's mind went hazy as she recalled her mother and the faint rosemary scent about her, the way she hummed the hearth's song before Sybil had ever heard it. How Henry sat by her side, the tender drone of his voice as he read to her. The way John stroked her hair as they lay in a field, basking in the warmth of the sun.

Strong hands were at Sybil's wrists, wrenching the rough rope free.

Pain flooded her body and she gave a gasping cough for air.

Finally free of their restraints, Sybil staggered forward on legs suddenly unable to bear her weight.

Reassuring arms came around her. "I have you."

She looked up and recognized the man who carried her as he navigated the fire-strewn pyre.

John Griffin.

"John?"

"I couldn't leave you." Gently, he set her on the ground.

Sybil gasped in a lungful of fresh air and reveled in the sensation of the cool, wet grass against her feet. "Thank you." Her voice was thick with emotion, with gratitude.

"God love ye, John Griffin." Kat hugged him first, then Sybil, catching her in an embrace that smelled of lavender and baking bread.

"Kat, you saved my life," Sybil said into Kat's riot of red curls.

Her friend released her, shaking her head. "Yer good heart did that. They just needed a reminder."

Anne stood solemnly aside, tears welling her large eyes. "I'm sorry."

"You didn't know how far this would go." Sybil took the young woman's hand and with the fullness of her heart said, "I forgive you."

Anne began to sob and Kat pulled the younger woman toward her.

"I wanted to do more." John looked up to where the eighteen lifeless bodies still hung, rain dripping from their limp feet. "I preached for days against the magistrate, against these trials." His jaw flexed, his face lined with remorse as he repeated, "I should have done more."

"You will," Sybil said.

He gave a single firm nod of determination. "I will."

The dais where Matthew Hopkins once stood was now empty, evidently having abandoned the magistrate to his fate. Another coward seeking only to save his own skin.

The younger guard approached, iron keys in his hands. He knelt at Sybil's feet and looked up. "May I?"

There was such reverence in how he spoke, affording her the courtesy of choice when she had been robbed of so much in those past weeks.

Throat too thick to reply, she simply nodded.

"Your mother saved my life." He unlocked the left shackle first. "I'd have died at my birth were it not for her."

Sybil put her hands over her heart, cherishing this memory of her mother as he unlocked the other shackle.

The iron fell away and the earth's energy poured into her, a beautiful note that picked up where it had left off. As if there had never been a separation between them. The sweetness infused her soul with love, with power, with strength.

And then Jacinda was there, and Sybil folded her into an embrace, breathing in the sunshine scent of her, her whole heart bursting. Jacinda wavered on her feet, face pale even as the clouds overhead broke away in filmy white threads.

"I tried," she said softly.

Sybil tightened her hold on her daughter. "You did well, my girl. You did well. And you sacrificed so much. I would never have asked—"

Jacinda smiled tiredly at her. "I know. But I would do it again. No matter the cost, I would always do it again."

When they finally pulled apart from one another, the guard was gone. But his story remained, another memory of her mother for Sybil to tuck against her heart.

A riot of emotions charged through her. Relief and gratitude to be saved, joy to hold her daughter in her arms once more. And sorrow.

Such intense sorrow for the horror brought on by the day. For the eighteen who had been so viciously murdered before the mob.

"This is not the place for a reunion," Sybil said sadly.

"Yet this is when we need one another most," John said, opening his arms to both of them.

Sybil fell into this embrace, as did Jacinda. They remained there, a broken family reunited, quiet, humbled by tragedy.

A howl of rage sounded in the distance as the mob caught up with the magistrate.

Sybil found her gaze once more pulled to the eighteen innocent souls, all lost. She only hoped there would be no more. One never knew how long spells took to manifest.

"I will speak against the abomination of witch trials to my dying breath," John said as he released her and Jacinda.

She reached blindly for his hand and closed her eyes in relief when his fingers folded around hers.

There would be no rest until the world was safe for them all. For the women who society felt were useless because they could not bear children. For the women who were too powerful for men to abide. For the women who dared reject men in positions of power. And for the men who dared stand by those women.

The world was not safe yet. But on this day, everyone had been forced to see, to remember. And if nothing else, it was a start.

CHAPTER SIXTY-EIGHT

Lilith

Lilith could do nothing more as Dragon strode away from her.

Even he could no longer see her, sense her.

She gazed down at her hand and saw nothing.

Was she doomed to walk the earth this way?

Alone forever?

The thought crushed her spirit.

How could she tolerate this nonexistence?

Dragon stopped suddenly. His ears perked up. Alert.

Hope clutched her heart so tightly, she feared it might pop. "Dragon?"

He looked over his shoulder and his green eyes met Lilith's. Fast as a shot, he was across the clearing and in her arms, purring and nuzzling her face with insistent headbutts.

Lilith laughed and cradled him in her arms, noting her skin was solidly visible against his sleek dark fur.

Jacinda had done it!

The details of how she'd pulled it off would likely never come to light, but she had done it.

Lilith was of this world once more.

"Lilith?" Asher's voice carried through the clearing.

"Asher," she called back, scrambling to her feet. "I'm here."

With Dragon racing by her side, she ran to the edge of the clearing as Asher burst through.

"I thought you were at work," she gasped.

He grabbed her in his arms as they met, swinging her into the air. "I thought I forgot something and came back."

She laughed. "Apparently it was me."

He set her down gently and studied her, eyes crinkling with joy. "You're safe. You're *you*."

"That might be the nicest compliment anyone has ever given me." She grinned up at him.

"I thought I'd never see you again."

"Well, you *did* forget about me," she teased.

"I…" He frowned. "Wait… The couch…"

Lilith gave a coy smile, one that smacked of I-told-you-so.

"I'll never forget you again." His tone was playful as he said it, but there was an earnestness to his gaze that went straight to her heart.

"Now, that's a promise I'll take."

He reached for her, cradling her face in his hands, his gaze dipping to her lips. And this time, when she closed her eyes and tilted her chin up, she was rewarded with the warmth of his mouth on hers.

That night, as Lilith faded to sleep, the perfume of honeysuckle guided her into her dreams.

Sunset gilded the sky in an array of golds and reds and oranges. Three figures strode together. A tall man, his frame lanky but strong, with a woman on either side of him. One was shorter with long red-gold hair and a bird soaring after her, the other with close-cropped dark hair; a horse loped alongside the trio.

A quiet hum filled the air with a sense of peace. Of love. Of belonging.

The woman with short hair turned around, hazel eyes meeting Lilith's across the field, across time and space. Her lips moved and the wind carried her words to Lilith like a whispered blessing.

Thank you.

CHAPTER SIXTY-NINE

So Mote It Be

August 12, 1647
Manningtree, England

Matthew Hopkins sputtered on a choked gasp that wrenched him from his sleep. A cough wracked through him, his body convulsing.

He swallowed to soothe the ache in his throat and lay back upon a pile of feather pillows, a veritable cloud of luxury.

While he hated being relegated to his home in Manningtree, he was grateful for his own bed in his state of illness. He did miss the travel though, the way those provincial towns welcomed him like a king.

An old bitterness resurfaced.

No one needed witch hunters anymore, deeming the task not only unnecessary, but barbaric. The injustice of how readily he'd been discarded eroded his soul like a canker.

They'd even accused him of witchcraft!

The accusation was preposterous.

No one wanted to hire a witch hunter suspected of being a witch.

He'd almost been made to perform the swimming test. The fools.

After such defamation, he was run out of any town he approached. Wrongly persecuted.

Horrendously unfair.

At least, even if he could no longer hunt down witches, others might do so in his stead. His publication of *A Discovery of Witches* had been successful and would spread word of the existence of their evil.

The income from the book had been a much-needed reprieve after the coin coming in from witch hunting had gone dry. Oh, and it had been lucrative.

A tickle stirred in the back of his pharynx.

Yes, quite lucrative indeed.

He cleared his throat.

Imagine what he might have made if he'd been allowed to continue.

A cough seized him, sending him into a violent fit that left him bent in half. Shaking, he leaned back on his pillows and wiped the sweat from his brow.

The breath wheezed and rattled in his lungs.

A woman's face rose in his mind's eye.

Sybil Brantham.

The handsome widow from Bury St. Edmunds. The one who later wed the vicar who had brought down the witch hunts with his outlandish sermons.

Her escape from the clutches of death had cost Matthew twenty shillings.

He dragged in a hard gasp, but the air felt too heavy, too thick to breathe. As if something were squeezing around his neck.

Another face filled his mind, the young woman who had been hanged. Her name alluded him, but her comely appearance was there, glowing with youth and beauty.

His lungs sucked against themselves, robbed of air. Desperate for it.

A choked sound came from his gullet, wet and inhumane.

His fingers skimmed the Flemish lace at his throat as he fought to loosen the strings that tied his nightshirt closed.

Panic fluttered at his awareness.

Breathe.

He needed to breathe.

Another face came into his mind. The hideous old hag he'd tossed into the River Lark. The one absolved of witchcraft when she drowned. Another loss of twenty shillings.

The pressure in his chest was unbearable. What the Devil was cutting off his air?

He clawed at his neck.

More faces. The old vicar who had been hanged the same day as the pretty young woman. And the man and wife. Then came the others in a flurry, every face, every life, the force around his throat squeezing tighter and tighter and tighter.

He clutched at the bedding, fingers raking over the fine Rennes linen sheets.

Those he'd killed poured through him as the life drained from his body.

Most were old. Poor. Vulnerable. Nearly all were women.

Twenty shillings in his pocket for each.

He was found the following morning by his maid, eyes bulging, tongue swollen and thrust between blue lips. Like the victims he'd condemned to be hanged.

A couple hundred furlongs away, in the town of Bury St. Edmunds, a similar discovery would be made.

Robert Walsingham lay prone in his prison cell, a hand clasped round his throat, his eyes squeezed out from their lids, a fattened tongue oozing between his lips.

Perhaps he might have been glad for his own death. The last two years of living had been difficult.

The honor of magistrate had been stripped from him, the people exercising their own rights under oyer and terminer in their outrage. Without the assizes, anarchy swung in all directions.

He'd been thrown into the stocks first. In that moment, everything he'd become—strong, authoritative, in charge—had been tossed away, and he'd once more been reduced to that scrawny child the other boys kicked around, the one the girls ridiculed, the one who brought his father such shame.

After, he was sent to prison and had moldered there since.

In the final few moments of life, Robert was forced to accept he'd never be a powerful man again.

Faces trailed through his mind's eye. The eighteen women and men he'd seen hanged that day, and the countless women he'd hurt with his words, with his hands, with his unmitigated gall to violate them.

As each face pressed into his brain, the air became harder to breathe. Too thick. Until, at long last, the stream of faces dwindled, and the life slipped from his body.

On an entirely different continent, Sybil woke in the middle of the night to a sense of peace. Her connection to the earth had faded after the mark on her arm disappeared. But in that blissful moment, she was bathed in the beauty of the earth, the soft, breathy sigh of an enchantment that had run its course to completion.

Sybil closed her eyes, savoring the embrace of that power. And the relief that the men who had harmed and killed so many would never do so again.

Her husband stirred beside her. John reached for her, drawing her against the familiar comfort of his warmth.

She closed her eyes and savored the tranquility in her body and soul.

They had begun their life in the New World, in a place called Maryland, where they could begin again.

There was peace in knowing that their girls would remain safe.

Not only Jacinda, born of her and John's love so long ago, but also the girl who Sybil had helped escape from prison. Little Maggie, who learned to speak again after all she had endured, a mother who was slain before her eyes, the unjust arrest under the accusation of witchcraft in her mother's place. The New World suited her, winning shy smiles from time to time, and a tentative curiosity that seemed to grow with each passing day.

The New World suited them all, a chance to start over. To live again.

And they would cherish every moment.

EPILOGUE

Lilith

One year later…

Dragon ran to Lilith before the crunch of tires on gravel could be heard in front of Brackenmere Manor.

Essie had finally arrived.

Lilith practically ran outside as Essie freed Amara from her car seat, wrapping them both in an all-encompassing hug. The vanilla-scented lotion Essie favored curled around that embrace, bringing with it a lifetime of memories of friendship, laughter, and more than a few bad ideas.

Lilith released them with a grin. "I cannot believe you flew all the way to England to see me."

"I would fly to the moon to see you." Essie set Amara down, and the little girl immediately bolted off with Dragon. "It's been over six months since you left Savannah. You know I can't go that long without seeing you."

After everything Lilith went through at Brackenmere Manor, she couldn't bring herself to return to Savannah for good. She'd gone back long enough to pack the old house on East Waldburg Street and put it on the market, selling it for a sum that would have made even Mama happy.

And speaking of Mama, selling that house cut the last of Lilith's ties to her. She'd walked around the empty building, feeling its vastness and a ghost of the missing part of Mama she'd never been able to find.

With that, Lilith was able to say goodbye to Savannah.

Sometimes roots could be an anchor, and Lilith was finally free to soar once she cut herself free.

Her heart was in England, in the land of her blood, in the ferns framing Brackenmere Manor, and in the little black cat who saved her as much as she'd saved him.

Essie glanced around. "Besides," she added in a low-key whisper. "I *have* to meet Mr. Darcy in person."

Lilith laughed and helped her friend with her suitcases. "He'll be here when he gets off work. I'll show you to your room. You okay with staying in the manor?"

"Are there still dead people moving around in it?"

"Do you want there to be?"

Essie looked appalled. "You know I do not."

"Good thing I almost got myself killed getting that taken care of for you then." Lilith winked. "No, they left when my birthmark did." She lifted her arm to show where the smooth skin was now absent the crescent moon shape she'd had all her life.

"Then if you're asking if I'll stay in your manor in the English countryside… I dare say, I don't mind if I do." Essie employed a terrible English accent as she spoke, one tinged with her Southern twang. "Is it really livable already?"

Lilith hauled the larger of the two suitcases while Essie collected Amara and tucked her neatly onto her hip.

"It's been a lot of work, and even more money, but yes, it's livable." Lilith beamed proudly up at Brackenmere Manor. A new coat of limewash covered the grime and made the darkness of the new roof stand out in stark contrast.

"So, you own this place now?" Essie asked as Lilith unlocked the door. "How does that work again?"

"Time altering," Lilith said in an exaggerated spooky voice with a wink for Amara.

The little girl giggled, revealing that dimple Lilith had always loved, the one that perfectly matched Essie's.

"Sybil didn't die by fire, so Robert Walsingham was never awarded the property. In fact, Asher was able to help me find the original deed showing it was in my family and ensuring my ownership. He's also been helping me with the rebuild on weekends."

"So, when's he moving in?" Essie lifted a brow.

Lilith shot her friend a look. "Maybe never."

"Come on." Essie groaned in exasperation. "You need your happily ever after."

"Asher and I are more of a happy-for-now kind of couple." Lilith put her hand on the door latch. "As for *my* happily ever after, I found it." She pushed the door open, revealing the restored Great Hall.

"A woman must have money and a room of one's own," she quoted Virginia Woolf as Essie took in the newly upholstered furniture, the massive hearth with those gorgeous Grecian statues, and the freshly polished floor.

Essie's mouth dropped open. "Lilith…this is incredible."

They went through each room, restored with a blend of old and new, a mix of Sybil and Jacinda, with some of Lilith.

The task had been considerable and costly. Funded through the investments that had made Lilith so wealthy, and through the sale of her home in Savannah.

They went up to Jacinda's bedchamber, where Essie and Amara would be staying, and found Aunt Jacqueline there, straightening a small basket of toiletries. She and Asher were now Lilith's neighbors, and she'd insisted on helping Lilith ready the manor for guests. She spun around with a smile. "Is this Essie, whom I've heard so much about? And sweet Amara?"

As they all hugged like old friends, Lilith couldn't help but smile at how Aunt Jacqueline's health had improved. What had been lost from her gifts had been made up for in the absence of the burden of her own legacy. There was a glow about her that seemed to emanate from within, leaving her cheeks rosy, her eyes bright, and her body as mobile as someone three decades younger. While she admitted to missing the hum of the earth, she still delighted in her garden.

"Skunk," Amara declared with a squeal of delight.

"'Mara, don't be so—" Essie gave a shriek. "It *is* a skunk!"

"Oh, that's Lord Wimbleton the third," Aunt Jacqueline said with pride as the little animal waddled after her, still her constant companion despite no longer having the earth's gifts. "Don't worry—he is a gentleman who keeps his smells to himself."

"The third?" Essie asked, dumbfounded. "There were two more?"

Lilith grinned. "Nope."

"As long as he doesn't spray," Essie said dubiously before turning to the room with its elegant four-poster bed and lush velvet covers and curtains. "But look at this place. Lil! You live in an honest-to-God manor. Call Eugene right now and tell him I'm not leaving. He's just going to have to move here with us."

"There is enough room for you all to move in," Lilith teased.

"Don't tempt me." Essie hugged Lilith. "Truly, this is amazing. *You* are amazing. I never thought I'd see you so happy."

The broad smile on her face showed exactly how glad Essie was for Lilith. A woman's greatest cheerleader was her best friend and Essie was the best they came.

Lilith warmed with love and appreciation for her dearest

friend, who had flown across the ocean—with a child no less—just to see her.

"Wait until you see the garden," Lilith said. "Aunt Jacqueline has been helping me."

"Want to see the garden, Amara?" Essie asked her daughter.

The little girl nodded her head vigorously, setting the beads in her hair clacking.

The garden truly was a sight to behold with vibrant blossoms of roses and bluebells, and, of course, Suffolk county's flower, the oxlip. Amid the lovely blooms were herbs of every kind for any spell that might be needed.

A blue butterfly floated around Amara while she sniffed one flower after the other, Dragon protectively at her heels. She giggled and chased after the pretty insect, running along the path, hands stretching for those lovely blue wings as it continued to remain just out of reach.

"Too far, Amara," Essie called.

But Amara didn't stop.

"I'll get her." Lilith jogged after the little girl, following her to the curtain of weeping birch trees.

A gut feeling made Lilith hesitate, waiting to see if Amara could cross the threshold into the honeysuckle clearing. The butterfly danced through the air, disappearing between the sagging limbs of the tree, and Amara followed.

Lilith ducked into the clearing in time to see her goddaughter exclaim in delight and reach for the sweet blooms that filled the air with their alluring fragrance.

The honeysuckle vine quivered and stretched to meet Amara's hand.

The crook of Lilith's arm tingled, where her birthmark used to be, a ghost of its presence that still lingered from time to time. A reminder of who she was, of what she had done. And what the earth still needed her to know.

Several new honeysuckle blossoms unfurled, releasing their lovely fragrance. Amara laughed, the sound tinkling and magical as a halo of light seemed to glow around her.

All at once, Jacinda's words came into Lilith's head.

I give you the gift of choice.

Suddenly, her words made sense.

She hadn't meant that Lilith could choose to keep their legacy going or not. She had given Lilith the opportunity to choose *who* would carry on the legacy. And there was no child in this world Lilith loved more than her goddaughter.

Of course, Amara couldn't relocate, but there would be time enough with their visits to England, and Lilith's trips to Savannah.

In the past, Lilith would never dream of inviting danger into the life of her beloved goddaughter. But this was not the past. And this gift was not binding.

Amara would grow into her own person, who knew who she was and what she wanted; a woman who would choose to accept the legacy or not.

The days of killing women for their connection to the earth, for the power they wielded, were not gone. Not entirely.

But they were changing.

Their world was one of empowerment, of strong women with even stronger voices, even for those who try not to listen. Now was a time for the daughters of the earth, needed more than ever to bolster the women of the world, to amplify those voices.

Now was a time to reclaim that power.

Now was a time of witches.

PAGES FROM THE GRIMOIRE

These pages were never meant to be released into the world. But they have been unearthed and altered for a modern reader, to allow for women of today to practice simple charms for healing, through body and soul.

There's a little magic in all of us. Embrace yours.

A Gentle Note: As with all herbal and aromatic blends, individual sensitivities may vary. If you plan to apply any preparation to the skin, consider testing a small amount on your inner wrist first and waiting twenty-four hours before use.

MOONLIGHT RELAXATION TEA

Harness the quiet gifts of lavender and chamomile to encourage calm and invite restful sleep. Best prepared at night, just before bed.

INGREDIENTS:

1–2 tsp dried lavender
1–2 tsp chamomile
Honey to taste

DIRECTIONS:

1. Steep herbs in hot water 5–7 minutes.
2. Whisper "A peaceful night" as you stir in the honey.
3. Sip with intent: breathe in calm, exhale your stress.

A SAFE HOME

Clear away stagnant energy in your home while ensuring your home and loved ones remain protected.

INGREDIENTS:

Distilled water
Fresh rosemary sprig
Basil leaves
10 drops sage essential oil (optional)
3 drops tea tree essential oil

DIRECTIONS:

1. Boil water with herbs and let cool.
2. Strain and pour into spray bottle.
3. Add drops of essential oils.
4. Very lightly mist doorframes clockwise and envision a green glow sealing the space.

LOVE YOURSELF BALM

A gentle balm for stressed skin and a weary spirit, scented with herbs long used for comfort and care. Perfect for giving love back to yourself.

INGREDIENTS:

½ cup olive oil
2 tbsp dried chamomile
2 tbsp rose petals
1 tbsp beeswax
10 drops lavender essential oil
5 drops geranium essential oil
2 drops tea tree essential oil

DIRECTIONS:

1. Infuse herbs in oil over low heat for 30 minutes and strain.
2. Melt in beeswax.
3. Add essential oils—more or less as you like the scent.
4. Pour into tin while saying "Comfort in self love."

SWEET DREAMS MIST

Invite intuitive dreams and a restful night's sleep with this blend of essential oils.

INGREDIENTS:

$^{1}/_{4}$ cup purified water
15 drops lavender essential oil
5 drops Roman chamomile essential oil
5 drops tea tree essential oil
3 small chips of amethyst

DIRECTIONS:

1. Combine ingredients in a dark glass bottle.
2. Shake gently before use.
3. Mist lightly around your pillow or bedside before sleep. For external use only; allow the mist to dry before lying down.
4. As you mist, open your heart and mind to receive the dreams the earth will send you.

STRENGTH AND GROUNDING TEA

Make sure your feet are thoroughly planted under you with this hearth-centered drink for strength, warmth, and grounding.

INGREDIENTS:

1 cinnamon stick
A pinch of cloves
5 allspice berries (dried)
A slice of orange peel
1 cup hot water
Honey to taste

DIRECTIONS:

1. Place ingredients in a mug and pour hot water over them.
2. Steep for several minutes.
3. Drink while warm.
4. Circle cup clockwise with a spoon and whisper, "Ground me in strength."

FRIENDSHIP TEA

Share this tea with a dear friend to nurture your bond with a gentle connection. Laughter while enjoying tea is greatly encouraged.

INGREDIENTS:

Hibiscus tea
1 tbsp rose petals
1 tbsp chamomile
Honey

DIRECTIONS:

1. Add rose petals and chamomile to hibiscus tea.
2. Steep in hot water for five minutes.
3. Sweeten lightly with honey.
4. Share with a good friend and relish the connection you share with a good laugh.

LET IT GO BATH

Let your emotional stress go with this soothing bath, good for the body and the soul.

INGREDIENTS:

A handful of Epsom salts
10 drops lavender essential oil
5 drops ylang-ylang essential oil
Fresh rose petals

DIRECTIONS:

1. Add ingredients to a warm bath.
2. Soak and breathe deeply for several minutes.
3. Visualize your worries dissolving into the water and draining away when you pull the plug.
4. Bonus: Collect rose petals afterward to bury in your garden and bury your woes along with them.

BOTTLED CREATIVITY

Embrace your creativity with this charm, blending warmth, memory, and intention to wake the muse.

INGREDIENTS:

Small jar with a lid (as pretty or fancy as you'd like it to be)
Citrine stones (very small)
Dried rosemary—just a pinch
Dried rose petals
Cloves
A small slip of paper with a creative word for inspiration

DIRECTIONS:

1. Place all items in the jar.
2. Secure the lid.
3. Keep stored in an area where you will need creativity.
4. When extra creativity is needed, hold the jar and whisper your creative word to yourself.

May these pages remind you what women have always known—that love is power, kindness is strength, and the care of a friend is the best gift life will ever offer.

AUTHOR NOTE

To those who like to read the Author Note before delving into the book, please know this note does include spoilers. Read at your own risk!

A Time of Witches is a story I have wanted to write for over twenty-five years. The idea first came to me when I was in high school and continued to have a recurring dream that I was being burned alive at the stake.

But I was also a dramatic teenager with an overactive imagination, and I immediately started thinking that maybe I was reliving a past life, or maybe even experiencing what an ancestor had endured. The idea to write this book has been poking at the back of my brain ever since.

To write this, I did extensive research on the witch trials in England, including traveling to Bury St. Edmunds in Suffolk, England, where one of the largest mass executions for witchcraft in England took place.

On August 27, 1645, eighteen men and women were hanged after Matthew Hopkins declared them witches. I wanted to include some of these real-life victims in my book. Those victims include: Mary Bacon from Chattisham, Mary and Thomas Everard from Halesworth (mentioned simply as Mr. and Mrs. Everard in the book to avoid confusion with too many Marys), John Lowes from Brandeston (the aged vicar), and Margery Spearham from Medham (known only as Margery in the book). I included as much knowledge about these victims as my research allowed.

Margery was the only character I incorporated a fictional element into. What I know of her is that Jacob Neech called her a "lewd woman who never went to church" and that her confession included her use of imps to protect her husband, who was a soldier at war. I imagined this woman as being young and beautiful, a woman who loved her husband. Unfortunately, attractive young women left alone are often the subject of unwanted male attention, and so I incorporated that into her story, though it was entirely fictional on my part.

It is important to me that these victims I have named are remembered.

Regarding August 27, I wanted to note that while we are under the Gregorian calendar, Sybil's timeline would observed the Julian calendar. This makes approximately ten days difference between 2025 and 1645 on that date. I tried to incorporate this into the story, but adding ten days didn't work into the plot and created pacing problems. That said, I chose to treat both timelines as sharing the same August 27 date rather than adjust the historical timeline.

Sybil is also a fictional character; however, her predicament of being burned alive is not made up. In September 1645, there was another victim in England named Mary Lakeland from Ipswich. Unlike the other victims, she was burned alive for the crime of using witchcraft to kill her husband, which was considered petty treason, resulting in the sentence to be burned alive at the stake. Unfortunately, she did die in this manner.

But on the note of Sybil, I wanted her to have a strong name tied to Bury St. Edmunds. Sybil Andrews was born in Bury St. Edmunds, a woman who fought prejudice to become a renowned artist in the early 1900s, specializing in printmaking. She was strong, independent, and worked as a welder during both world wars.

Unfortunately, Matthew Hopkins was a real person. Between 1645 and 1647, the self-proclaimed Witchfinder General operated across parts of England, accusing people (mostly women) of witchcraft, resulting in the deaths of an estimated 112 people. His methods included food, water, and sleep deprivation, the walking test, and the swimming test—all of which were not considered torture at the time. The prickers were unfortunately part of history as well, townswomen who were paid to strip and shave victims in their search for witch marks.

Eventually, the people turned on Matthew Hopkins, saying maybe he was a witch. Rumor has it, he was threatened with the swimming test. In his forced retirement, he wrote *The Discovery of Witches*, a manifesto on how to identify witches. He died August 12, 1647, of what was presumed to be tuberculosis. I tied his death in real life to a spell fulfilled by Sybil to make him suffer as his victims had.

Magistrate Robert Walsingham was a fictional character, but representative of many men in places of authority that I read about while doing research for this book. Justice was served to him as well in the same fashion.

My trip to Bury St. Edmunds was filled with valuable information, provided by Moyse's Hall Museum and the incredible Bury St. Edmunds Tour Guides group, who kindly featured me in a local newspaper for having completed a record number of back-to-back tours.

Part of this trip also included a stop into The Nutshell (dubbed the smallest pub in Britain), where it is rumored the nails and hair of accused victims were kept in the basement to ensure the victims were not able to be buried whole, which restricted them from getting into heaven. I did go to Thingoe Hill while there as well, which is now part of a highway system with a series of apartments nearby. But knowing its history, there was a haunting sense to the area.

Lilith's story was also an important one for me to share. So many women of my generation were taught to always be sweet, never get in the way, and try not to be a nuisance. What's more, women feel this pressing expectation to get married and have children. But that isn't every woman's dream. Lilith's journey is about reclaiming a voice shaped by generations of silence, and learning that power does not require explanation or permission.

To ensure authenticity, I also went to Savannah, Georgia, for my research. While there, I stayed at the Catherine Ward House Inn, which I used as a model for Lilith's house and am so grateful to Sonja for taking the time to talk to me about the care and keeping of historic homes in Savannah to make my references more accurate.

As you all know, I'm a huge lover of local bookstores and I adore E. Shaver Booksellers in Savannah. I used E. Shaver Booksellers' store as a model for Shelver's Books in my story. If you're ever in Savannah, I highly recommend you pop by and check out their books and adorable cats. A side note that none of their cats have tummy issues that I know of—that was thrown in for a little humor and my own experience as a cat mom with two very sensitive babies.

On the note of cats, I very much want to address black cats. I am the mother of a black cat myself. He actually was the model for Dragon, and so very special to me as a result. Gunner very seldom meows, but simply chirps and coos and is just the sweetest little guy. Black cats have had a bad reputation for centuries, being seen as wicked or bad luck or the Devil's tools. Even today, these superstitions persist, and black cats are often passed over for adoption because they are considered less photogenic than other pets. The horrors that have been inflicted on black cats absolutely breaks my heart, and I refuse to share that information as it's too awful. I've always been an advocate for adopting over purchasing animals and highly encourage people to consider black cats as they are so often overlooked in shelters and humane societies.

Two animals in this story also are very special for their names. While writing this book, I offered two giveaways to name an animal in my book. One to support the Ashland Public Library and the other for HALO Havanese Rescue. Asher's grumpy dog, Toby, was named by Kristen Ahern and her daughter after their own dog, Toby.

Sybil's horse, Brixton, is there to detail the original horse racing done in Newmarket (by Charles I) before the established horse races implemented later by Charles II with Brixton being a rescue racehorse. As the mother of an equestrian, I wanted a former racehorse to have his own happily ever after. Chris Doyle and her granddaughter, Luci, made naming this horse extra special. Luci is an equestrian as well and Chris used naming Brixton as a means of connecting with her granddaughter over her love of horses. Together they researched the Newmarket horse races and names that would be period appropriate before settling on Brixton, which means strength, stability, and a sense of belonging. I wanted all "familiars" to have a quality of their humans in their personalities and these fit Sybil so well. Thank you to Kristen, Chris, and Luci for making these animal names so wonderful!

To ensure the herbs used in this book were correct, I studied holistic healing from history and today. I subscribed to the

Apothecary At Home subscription box and learned so much for this book through them. I also paired this research with historic herb remedies from texts dating back to the 1600s.

The magic in this book is fictionalized and symbolic, inspired by—but not meant to represent—historical or modern practice.

Any mistakes made in this book are entirely my own. I do extensive research for all of my books, but ultimately did not live in the 1600s myself.

The most important aspect of this book was to reflect on how women were persecuted, women who did not have wealth, women who had too much, women who were too pretty, women who were not pretty enough, and older women who society felt had nothing left to offer. I wanted to give those victims of the witch trials a voice that resonated through the modern world, to empower them through time.

I hope you've enjoyed this book that has been lodged in my heart and mind for so long. As with all of my books, it is truly an honor to get to share people's lives in history through my work.

ACKNOWLEDGMENTS

The act of writing a book involves so many people who offer their time, expertise, and heart. I'm always grateful for the acknowledgment section, where I can thank everyone who helped make this book what it is.

First of all, to my incredible readers, who are always so excited for my next book, who connect with me at events and online, and who write the most amazing reviews that help me through my tough writing days—thank you. You are the reason I am able to write these books at all, and I'm immensely grateful to you.

I'm absolutely indebted to the fabulous team at Hanover Square Press who make literary magic happen in the best possible ways: Grace Towery, my wonderful editor, whose advice helped make this book shine; Leah Morse, who coordinates fantastic events that allow me to meet so many readers; Brianna Wodabek and Brenann Francis, who find the best ways to spread the word about *A Time of Witches* so readers can discover it; and Eden Railsback, for always being there whenever I reach out. Thank you as well to the design team for this absolutely gorgeous cover—I'm completely in love with it. I've been so fortunate to meet the HarperCollins teams in both New York and Toronto and know that a whole village stands behind me. To Angela Melamud, for working so hard to get my book in front of readers and for being a wonderful cheerleader for my work. Finally, to my incomparable agent, Kevan Lyon—I can't imagine this writing journey without you.

I couldn't do this without the support of my family and friends. Thank you to John, who embarked on the trip to Bury St. Edmunds with me for research and who keeps the chaos under control while I'm doing events or racing toward a deadline, and to my girls, who are always so proud of me. Thank you to my parents and brothers for their constant love and support. A huge shout-out to my mom for reading through this book with her eagle eyes and for watching the kids and cats while John and I were on our research trip.

Thank you to my bestie, Eliza Knight, for always being my own real-life Essie. To Heather Webb, who read this story raw before anyone else laid eyes on it and offered wonderful feedback. To Tracy Emro, for always being such a fabulous sounding board for ideas and for your great suggestions. And to Alyssa Matesic, for your edits on this story and suggestions that helped it shine.

Research is so important, and I had some amazing experts who helped bring this story to life: the incredible Bury St. Edmunds Tour Guides team, especially John Saunders, for coordinating so many tours; Dan Clarke at Moyse's Hall, for taking the time to share so much about the exhibits and the history behind them; Sonja at the Catherine Ward House Inn in Savannah, for letting me pick her brain about the care and keeping of an old home; and Jessica Osborne at E. Shaver Books, for taking time out of a busy day to chat with me about running a bookstore so I could portray it authentically in the story.

This book was particularly special to write while I was completing my MFA in Creative Writing through the low-residency program at Drexel University. I'm so grateful to my amazing cohort for their input and for the many times they read about this book over the last two years of our program together. Your insight is embedded throughout this story.

Thank you to my amazing agent sisters, the Lyonesses, for the constant love and support, and to the wonderful group in my Secret Story Society for always being there with enthusiasm, encouragement, and thoughtful suggestions for my book ideas.

And finally, a heartfelt thank-you to librarians and booksellers, for creating such enchanting places where readers can discover the perfect book. You hold the best kind of magic in your hands, and I'm endlessly grateful for all you do.

To the book bloggers, reviewers, and Bookstagrammers—you are incredible. The number of books you read, the time and care you put into your reviews and posts, and the way you help create book buzz is extraordinary. Thank you for your support and encouragement, and for the many books on my TBR and read list that found their way to me because of you.

I am truly beyond grateful.